LINDA HUGHES

WAKING INNIS BREE

HIGHLAND LEGACY ROMANCE

With gratitude to my Scottish Highlander ancestors.

"Admiring Nature in her wildest grace,
These northern scenes with weary feet I trace ..."
Robert Burns, 1787
Written in the parlour of the Kenmore Hotel, Scotland.

CHAPTER 1

*C*lover tickled her bare toes as she trotted across the verdant meadow. Stopping to pluck a wild yellow primrose and sniff its sweet aroma, she placed it over her ear, satisfied it gave her a country air he'd adore. She hurried on. After all, her hunk of a sexy lover awaited by the stream.

The field merged into a copse of Scots pine trees that provided a silken carpet of fallen needles underfoot. Her heart fluttered. Her grin widened. Her cheeks flushed. She ran as fast as her legs would carry her, causing her long, loose, raven black hair to frolic about her face and the skirt of her delicate sundress to mold itself to her thighs. Her skin vibrated with heightened sensations, having come to full attention in anticipation of what was to come.

Emerging from the trees, she could finally see him there beside the burbling brook, the sight causing her to come to an abrupt halt to savor the magical scene. He didn't see her yet, his head bowed as he stepped into the stream to rub refreshing water over his sinewy bare torso, glistening in the sunlight like a gilded god. His unruly red hair shone like coiled copper. His green and brown tartan kilt billowed in the breeze, inviting a glance at what jewels hid within. She swallowed hard, doing her best to stay sane.

He looked up and saw her, bright blue eyes meeting emerald-green eyes as they drank each other in. Jamie Fraser's luscious lips parted in invitation, belying his besotted love for his one and only, his Innis Bree MacIntyre.

INNIS BREE JERKED awake with a snort. Embarrassed, she swiped a droplet of drool off her lip. Half a dozen other faculty members turned around to stare, two frowning, two snickering, and the other two only half awake themselves. They quickly turned back to their monotonous boss, the dean, who droned on in the front of the room.

Innis Bree's friend Kathryn, sitting one seat away at their round table, tossed a playful thumbs-up at the clumsy awakening. The chair between Kathryn and her sat empty, their buddy Rama having vacated his seat.

Straightening her spine, she inhaled deeply and pried her eyes open as wide as a frog's to try to pluck her brain out of its dreamy trance and plant itself back into reality. The enticing image of sexy Jamie Fraser – actor Sam Heughan, actually, on the TV series *Outlander* – sadly faded away. She dismissed a fleeting worry that maybe it was strange that she always dreamt about a fictional character rather than Walter Morton, her real-life fiancé who she'd be pledging her life to in one short week.

She looked around for Rama. Ah, there he was at the blessed coffee station at the back of the big room that was filled with tables occupied by the college's history department faculty members. Rama poured three cups of coffee, one undoubtedly for her, and headed to their table, somehow managing to juggle all three mugs of steaming brew, belying his days as a server at an

2

IHOP restaurant while in grad school. He waggled his bushy, black eyebrows at the women. Innis Bree couldn't help giggling. Without Kathryn and Rama, she'd be doomed. These interminable, twice-a-week, senseless meetings drove her to drink.

Coffee. Barrels of coffee.

"Here you go. Elixir of the gods," Rama whispered as he slipped into his seat. He handed her a mug, gave Kathryn one, and sipped from his own.

Innis Bree held the hot cup in both hands and raised it to her face to inhale the delight. "Thank you my wonderful, dear, thoughtful, angel, superhero friend. You have saved my life," she quietly cooed.

Kathryn leaned over with a hand up to the side of her mouth for imagined privacy. "I swear she's more long-winded today than usual. Yes, we know she's the boss. No, we don't need to hear about it over and over and over again." She rolled her eyes, shook her head, and returned to her coffee.

The "she" Kathryn spoke of was one Dr. Monica Smith, dean of the history department at North Carolina College, an unhappy woman who insisted on proving to her minions that she held reign over them. As if they didn't already know, what with the tongue-lashings most of them got on a regular basis. However, Dr. Smith did have a few faculty pets who groveled at her feet, suck-ups resented by the rest of them.

One of the perky pets bounded out of her seat when the dean motioned for her to take charge of the meeting, at this juncture a slide presentation about how to fill out required forms, something all except the latest hires had done a hundred times. The dean, surprisingly, slipped out a side door.

Innis Bree choked on her coffee a minute later when said dean tapped her on the shoulder, apparently having returned to the room through a back door.

"Come with me," the stern woman commanded.

Feeling like a kid being summoned by the principal, Innis Bree had no choice but to follow the waddling woman out the door and down the hall to her office, a room Innis Bree, like so many others, had been called to many times. Her boss pointed at the chair in front of the cumbersome wooden desk, so she plopped down. Again.

Dr. Smith waggled her ample fanny into her padded seat on the other side of the desk, placed her forearms on the wood, and clasped her hands. She reminded Innis Bree of the evil Ursula in the *Little Mermaid*. One long forefinger shot out to point at her target.

"Innis, we have a serious problem here."

Innis Bree opened her mouth to correct, for the dozenth time, the misuse of her name. The dean always said "In-ISS," even though she'd been told it was pronounced "IN-iss," the American version of the Scottish name, in honor of her dad's heritage. It was an inherited family name and the middle name, Bree, always went with it. That fit the bill for her North Carolinian mother, as the use of first and middle names was a common Southern American tradition. Innis Bree didn't get a chance to say anything, though, before her boss spat a question at her.

"Do you have a medical condition I need to know about? You fell asleep in our meeting today."

"Um … Hmmm …." She mulled that over. This might be a chance for an exquisite excuse. What might she have? There was a sleep disorder where people nodded off at all times of the day, but she couldn't remember what it was called. If she'd been diagnosed with it, she'd know. Medication – that might be it. Some prescriptions made people drowsy. What might she have that required pills? Allergies? PTSD? An STD? She entertained herself with the possibilities.

"So, no medical condition. Partying too late at night, perhaps?" Her tormenter took on an exaggerated tone of degradation. PhDs be hanged. This dean talked to most of her highly educated, highly skilled, highly experienced faculty as if they were miscreant four-years-olds.

Innis Bree swallowed, lifted her chin, and decided to forge ahead like the strong woman she was. Or hoped she was. Or maybe only fantasized about becoming. "Dr. Smith, I mean no disrespect, but most of us at the meeting have filled out those forms many, many times. We don't need further instruction about how to do it. I was bored. I nodded off." She thought it prudent to skip the part about dreaming that steamy Jamie Fraser was her lover. "That's all there is to it. No medical condition. Certainly no partying. Perhaps that training could be provided in a workshop for new faculty members, and the rest of us could use the time for lesson planning, grading, and replying to student questions."

The minute she shut up, she knew she'd made a grave error. The purpose of those meetings wasn't to train anybody. They were for everyone to understand that Dr. Smith owned them like slaves.

She watched as the woman's pseudo-calm exterior percolated into rage, a crimson anger creeping up Monica Smith's neck and exploding across her cheeks. The pupils of her beady eyes contracted to pinpoints. Her scalp shifted upward as her eyebrows shot up.

"Dr. MacIntyre, you're being impudent and disrespectful. What is your career goal here at North Carolina College? You don't seem to be keeping your future in mind."

Innis Bree knew that meant she was a peon who had to follow the ridiculous rules or be kicked out. She stared the woman down, thinking, *My career goal is to fulfill my dream of not working with you.* What came out of her mouth was, "My goal is to do my job without being harassed."

"Harassed? Harassed! How dare you accuse me of harassing you." Monica Smith bellowed and, with outstretched arm, pointed at the door. "You're fired!"

Innis Bree blinked. "What?"

"Now. Out. I don't ever want to see your insolent face again!" The dean seethed as she shot up out of her chair so quickly it banged against the bookcase behind her.

Bumfuzzled, Innis Bree stumbled out of her seat. "Wait. Wait. You can't fire me like this. I have a contract for next year. This semester isn't over for another week. You can't leave my students in the lurch like that for final exams. You can't fire me because I nodded off at one of your stupid, coma-inducing faculty meetings that you only hold to prove you're the boss of us."

Uh-oh. Now she'd done it. She raced out of the room and slammed the door shut just in time to let it shield her from a flying book aimed right at her. The tome could be heard crashing against the other side of the door and tumbling to the floor, accompanied by a howl from the pitcher.

Stunned, Innis Bree glared wild-eyed at the administrative assistant who sat at a desk next to the dean's door. The frail young woman, so kind-hearted no one knew how she withstood her boss's abuse, appeared to be stricken with fear.

"Hurry!" she insisted. "Go!" She stood up to place herself between the dean's door and Innis Bree, arms spread out like a school safety guard.

Innis Bree had no choice but to flee.

DELINA'S EXOTIC, kohl-lined, earthy brown eyes widened in confusion. "Wait. No. She can't fire you like that. Can she? What a bitch! You need to go over her skull and file a complaint."

"It's 'above her head,' dear." Rama gently corrected his wife, who didn't yet know all the nuances and phrases of the English language. They came from Malaysia, an arranged marriage that had thankfully worked out. He'd been in the States for seven years, she for three. He picked up her delicate hand and kissed the back of it.

"You two are such lovebirds." Kathryn sighed. Married for twenty years, with two teenaged boys, she occasionally commiserated about how her husband wasn't romantic anymore. "I'm jealous, you know. My husband hasn't kissed my hand in years. Oh wait. He never did." She tittered and sipped on her ginormous frozen margarita. They all knew she loved her man, having determined she wanted to marry him the first time she ever laid eyes on him in class while in college.

The four of them sat in their favorite bar, Paddy's Irish Pub, located close enough to campus that they could leave their cars in the faculty parking lot and walk over every Friday after work for happy hour. Delina had joined them after her shift as an office manager at the local hospital. The women all drank margaritas while Rama nursed a bottle of Bud.

Innis Bree sucked down the last of her drink and stared at the wide empty glass with its annoyingly cheerful yellow lemons and flowers painted on the sides. Without looking up, she moaned, "Maybe she 'can't' fire me, but she did." Her unsteady gaze returned to her friends. "I worked my fanny off to get this far. All those years of school. All that studying. All that research. I'm only thirty-two, and now I'll never find another job as a professor."

"Now, honey," Kathryn insisted, reaching over to pat her arm, "don't think like that. First of all, Delina is right. You need to go over the bitch's head – although I like skull better – and file a formal complaint. Never mind that it isn't proper protocol. Do it anyway."

"Yes. At this point, you have nothing to lose," Delina insisted.

Rama nodded. "Even though she won't give you a recommendation, there are a hundred other people who'll give you rave reviews. Professors. Deans. Administrators. You know that, don't you? Everybody loves you."

"In fact," Kathryn said, "I'm sure that's why Fuhrer Smith hates you. You're loved and she's hated. Except for those brownnosers."

"What's a brownnoser?" Delina asked.

"Oh. Um. Hmmm. How do you explain that?" Rama entreated his two American friends for help.

Undeterred by the nature of the topic, Kathryn explained in her usual straightforward manner. "Historically, the phrase began in the American armed services in the 1930s and meant to follow someone so closely as to stick your nose up their ass."

"Eee-www!" Delina's hand flew to her chest, and her nose crinkled. "That's gross."

"I know. But even though it has such a gross origin, it no longer has such a vulgar connotation. Probably because most people don't know its origin. Now it simply means somebody who does anything they can, to the point of being sickening, to please a superior like a teacher or boss or parent. The big word for it is sycophant."

Innis Bree and Rama exchanged a knowing glance, enjoying their friend's penchant for providing a lecture at any opportunity. Kathryn may as well tattoo her forehead, *I will teach anyone, anywhere, anytime.*

"Back to Innis Bree's dilemma," Rama interjected. "You haven't had a chance to tell Walter yet, have you? Where is he, by the way?" He looked at the door. "He's usually here by now."

It was true; her soon-to-be hubby always joined them for their Friday celebrations at the end of the workweek. But Walter was a no-show.

"I don't know where he is." She shrugged helplessly. "He isn't answering his phone."

"I'm so excited about your wedding," Delina chirped. "I love our maid-of-honor dresses."

"I'm excited about the wedding, too," Kathryn said, "our dresses aside. I'm even more excited that you two are going to Scotland for your honeymoon to look up your ancestors. That's as romantic as it gets for a historian."

"Yeah, it is." Innis Bree couldn't suppress a grin, the thought of the long-awaited trip momentarily superseding her devastation over being fired. "I can't wait to see my ancestors' hometown. Walter's, too. His is Inverness. He's as excited as I am." She brightened. "Surely, everything must be okay. Last-minute CPA stuff must have come up. His accounting business is booming, you know." Quickly dismissing her concern over his tardiness, she switched topics. "We're gonna get my ring in Scotland. That was his idea. He said that would make it more special. He's so romantic." She held out her left hand and jiggled her bare ring finger.

"That smile," Kathryn mused. "You're hoping for the most romantic time of your life in Scotland, aren't you?"

"Yup. A girl can hope, can't she?"

Nope. It turned out a girl could not hope, after all.

CHAPTER 2

*I*nnis Bree stepped off the train and onto the Pitlochry, Scotland, platform, wrestling with her roller bag, tote bag, and purse along the way. Few people disembarked – two teenagers, an elderly couple, and a man and his dog, all seeming to be locals.

Before the train had come to a full stop, passengers had huddled together at the door, and a fluffy dog nudged her leg. She'd asked if she could pet it.

In his charming Scots accent, its owner had said, "Aw, to be sure. He's about the friendliest laddie alive. This here is Winston. He's a Shetland Sheepdog, a Sheltie."

She adored the man's brogue, the way he pronounced about "aboot" and spoke with a lilt. She felt like Dorothy in *The Wizard of Oz*, certainly not in Kansas – or in her case North Carolina – anymore.

"Hello, Winston." Innis Bree had stroked his Sheltie's soft white ruff, which garnered a slobbery lick of her hand.

Now, as she stood on the platform and everyone else scurried away, only Winston turned to look at her. The man whistled and the canine whined, not wanting to leave his new friend all by herself. His human said, "Come on now, laddie," and Winston obediently, albeit reluctantly, obeyed.

The train left the station and disappeared down the tracks, the whirr of its engines fading away as it went. Innis Bree stood in silence, utterly alone.

"Great honeymoon," she groused to no one.

Feeling lost, she looked around, not surprised that her scheduled ride, some guy named Clyde, wasn't there. Everyone on earth had abandoned her.

The depot was a rather gloomy Victorian-era dark stone building with fancy trim and tall chimneys. A sign on the door read, "Back on an hour," probably for lunch she surmised. A footbridge spanned the double set of train tracks to a platform and a smaller, cheerier, blue-and-white building on the other side. It appeared to be closed, too.

She held her hands up to the depot window to peer into the empty waiting room. Despite the sign, she tried the doorknob, to no avail. Lush foliage surrounded the buildings and a bird chirped nearby, the only greeting to be heard. Or perhaps it had been a note of disdain at her being there.

A short side road led to the village of Pitlochry. She could see enough of the town, nestled as it was in the central highlands of Scotland, to see that it was a picturesque historic village.

And all of that was to have been shared with Walter. However, there was no Walter anymore. He'd failed to show up at their wedding, leaving her standing at the altar all gussied up in a big gown and big hair and big dreams without a groom.

So that was that. She didn't try to get him back. Who'd want a man who would do that to her?

She'd come on their "honeymoon" alone because there was no way she'd let her long-awaited maiden trip to Scotland be spoiled simply because she'd unceremoniously been dumped by the man she'd been ready to cleave her life to until one of them croaked, not to mention that she now wallowed amongst the unemployed. Money be damned, she'd decided. Most of the trip had been prepaid by Walter, anyway, and she wasn't about to let the jackass get a refund.

So she'd bravely come across the big pond by herself. Now, however, she felt anything but brave.

That randy Jamie Fraser hadn't materialized, either. She couldn't help lambasting herself with that thought, piling failed fantasy on top of real-life misery. No one, apparently, was going to show up to save her or so much as help her out.

"Well," she mumbled, squaring her shoulders in determination, "I'll have to do it myself."

She sighed, suddenly overcome with a heavy dose of imposter syndrome. Strong? Doing it all by herself? She could handle that in her work, despite Dean Smith's accusations. But standing here alone facing her crappy personal life? Alone on her honeymoon? Not so much. In fact, not at all.

She hefted her purse onto her shoulder, secured her tote bag onto the top of her roller bag, and hauled it all around to the other side of the building to check out the parking lot to see if her driver was there. Not one car sat in the few spots. She'd have to schlep down the lane to a shop or café or pub to inquire about hiring someone to drive her to Kenmore, her ancestors' ancient home-town thirty minutes away, her destination. Too remote for train service, a ride was necessary to reach the village on Loch Tay.

She'd made it halfway down the side road when a shiny red Citroën whipped by, gravel spewing as it careened to a stop in front of the depot. A man jumped out, left the door open, and jogged around the building to the platform. She'd been told that her driver Clyde was a large, balding, middle-aged gent who'd be wearing a kilt and driving a black sedan.

This dude certainly wasn't Clyde, not with his unkempt black hair, medium height, and scroungy jeans and tee shirt. He looked about her age, thirty-something. She stood at the side of the road, looking back at the station to watch him.

Angry. That was her first impression. He'd come to get someone who hadn't shown up. Touché. Join the club.

She started to trudge toward town again when it hit her. She turned around and hollered. "Hello! Are you looking for me?"

The man, now standing at the side of the depot, lit up a cigarette, which surprised her. What did he think this was – 1955? Nobody in their right mind smoked anymore.

"Nae," he yelled. "I'm looking for an American couple." His deep baritone voice with its clipped Scottishness intrigued her. Yup, angry. The compulsive drag on the cigarette said so, too.

He reminded her of one of those ne'er-do-well bad guys in an old movie. A young Sean Connery in *The Frightened City*. Or more recently, Colin Farrell in anything if he wore jeans and had tattoos on muscular biceps that peeked out from the short sleeves of his tee shirt.

"That's me." She waved – uselessly, she realized – and headed toward him. "I mean, I'm the only half of the 'couple' who's coming. You're here to take me to Kenmore?"

She reached him as he tromped over to stand by his car. He leaned onto the vehicle, cocked his head, and pointed at her with his little cindering stick. "So the other half o' your 'couple' buggered off, eh?"

She wasn't sure what that meant but figured she got the gist. "What makes you think that?" The defensiveness in her tone surprised her, but she couldn't let it go. "Maybe I told him to 'bugger off.'"

He squinted and took a long draw on his cigarette, smoke twirling its way up to veil his deep lake-blue eyes. "Huh. You stick with that story if you want to." He flicked the cigarette down and stomped it dead. "Come on, I'm your ride." He motioned for her to get in as he took her bag and plopped it into the trunk, "boot" as she knew it was called here.

Not happy to be sharing a ride with this surly dude, she had no choice. *If Walter was here ...* No, she reminded herself. Walter was not there and would never be there. She had to stop thinking about "what-if Walter." She got into what felt like the driver's door, seeing that in the British Isles the driver sat on the right and vehicles drove on the left side of the road. All backwards from home.

Her whole life had twisted backwards from what she'd expected.

The driver dude took off with such a roar she felt like an astronaut on take-off, her head flinging back onto the headrest. At the end of the lane, he turned onto the main street and, thankfully, slowed down. It took five minutes to reach the edge of town and turn onto a country road.

"I'm Innis Bree," she said by way of trying to start a conversation.

He didn't so much as glance at her. "I figured you weren't the Walter who made the reservation." He guffawed.

Oh lordy, she thought, he thinks he's funny. This was gonna be a lo-o-ong thirty-minute ride.

He didn't offer his name, so she gave in. "And ... you're not Clyde."

"Nae. That I am naw." He stepped on it to speed up.

She knew "nae" meant no and supposed "naw" meant not, given the context. He said "fer" instead of "for" and "yer" for "your." This would take some getting used to, but she liked it.

But she didn't like that he hadn't answered her question. Bobbling her head in agitation, she said, "So, you are ...?"

"Your substitute driver, only here because my blimey brother-in-law Clyde sprained his ankle an hour ago and my sister begged me to fetch you. She doesn't want Clyde's driving reputation to get a black mark."

Something about that Scottish accent got to her. The incongruity of being fascinated by the way this particular man talked confused her. It made no sense to be taken by the voice of such a grouch. She shook it off, asking, "You mean I'm supposed to give you a good review?"

"That's the idea. Think o' poor Clyde with a big cast on, pitifully stumbling all o'er the place."

He took a corner so fast it flung her into the door, and she flinched automatically when it seemed they turned onto the wrong side of the road. This left-side driving thing would take some getting used to. They straightened out, and she thought it best to calm down by taking in the lovely scenery.

They were in remote country now, with almost no traffic. Sprawling farmland fronted green highland mountains, the Grampian Mountains she'd read in her research of the area. She could see why her ancestors had been drawn to the Appalachian Mountains in America. This looked similar. In fact, geologists reported that eastern North American and western British, Scandinavian, and African mountains were once the same range, torn apart over millions of years, with the Atlantic Ocean forming in between.

Here pastures spread out amongst farmhouses, with sheep and "coos" grazing, exactly as she'd imagined rural Scotland. Some of the farmhouses were constructed of fieldstone, with the stone fences she'd always seen in pictures.

She pointed at a stand of highland cows, "coos" they were called, at a fence right by the road, ginger-colored cows with big horns and bangs that hung over their eyes. She'd read all about them and asked Not-Clyde to stop, but he wasn't having it.

"My sister Jenny will string me up alive if I dinnae deliver you safe and sound. Ne'er get too close to a coo unless you ken its personality. Those horns can be deadly."

"I want to meet your sister. She sounds like my kind of gal."

He huffed. Whether in jest or disgust, Innis Bree couldn't tell. "She's a pip, to be sure," he said, still leaving her in the dark. "She wouldna want you down by those coos, either. It's muddy along those fences. You'll ruin your new trainers. Why do Americans buy brand new white trainers for traveling, knowing they'll get ruined?" he scoffed.

If he hadn't pointed at her sneakers, she wouldn't have known what he was talking about. She hated to admit he was right. Her new white Nikes were already dirty and scuffed from airports, airplanes, and trains. They'd be trashed in no time. She'd packed light, so the jeans she wore, one of two pairs she'd brought, would take a beating, too.

She didn't answer him and glanced at his footwear. Muddy boots, so who was he to talk? She didn't point that out, though, deciding to salvage whatever shred of civility might be possible in this situation and quite proud of herself for it.

Ignoring the rude ruffian, she looked out the window to enjoy the view some more.

By the time they pulled up to the hotel on the main street of Kenmore, the silence between them may as well have been a coo sitting there. They both got out without saying a word. He plopped her bag onto the sidewalk and jumped into the car.

She hollered, "Goodbye, Not-Clyde."

He sped away.

"Well, that was interesting." She considered the dust that billowed in his wake.

"Hello, Innis Bree."

The sound of her name pronounced in Scottish soothed her soul as she turned around to find an elderly woman at her side. Here it was "EE-nish," and the "r" in Bree had an enchanting trill. A little sprite of a thing, the woman had glorious spiky white hair and wore a colorful flowy dress. Long, angular earrings hung from her dainty ears, and bracelets jangled as she gestured.

"I heard Laird would be bringing you in. Grumpy, isn't he? 'Crabbit', we call it." The woman chuckled and swished a hand in dismissal. "Pay him nae mind. He's been that way e'er since his wife left him last year for an actor in London."

"Ah. Crabbit describes him perfectly." Innis Bree smiled at the friendly woman. "You're Ailsa. I'm so glad to finally meet you." She held out her hand.

Ailsa wrapped her arm through Innis Bree's instead of shaking hands. "Me, too."

"I'd have known your voice anywhere. I've so enjoyed our phone conversations."

They'd talked twice since Innis Bree found the genealogist on the internet two weeks earlier. Ailsa McCauley's soft Scottish lilt was indelibly endearing. A widow, she lived with her invalid mother, and "ancestry quests," as she called her family history searches, were her passion.

Ailsa guided the foreign visitor to the center of the empty street and swept her arm out to emphasize the village and its loch, turning all the way around to take it all in. "How do you like this place where your ancestors lived and worked and worshipped and played and died?"

Innis Bree slowly circled, mesmerized as she took in the homeland of her forebears. "It's even better than I imagined, prettier than the pictures." Although grey-tinged clouds tumbled across the sky, occasional sprays of sunlight struck the earth, highlighting the scene before her. The gentle breeze felt cozy. The scent of fresh loch water and the abundant roses in window boxes filled the air. She felt entirely at ease, as if suddenly returning to her own hometown. Ah, it felt as if, she realized, her ancestors greeted her warmly.

18

The village had been built on a peninsula that jutted out into Loch Tay on two sides with River Tay on a third side, an idyllic setting. Loch Tay was a deep, fifteen-mile-long lake known for good fishing. A few small boats dotted the water in the distance.

She'd been studying up on the area for two months. Down the street and up a path she could see the church, a "kirk" as churches were commonly called here, with its tall Celtic stone cross out in front of the gate. According to the baptism records she'd found on *ancestry.com*, her ancestors had been baptized, confirmed, married, and mourned at death in that very building. One had even been chastised by the priest for calling his neighbor a witch.

Across the street from where she stood were a stone building, a road that led to the shore of the loch a block away, and a long white building for businesses, including a combination post office and general store. When she looked to her side, at the end of the main street sat a large stone arch announcing Bridgmoor Castle.

"The castle is privately owned," Ailsa said. "We're naw invited in. However, your room at the hotel is all ready for you." They turned around to take in the Kenmore Hotel, a two-story white building with black trim.

Innis Bree read the sign. "Kenmore Hotel, Scotland's oldest inn, established 1572. Wow. It's been here since the days of my ancestors and Shakespeare."

"He was ne'er here, but in the pub you'll find a connection to Robert Burns." Ailsa pointed at a door on the right side. "They have excellent food there, too. The hotel is here." She gestured to the door on the left. Innis Bree secured her purse on her shoulder, grabbed her bags, and followed Ailsa inside.

Quaint was the word that sprang to mind. Charming. Authentic. Historic. The interior of the hotel was all the things she'd imagined. Beautiful well-worn carpets. Antique furniture. A wide opening to the adjoining pub, the "parlor" she saw it was called.

A friendly clerk checked her in. Ailsa accompanied her to her room and said she'd come back mid-morning the next day. Even though it was only afternoon, traveling halfway around the world, contending with a grumpy driver, and adjusting to the feeling that her ancestors surrounded her had made this a mightily exhausting day. Within ten minutes she slept like a baby.

CHAPTER 3

"*I*nnis Bree. Och, me love, yer finally here! I've been waiting fer so long. Yer as bonnie as e'er. Come to me. Come to me, Innis Bree ..."

She bolted upright, awakened by a man's deep voice with a thick Scottish accent.

"Jamie?"

No, of course not. That was stupid. Jamie Fraser was busy with that brilliant and beautiful Claire, his wife on TV.

"Who in blazes was I dreaming about?" she groaned.

He'd said her name with such emotion, "Eee-nish Bree," with that long trill of the "r." Rubbing her temples in an attempt to clear her head, she couldn't get a fix on an image of the man. Only the Scottish voice and a vague picture of outstretched arms came to her. He'd been begging her to come into his embrace.

"What a silly dream," she concluded.

Wide awake now, she pulled down the white cotton sheet and comfy white comforter and got up to find her phone to check the time. The screen glared up at her: 3:30 a.m. She'd slept a full twelve hours, much needed rest after her journey. But after traveling so far, the change in time zones wreaked havoc on day and night. Her brain was still in North Carolina while her body was four thousand miles away. It was bedtime at home, but she'd already slept her fill.

At the open window that looked out onto the backyard, she stuck her head out to take in the view. Moonlight glistened on the river that wound its way to the loch. Crisp night air enlivened her, inviting her to leave the confines of her room. She hesitated. She'd never go out at three-thirty in the morning back home, even though she lived in a relatively safe place. Nothing, however, was entirely safe. What about here?

Caution be damned. Certainly it wouldn't hurt to simply step out into the fresh night air. She quickly cleaned up, threw on some clothes, and left her room. Downstairs, the reception desk sat empty, and the pub was closed. The inn seemed to belong to her and her alone, an eerie yet invigorating feeling. She wondered how many times her forebears had been in this very place, usually the men at the pub, no doubt. She went out the front door and only after it clicked shut behind her did she realize it had locked her out.

With no option now, she decided to explore the village. The full moon journeyed toward the horizon, providing a delicate swath of light casting mysterious shadows in the witching hour. A few buildings had on outdoor lights, and she had her phone should she need a flashlight.

Testing the limits of her bravery, she looked around, fear somehow enticing her to feel vibrantly alive. Drawn to the church, she walked up the street and paused at the tall Celtic cross that stood at the front of the property, which had appeared benevolent in the daylight but had become menacing in the night. Morbid curiosity forced her to pass by the cross and through the arbor that served as the gateway to the church. The church's unusual clock tower glared down at her with ... what? Welcome? Disdain?

Caution? She didn't move, not knowing what to do – try the church door or run. A wan ray of moonlight struck the graveyard alongside the church, solving her dilemma.

"Whoa. Too spooky." She turned on her heel and hightailed it back to the main street where lighting expelled the gloom. Feeling fortunate to have escaped the daunting church and its graveyard ghosts, she roamed around the few blocks that made up the business section of the village, ignoring the gate to the castle to which she, along with everyone else apparently, was not invited. She ambled down the street that took her to the nearby shore of the loch.

Moonlight ricocheted off the rippling water, creating a merry dance on the surface that made it easy to imagine a Loch Ness monster out there. A bench provided respite, so she sat down and studied the sky. Diaphanous clouds slid across the moon to mute its glow but slipped on by, and the orb shone down on her once again. A slight wind came and went. An owl hooted. Peacefulness swept through her. This felt like home, a romantic notion, she knew. She'd been so fascinated with her ancestors for so long, she felt like she'd lived right there amongst them.

After pondering her mysterious heritage, she realized dawn had begun, the start of a new day. She'd read how Scotland was so far north summer days were seventeen hours long and, therefore, nights were short. Dawn and dusk tended to linger with a gray, sluggish tinge called the gloaming, the term especially used at dusk. That tinge, however, dispelled the imaginings of scary things going bump in the night. Her sense of bravery rebounding in the growing light, Innis Bree became intrigued by what might lay down a dirt road over a knoll. Walking away from town yet making sure it was still visible should she need to run for safety, she rounded the small hill and stopped to survey the woods ahead.

A battered old truck drove up from behind and pulled alongside her, something that would have freaked her out at home. Here it seemed okay, especially when an old gent poked his head out the window.

"Miss, fit like are ya?" he asked. "Lost, maybe?"

"Oh, thank you for asking. I'm fine. I couldn't sleep and decided to take a walk."

"Och, yer at the hotel then?"

"Yes. I accidentally locked myself out, so I decided to take advantage of the chance to look around."

He stared for an eternity before responding. "An American, eh?"

"Yes."

He nodded as if that made sense to him, an American woman stupid enough to lock herself out and wander around in the dark of night. "Can I give ya a lift? Ya've wandered a wee bit far."

"No, thanks. I need the exercise after my long trip."

"Aye. I see. Well, dinnae stray fer too long." He pointed up at the sky. "A storm is brewing."

She looked up. There were a few non-threatening clouds, nothing to worry about. "Thanks for the warning."

He started to go but stomped on the brakes when he saw her glance down a two-lane dirt trail that veered off into the woods. He called out to her, "I dinnae think ya should go down there, lass. It's full o' brambles. Best be headed back." With that, he nodded and drove away.

She watched his truck jounce along the road until it disappeared. She'd picked up another new Scottish word, "dinnae." It apparently meant don't. He'd said, "I don't think you should go down there." That only served to make her all the more curious about was down there.

Up above, pale pink streaks erupted across the sky, the promise of the rising sun. On her left sat the trail through the woods she'd been warned against. Before she knew it, she'd taken the road less traveled and topped a hill that graced her with a spectacular view.

She gasped. "Holy moly, look at that!"

Dawn crested the horizon and broke through the scattered clouds to cast pink and lavender rays upon a mansion, dilapidated and forlorn, yet astounding in its very existence. Unable to resist, she worked her way through brambles and trees to reach the gravel drive in front of it. Magnificent or monstrous, it would be hard to say. Both, she decided. It was a rectangular, three-story, brick structure in the eighteenth-century Georgian style, what was called the colonial style in America.

Clearly, no one lived there. Half the roof had fallen in long ago, but the brick and stone walls on that roofless side remained, ivy-covered structures casting long shadows in the dawn of the day. A brick chimney seemed unfazed by the destruction around it, looming tall and proud. The large windows on that side held no glass. A side door no longer had a door, only a gaping hole.

However, from the main entrance on, the other side of the building remained in quite good shape with the mullioned windows intact, some with stained glass, and a slate roof that appeared to be whole and hearty. The chimney on that end of the house seemed sturdy.

Thunder burst overhead, its rumble rolling across the sky like a low-flying jet.

"Crap! Why didn't I listen to the old guy?" Without thinking, she scurried through the doorless side entry, found a door leading into the intact part of the house, and scrambled inside. Without a second to spare, she skooched into a corner by the front door in the main hallway as a torrent of rain erupted outside. Shivering, she wrapped her arms around herself and derided herself again for not listening to the wise, old, local chap who knew what he was talking about.

Glancing around, even in the dim light, she could see that this had once been a magnificent mansion. Unfortunately, she had no time for gawking. The downpour on the roof became deafening.

More thunder clapped. Blinding lightening flashed, causing her to shield her eyes from the window at her side. Somehow, however, she managed to hear a vehicle pull up and screech to a stop. Peeking out the window, through the rain she could see the blur of a truck. The old man? Or was it … someone else?

"It must be the old guy," she reassured herself.

A hunched figure got out, opened a wonky umbrella, and covered himself as he jogged up to the house.

"Wait," she whispered, worried now as she spied on the figure that moved too nimbly to be the elderly gent. Trepidatious at the appearance of a stranger out of nowhere in this remote place at this hour, she squatted down, trying to become invisible.

He disappeared from her sight as he went through the doorless doorway and the door into this part of the house. She could hear his long strides on the marble floors until he came upon her and stopped. He lowered his umbrella.

"You!" She hadn't meant to sound so petulant. But really, was this the only savior around? Apparently so. Not-Clyde – what had Ailsa called him? Larry? Leonard? – stood there frowning at her.

"Come on. Let's go," he growled. He put out a hand to pull her up. She didn't take it.

"I don't want to go with you," she snarled.

Dramatically spreading his arms out wide, the umbrella dripping a puddle on the marble floor, he said, "I'm all you've got."

She didn't move.

"Okay then. Suit yourself." He turned to go.

"Wait."

He turned and cocked his head, studying her as if he might abandon her anyway, an act to irritate her, no doubt. He held out his hand again. She ignored it and slid up the wall by herself. Nonplussed, he motioned for her to join him under the umbrella. When he wrapped his arm around her shoulder and drew her in tight, Innis Bree's knees went weak. The feel of him so close, even in this impossible situation, turned her whole body to mush. Her brain went AWOL. Why on earth would she react like this to such a grouch? She had no answer.

He walked her to the passenger door of his truck and opened it, hollering to be heard over the din. "Shove them o'er." He pushed her inside and slammed the door.

A lamb and a Sheltie stared her in the face.

"Baa-aa," the lamb complained in a high-pitched whine, not one bit happy about having been pushed over. The dog merely stared her down. The pungent smell of wet animals overtook the space.

He'd left the truck running and the American country song *Heart Like a Truck* played. Apt description of the man.

Not-Clyde-Larry-Leonard closed the umbrella outside his door, jumped in the truck, threw the tattered thing on the floor, and slammed his door shut. He got mighty wet in the process.

"There are a sheep and a dog in your truck." She couldn't help being amused by the absurdity of all this.

The lamb bleated loudly in disapproval. The dog hadn't made up its mind yet, looking her over with almond-shaped brown eyes. It was an old truck, so old it didn't have a console in the middle, leaving the front seat open all the way across, like a backseat. The four of them were crammed in like sardines.

"The lamb is Olive. This here is Maisie. They'll get used to you."

With an aggravated punch of a button on the dashboard, he turned off the music. Maisie nuzzled him. Innis Bree was surprised by the grump's affectionate fluffing of the dog's ruff before taking off.

They went down a gravel drive that was wider than the dirt one she'd walked in on. She could see that she'd taken a side road, like an old service entrance.

Carefully petting the lamb's head to try to get into its good graces, Innis Bree asked how he'd known she was at that house.

He shook his head in disapproval, his wet black hair falling in waves around his face. A rivulet of rain dripped down his fore-head, and she watched as he brushed it away, reluctantly admitting to herself that he was handsome. Maybe not a Jamie Fraser knock-out stud but close.

"Maisie and I went out looking for Olive and saw you walk out o' the trees and into the house. Snoopy thing, eh?"

That voice again – it got to her, drilling right down to her core. *Hang on, girl. Get a grip,* she admonished herself. What he actually said might have been offensive, but even with his hand over his mouth he couldn't hide the smirk that created an inviting line down each stubbled cheek.

"I, well, I woke up in the middle of the night," she said, doing her best to act like a normal human being who wasn't obsessed with everything this man said and did. "I stepped outside, acciden-tally locked myself out of the hotel, and decided I might as well go exploring."

Maisie jostled Olive for territory, shoving the lamb out of the way so she could lay her head on Innis Bree's lap. Big puppy eyes looked up in longing. Innis Bree couldn't help but obey and pet the girl. The canine's tongue flopped out as she slobbered on Innis Bree's jeans in delirious delight.

"See? I told you she'd get used to you." Her reluctant rescuer drove with one hand and held Olive with the other. "This wee lamb went wandering in the night, too," he explained. "She wasn't there when I opened their pen this morning. I'm a sheep farmer, in case you haven't guessed."

"Ah, I see." She'd wondered what that faint aroma had been when he'd picked her up at the train station. Now she knew. It was sheep farmer smell. Wool and all that. His allure waned. She wondered if Jamie Fraser had smelled bad, too, when Claire first met him. "Thank you for picking me up at the train station in your red car. This is a bit crowded," she teased.

"Naw my car. 'Tis my sister's. My brother-in-law Clyde, as you ken – as you 'know,'" he corrected himself for her sake, "was in a wee fender-bender. Naw his fault, mind you. That's when he sprained his ankle. Jenny didna want me picking you up in this 'rattle-trap,' as she calls it."

"I see." She struggled to keep the conversation going. "You like American country music, huh? So do I."

He huffed. "Dinnae worry. I like bagpipes, too."

So much for an amicable discussion about music. "Hey, who owns that mansion?" She jabbed a finger behind them.

"You're about to find out, from what I hear. I'll let Ailsa tell you all about it."

He pulled up in front of the hotel and looked at her so intently her body became acutely aware of his masculinity. Mush, again. Slow down, she told herself. Just because she was alone and lonely – and yes, horny – didn't mean she had to fall for the first human being with testosterone who came along, especially such a testy one. And who smelled like a sheep farmer. And who didn't even like her.

She'd hated him only minutes ago, but suddenly his sex appeal trumped his cantankerousness. If he grabbed her for kiss right now, she'd ...

"I need to apologize," he stated flatly without a hint of romantic attraction. "I was rude when I picked you up at the station. I'm sorry. 'Tis a busy time at the farm, lambing season ending, and I was annoyed as hell at my sister for guilting me into leaving. It wasna about you."

"Yeah. Sure. They always say that. No, just kidding. It's fine." It hadn't been at the time, but now with his manliness overshadowing any cogent thought, it was indeed fine.

He reached for the umbrella, as rain still pelted down, and held it out to her. "Here. Take the brellie."

She took it but didn't open the door. "Thanks. For everything. What's your name again? You never told me."

"Did I naw?" That grin again made her stare. He didn't seem to notice or, worse yet, care. "I'm sure you'll hear enough about me from Ailsa and the gossips in town. Now go. And stay out o' strangers' mansions from now on."

She threw him what she hoped was a flirtatious glance, although she wasn't sure what that might be. Olive baaed in return. Maisy barked. Innis Bree hopped out and hurried inside where she went to the window and watched Not-Clyde-Larry-Leonard's truck fade away in the rain.

"Damn. I wish I could remember his name."

"LAIRD BARTHOLOMEW BLYTH," Ailsa told her when Innis Bree asked the name of the brash man who'd now given her two rides. The genealogist took the last bite of her scone and sipped her tea. "It's an old family name," she explained as she wiped her fingers on her napkin. "He's the fifth Laird Blyth in his family tree. You say he gave you a ride again this morning?"

They sat at a table on the back deck of the hotel, a fine summer morning gracing them with pleasantness after the storm. The earth smelled fresh and renewed; iridescent hues of blue painted the sky; the river calmly ambled by. The absence of wind made it possible to work with Ailsa's research papers without them flying off.

"Yeah," Innis Bree said, answering Ailsa's question. "I fell asleep as soon as you left yesterday and woke up in the middle of the night. I came outside and wandered around, and by daybreak I was at that dilapidated mansion out there." She pointed in the direction of the mysterious house.

"Oh my. Laird found you out there?"

"Yes. He'd been looking for a lost lamb. Who owns that place?"

Ailsa's face lit up, amused. "He does, love." She chuckled. "You trespassed on Laird Blyth's property. I'm surprised you're still in one piece." She waved a hand in dismissal, chuckling. "Och. He's naw that bad. In fact, most folks around here admire him for the way he's worked so hard to buy that land. You see, it once belonged to his family, was stolen away during the Highland Clearances, and he wanted it back to save it from the 'green laird' who's bought the castle and its land."

"What's a green laird?"

Ailsa shook her head. "A green laird is a blessing to some and a curse to many. Mostly they're foreign investors who buy up highland land to 'save' it from what they consider to be environmental change. You see, for a couple hundred years, a lot o' highland castles and mansions have been owned by generations o' wealthy Scottish and English families who used them only for sport, like grouse hunting, for example. To attract the grouse, they'd burn heather and destroy forests, that kind of thing. These rich landowning families, however, have run out o' money and are selling. In come the environmentalists."

"That sounds like a good thing."

"Nae. As you say, it sounds good, but there's more to the story. The hunting grounds needed caretakers. The homes, only lived in occasionally for sport, needed caretakers. Workers were needed when owners were in residence. Local people had jobs. Without that, the jobs are gone. It chaps our arses that outsiders have come in and decided what to do with Scottish land and, in the process, have taken away jobs."

"Is hunting like that still popular? It seems like an old-fashioned thing."

"You'd be surprised. But, aye, for the most part, it's going by the wayside. The locals know that. They simply want what's best, not only for the land but for our people, as well. They believe compromises can be made."

"Like what?"

"The best o' all worlds would be if we could return more to farmland. Coos, sheep, crops. That's why folk around here admire Laird Blyth for what he's doing. He's been successful at it, but that's not a sustainable living for everyone. Another alternative is a golf course. There are heated arguments about that, as the land would be greatly manipulated. It would also, however, be well tended and would provide jobs for locals. There would be golf course jobs and increased visitors to the community. To me, that seems like the best compromise. Foreign green lairds tend to buy the land and close it up for their private use. End of story."

"Is the owner of Bridgmoor Castle a green laird?"

"Hardly. His bum's oot the windae, as we say, because he talks such rubbish. He claimed to be one when he bought the place, but he's no more a green laird than I'm a white virgin. Something weird goes on in that castle. I can feel it. So can other folk. But enough o' that. That's not why we're here. I have an amazing story to tell you about this area and your family in it, so sit tight. I'll start at the beginning. You're in for quite a ride."

Innis Bree polished off her croissant and tea as she listened. She was growing quite attached to this energetic woman whose brilliance she admired and whose style she adored. She wondered if Ailsa had always been this vibrant or if that was something she'd acquired with maturity. She guessed the older woman to be in her seventies but wasn't about to ask. Today, Ailsa wore slim jeans, a ruffly white blouse, dangly earrings, and her bracelets. Her spiky white hair was tied off her face with a colorful bandana. Innis Bree wanted to emulate that style, acutely aware of having become quite the mouse during her years in academia. With her jeans, plain blue top, simple stud earrings, and hair pulled up in a ponytail, she felt like Plain Jane. Walter had liked her that way. Last time she looked, however, Walter was nowhere in sight. She wasn't sure why she'd ever let that man dominate how she looked and wasn't about to ever let it happen again.

To add to her feeling of freedom, she couldn't believe she was finally here in Kenmore, learning about her heritage. Her desolate self-pity had ebbed and flowed with each passing hour since arriving, her initial devastation over being dumped not forgotten but slipping into stretches of not feeling life-shattering. Even being unemployed sometimes seemed less harrowing.

Her ancestors had survived life's travails. She would, too. Right?

Ailsa had been digging into the MacIntyre family ever since Innis Bree found her online. Innis Bree had been doing family research for years, culling out whatever she could find online. She hadn't found many details, though. Some things, Ailsa informed her, could only be found in the original historical records.

"Not everything is online," Ailsa explained, "like some people believe. The kirks – churches – usually kept good records, but for small villages like this, they haven't been put online. None o' this ..." she pointed at her stack of papers "... is online. Besides, you need to go to the places where your ancestors lived to feel their souls. That's why it's so wonderful you're here."

Innis Bree sometimes felt those old souls. Were the essences of her forebears' souls a part of her? Was there such a thing as ancestor memory? Was it in her DNA? That left her wondering if the enmity and attraction, the push and pull she felt for one Laird Blyth, a sheep farmer who had absolutely nothing to do with her life, was inherited. She dismissed the frivolous thought. How could it be?

"Let's take it in order, so it'll all be easier to understand. The first documents we have are from the 1600s," Ailsa said. "A copy o' kirk baptisms." She slid over a sheet of paper with old-time cursive handwriting Innis Bree had to struggle to read, it was so dull and loopy and fancy.

It took a minute for her to attempt to read aloud. "It says Gill...i...'"

"Gillimichell." Ailsa helped her along.

"Ah. Okay. 'Gillimichell McIntire, baptized, May 20, 1670.' Wow. That's a long, long time ago."

"Aye. Now, can you make out his parents' names? They're right there." She pointed to a spot on the paper.

Innis Bree hunched over the document, consumed with fascination that she looked at a record of her forebears from three hundred and fifty-three years ago. "John Philip MacIntyre, born 1640, and Margaret ... I can't read her last name ... born 1650."

"Keep in mind as we go through these documents that sometimes your family name is spelled M-c-I-n-t-i-r-e. That's very common in these records. In fact, you can find the same person's name spelled a variety o' ways. Spelling wasn't unified or e'en considered all that important until later. I cannae, I can't, make sense o' Margaret's maiden name either. It looks like N-c-v-y-l-l-e-n. 'Tis probably M-c or M-a-c something, but I cannae make it out."

"Aw, poor Margaret. She's lost to history."

"Naw entirely. You're here, and you're her offspring, way down the line. Margaret lives on in you."

"That's an amazing thought."

"Indeed, 'tis. Now, I have been able to verify your connection to these very MacIntyres. Not only through records. Your DNA that you submitted to *ancestry.com* shows us that you have ties to this very family, to others who can verify their ancestors came from this very village. So, naw only does your paper trail bring us right here to Kenmore, science does, too."

"It's incredible that this can all be figured out."

"Aye. Now, here's something interesting about John, your nine-times great-grandfather. When he was only ten years old, he was listed on the muster roll for the Battle o' Dunbar in 1650." She slid over a document labeled *Muster Roll*.

"1650. That's amazing."

"Here's the proof. See his name right there?" Ailsa pointed it out. "It was a fight between the Scots and the British for control o' Scotland. It pre-dated the time o' the Jacobites, who you've probably heard about. The Jacobites became organized in about 1707 and fought for many years for independence. In the end, they lost at Culloden in 1746. But the fight for freedom had been going on long before that, as we see here, like in the Battle of Dunbar."

"I do know about the Jacobites. I'd like to say I learned about them in history class, but the truth is it's been television shows and movies. My doctorate degree is in American history, so I'm afraid I'm woefully uneducated about most of this."

"The Scots lost the Battle of Dunbar – badly. It's lucky your ancestor John made it home. Most Scots dinnae. I thought it must be a mistake that John was listed because he was so young, so I did some digging and found that young male relatives o' warriors often went with them. Interestingly, no other MacIntyre is listed, no matter how 'tis spelled. So, John might have been with an uncle or something. Whether the young ones fought, I dinnae ken. I doubt it. Men probably took their laddies to help with camping and care o' weaponry and horses, and to teach them the ways o' war, like an apprentice. Mostly, they were passing on the fervent belief that Scotland should remain fore'er free."

"So, I have an ancestor who was a boy watching Scottish patriots fight for independence and teaching him to do the same."

"Aye. Alas, that's as far back as I could find. But that battle isna the only thing that's so interesting. Read this." Ailsa slid an open booklet across the table. "This is also from the kirk. 'Tis what I told you about on the phone."

Innis Bree scanned the page, then read. "The Session is shown in its judicial role when Eslpeth McGorrie complained of being accused of witchcraft by John MacIntyre. Both rebuked." She blinked. "Whew. There it is right there. Old John believed in witchcraft."

"That was common around here, e'en well into the 1700s. And it turns out that your John, who was the village blacksmith, was the first to witness a strange event when the waters o' Loch Tayside, as it was called then, retreated fifty yards from the shore. It's been documented that many thought the devil did it, with assistance from a witch. John must have believed that, too. The water eventually returned, and no one has ever known why it receded. It's called 'the troubling o' the waters.'"

"How weird."

"It gets weirder and e'en more fascinating, which brings us to how your branch o' the family ended up in America. We know that John and Margaret's son, Gillimichell, your eight-times great-grandfather, who was born here, died in the Virginia colony in 1720 at age fifty. Are you ready?" Ailsa threw her an impish grin.

A young server with rainbow-streaked hair appeared and asked if they wanted more tea. Both said yes.

"I like your hair." Innis Bree was accustomed to colorfully dyed hair. Her students often surprised her with their creativity in that regard.

The teen brightened. "Thanks. Me mam hates it." She took the empty pot that sat on their table and left to fetch a fresh, hot pot.

"Ma'am?" asked Innis Bree.

"Nae, dear. Our 'mam' is m-a-m. It's 'mum' to the English, 'mom' to Americans, and I don't know what else around the world. It's 'mother.'"

"Ah, okay, I get it. Where I'm from, that's very formal, used as a sign of respect for any woman, usually older."

"Well, it better be a sign of respect here, too, if we're talking about mothers. Okay, so, here goes – the MacIntyre family tree," Ailsa said.

She proceeded to dazzle Innis Bree with her knowledge. The long-ago connections amongst local families were indeed surprising, with the area's clan chief, one Clovis Campbell, thrown in for good measure.

Two hours and another pot of tea later, the two women were ready for a stroll to the kirk graveyard to peruse family headstones. Ailsa had more information to share, but a person could only absorb so much heady stuff before the brain started to rebel. Physical activity was called for in time. Innis Bree certainly knew that from teaching college students.

Little did Innis Bree expect that a walk in a place of the dead would enliven her life with a confounding surprise.

CHAPTER 4

A car drove by, stopped, and backed up, drawing their attention away from the MacIntyre headstones they'd been examining. The silver Mercedes convertible parked in front of the church, and a tall blond man in spiffy pressed pants, a crisp salmon-colored polo shirt, and leather loafers, sans socks, hopped out. Innis Bree threw Ailsa a questioning glance when he waved at them and headed in their direction.

"Excuse me, ladies. May I have a word?" He walked up to them with a flashy smile, his teeth so white they could compete with newly driven snow. "Hello, Ailsa. Good to see you again." He extended his hand and Ailsa accepted, albeit not too enthusiastically.

"Hi, Rory," she muttered.

"And you're the American I keep hearing about." He moved on to Innis Bree and stuck out his hand. "I'm Rory Skeffington, also an American. I hear you're a history professor in the South."

She placed her hand in his and looked up – way up – and thought she'd never seen a more perfectly sculpted face. Money, no doubt, helped with that. Big bucks aside, the results were stunning. Thick, nattily cut hair. Symmetrically square jaw. Shaven skin so smooth it could be a baby's bottom. Eyes the aqua color of the Caribbean Sea near an island shore.

"Yes, that's right. I'm Innis Bree," she managed. "Although, I've only been here a day, so I don't know why you're hearing about me."

He held her hand tight, no sign of letting go. She slid her hand out of his.

He let loose with a hearty laugh. "The gas station has a clerk whose husband saw you on the road by the loch at daybreak. Said you were taking a walk after locking yourself out of the hotel. Everyone in the place had a good chuckle over that."

His American accent said east coast but not thick New York City or New Jersey. It was more neutral, the "standard American English" often taught to newscasters to eliminate twangs and nuances.

"Ah, the nice older gentleman who offered me a ride," Innis Bree said, her own gentle Southern accent obvious to her after being aware of his speech. "I'm glad I provided entertainment." The thought of the local folks laughing at her somehow seemed fun rather than insulting.

He looked at his Rolex. "I'm hoping you ladies haven't had lunch and can join me at my place. I was on my way to partake. My cook is a miracle worker and won't have any trouble with company. It'll be my way of welcoming another American to the village."

The women exchanged glances, transferring a mutual unspoken message. The historian in each of them wanted to see the inside of that castle, and this might be their only chance.

"That's fine with me." Ailsa spoke up first. "Innis Bree?"

"Sure."

"Wonderful," he said. "Does right now work? It is lunchtime."

The women checked with each other again and nodded.

"Right this way then." With a grand gesture, he motioned for them to join him in his car. Innis Bree jumped in the back, and Ailsa took the front passenger seat. Before leaving, Rory pushed a button on his dash, a phone rang through, and a woman with an American accent answered. "Belinda, I'm bringing two guests for lunch. We'll be there in five."

He took off, and with the castle gate being a mere two blocks away, it only took half a minute before he hit a clicker on his visor to open it. They drove up a curvy driveway as the gate automatically closed behind them. Over a slight hill and suddenly they were presented with an enormous castle.

"It's beautiful, isn't it?" Rory boasted as he drove.

"Aye, a perfect example o' the neo-Gothic style o' the 1700s," Ailsa noted. "I've researched it many times, having lived here all my life. I've only been inside once, thirty years ago when they had tours."

Innis Bree wasn't familiar with neo-Gothic style but figured the square center with a round tower on each corner, plus a wing extending out on each side must be it. She did know that although the gray stone walls and towers looked ancient, the abundance of windows gave away the fact that the structure was no more than three hundred years old. Older castles were more fortified, with few windows and small ones at that, making it harder to be penetrated during battle.

Innis Bree's first impression was mixed. It certainly was grand. But she couldn't picture actually living in the thing.

"Bridgmoor Castle was built in the 18th century by a succession o' Campbells, who built on what was once an older castle, built by their ancestors in the 1550s," Ailsa explained as Rory pulled up in front. "The only original part o' the building is the cellars underneath it all."

"Yes," Rory said. "There are a few original pieces of furniture and artifacts, especially in the entry, but most of that stuff was sold long ago from what I understand, when these Campbells went broke. I know the place is huge, but I promise there's a very comfortable main living area. You'll see."

He parked and hopped out. A valet appeared and opened the women's doors, offering each a hand in turn to help them out.

"Why, you're Jeffrey Swain, Millicent's son," Ailsa said to the valet. "In the military for several years and come back last year. It's good to see you again."

Jeffrey seemed uncomfortable, his jaw clenched as he replied, "Aye, Mrs. McCauley."

Innis Bree wondered if he was unhappy working there. She certainly understood what that was like.

"Jeffrey, I'll need the car again in an hour," Rory said. "No need to move it. The ladies and I are having lunch."

Jeffrey nodded without comment and scurried ahead to go up the steps and open the elegant front door.

Rory and Ailsa started up the steps. Innis Bree paused to take in the spectacular view. "How much land is there?" she asked.

"A thousand acres," Rory answered. "It had been many thousands at one time."

"It's beautiful!"

The Grampian Mountains rose in the distance. The River Tay and another river joined together not far away. Splotches of heather and gorse dotted the land that meandered into the manicured lawn. She turned and in the other direction could see Loch Tay, no more than a mile away. It was a spectacular setting. Imagining what life had been like on this very spot more than three hundred years ago when her ancestors lived in the village boggled her mind. More so, five hundred years ago when the original castle was built. For all she knew, her ancestors had been here then, too.

Forcing her mind to burrow its way back to reality, she joined Ailsa as they stepped over the threshold. They thanked Jeffrey, who held the door open for them. He nodded again, apparently his preferred form of communication. Not much for words, that Jeffrey.

They entered an enormous foyer, and the sensation of having stepped back in time washed over Innis Bree. The room had a curved grand staircase that led to a second-story walkway with heavy, golden oak doors that secreted several rooms. The banister, balustrade, and balusters were also oak. The ivory-colored plastered walls in the foyer and up the staircase were covered in colorful clan flags, ornate crisscrossed swords, and dark portraits of staid figures dressed in stiff, fancy attire.

A lush red and gold Persian carpet covered the flagstone floor. Innis Bree shuffled her feet on the carpet. It felt so thick, she surmised it was new, although period appropriate. The room itself and everything on the walls appeared to be original to the Campbell era.

Innis Bree never knew quite what to feel in a historical room like this. She didn't know if she should be fascinated that the past surrounded her or a bit moribund that all the people in those pictures were dead and buried.

Rory pointed to a portrait of a heavy-set man in a kilt and wrap in forest green and light blue tartan plaid. A large sporran – she thought that was what the purse-like thing hanging at the dead man's waist was called – bore a large, silver metal clasp and a shock of fur. "That's the last Campbell to be influential in the area. He inherited the estate and the power of clan leader but died childless. So, having no heir, the place fell into the hands of an array of family members, and the power of the Campbells waned until the estate had to be sold in the 1990s."

Innis Bree and Ailsa stood there speechless, steeped in the past.

"I brought you in the front entry so you could get a feel for the place," Rory said. "We'll move into my informal dining room for

43

lunch. Afterward, I have to leave for a meeting, but Jeffrey can give you a tour if you'd like."

"I'd like," Ailsa said as she circled around to take it all in.

"Me, too." No way was Innis Bree going to let herself be left out.

"We can take a quick glance at one room I think you'll enjoy before we carry on." He opened the carved double doors that were straight ahead from the foyer. "The formal parlor."

Heavy, bold blues and greens overpowered the room from Innis Bree's point of view, but again, it was appropriate for the 1700s. Brocades, velvets, and silks upholstered the furniture and curtained the windows. Tufted divans, chairs, and an ottoman filled the space. A harpsicord sat near the massive fireplace. Tapestries pictured hunting scenes. However, everything looked new, and the room didn't have the scent of aging. Indeed, it smelled like heather.

"You've redone the room according to its original state," Ailsa noted astutely.

"Yes. Part of the fun of owning a castle is keeping the over-the-top décor, don't you think?" Quite proud of himself for his prize, Rory chuckled with delight. He backed out of the room and turned toward a long, dark hallway with an arched coffered ceiling, more portraits on the walls, and another flagstone floor covered in a Persian rug. "This way, ladies." He led them down the hall, chattering about how his business was headquartered in New York and he only had a chance to visit the castle for three or four days every couple of months. His primary residence was a brownstone in Manhattan. He had an estate on Long Island, too, on the shore. "And, of course, there's my cottage complex in the Caymans."

"O' course," Ailsa quipped.

Innis Bree had no idea what a person did to have that much money. Whatever it was, she didn't know how to do it.

He pointed things out as they went, including a ladies' loo.

"We'll pop in here and freshen up before we eat," Ailsa insisted, taking Innis Bree's arm and pulling her toward the bathroom.

"Certainly," Rory said. "Lunch will be right in here. Join me there." He pointed to a door at the end of the hall and headed in that direction.

Ailsa hustled Innis Bree into what turned out to be a large public bathroom.

"Hey, what's this?" Innis Bree asked as she marveled at the tiled, marbled, and mirrored room with half a dozen stalls and a bank of sinks, all fitting with the era of the castle.

"From the 1920s to the '50s, the owners conducted tours. They had to install public loos. But that isna why I brought you in here. I want to warn you about Rory. He's the phony green laird I told you about, a billionaire who's used to getting his way. Worst o' all, he's a heart-snatcher. And a body-snatcher. He's tried to bed every pretty female that moves around here. Succeeded with a few, from what I hear. And those visits he makes every month or so? Usually, he brings a different chickadee with him every time. They never leave the castle. Folks worry he's doing something nefarious in here with them. I'm telling you, be careful."

"Oh, Ailsa. He doesn't care about me. He invited us because I'm a history professor. He wants to talk history."

"Huh! Nae. You aren't really that naïve, are you? I've known him for the year he's owned this place. He knows I'm a historian, and he's ne'er invited me to lunch before. And I told everyone at our last town meeting that a history professor was coming. He was there and coulda arranged lunch with me then. But nae. He had zero interest until he saw you in the graveyard."

Innis Bree didn't know if she should be flattered or frightened. "Thanks for the warning. I'll be fine." She sloughed it off. Surely, this billionaire wasn't interested in little ol' her.

"Well, you've had that heartbreak and might be vulnerable. Dinnae fall for his balderdash bullshite."

Certainly Ailsa must be overreacting. Besides, Innis Bree didn't like the insinuation that she might be dumb and blind after being jilted. She knew Ailsa meant no harm, but this piece of advice could be dismissed. Dismiss it, she did.

Rory turned out to be a charming host, even winning over Ailsa, it seemed. He told rollicking stories about growing up in New York City and some of his faux pas when adjusting to Scottish life. He asked questions of both women about their work.

Ailsa became animated as she explained the genealogical work she often did with Americans who had ties to the highlands. Innis Bree noticed that her Scottish lilt became less prominent when with two Americans. Accustomed to American English, Ailsa adjusted well to it, incorrect as it may seem to her.

When Rory turned his attention to Innis Bree about her work as a history professor, she admitted she'd recently been fired. He immediately took up her defense.

"No!" He clapped the table. "How unfair. Well, surely you won't have any trouble finding another job, a better one, in fact."

If charm could drip, his was a waterfall.

Innis Bree liked him. A lot.

When it was time for him to leave for his appointment, he took her aside. "How would you like to play princess for an evening and have dinner with me here at the castle tomorrow night?"

She accepted. After all, what woman in her right mind would refuse a man who looked like Prince Charming, lived like a king, and owned an honest-to-God castle in Scotland?

If only Walter could see me now, she thought.

"KATHRYN, you won't believe this. I have a date tomorrow night with a billionaire who owns a castle! Do you believe it?"

Silence sailed across the Atlantic Ocean.

"Kathryn, are you still there?" Innis Bree checked out her phone to make sure they were still connected.

She sat curled up in the chair in her room, the afternoon sun providing a golden glow through the window. She'd called knowing that with the five-hour time difference, her friend would be at the college but didn't have a mid-morning class to teach.

"Um, yeah," Kathryn finally said. "Is he, you know, Dracula or a vampire or anything?"

Innis Bree laughed and told the story of meeting Rory Skeffington.

"Wasn't that an old movie with Bette Davis and Claude Rains? *Mr. Skeffington.* She played a horrible character."

"Well, this guy is not a horrible character. He's a dream. I wish Walter could see me with him." She didn't elaborate to reveal the daydream she'd already had of becoming engaged to one of the wealthiest men in the country, showing him off around her hometown, and running into Walter and his new girlfriend, whoever the bitch might be. Adding to the glorious satisfaction of her fictitious confrontation, Walter, being a good half foot shorter, would have to look way up into Rory's perfectly molded face. Rory's bright, shiny teeth would beam down at the littler man as if he were a mere peon in the presence of a mighty king.

Dismissing the rich guy, Kathryn wanted to know what Innis Bree learned about her heritage. The history professor was far more interested in the lives of dead people than in the life of a living rich dude.

"By lunchtime, I'd learned so much." Innis Bree explained what she'd discovered that morning. "Then, when we came back from lunch, the most amazing thing happened! Ailsa showed me a document from 1700. It was my name, Innis Bree MacIntyre, right there, over three hundred years ago. But here's the most interesting part. It was a church record that said a Duncan Campbell –

that family ruled the clan – this Duncan accused Innis Bree of being a witch!"

"What? That's amazing! What happened to her?"

"We have no idea. We're gonna work in the church cellar tomorrow, looking up more old records to see what we can find. What we don't know is how that Innis Bree's name from way back got passed down to me. I know my great-grandmother and her great-grandmother had that name. But why? Was the original woman something special? At one time, did family members think she was a witch? We don't know."

Kathryn made Innis Bree promise to call her as soon as they found out more. They chatted for a while longer, with Kathryn doling out a word of caution about the rich guy, echoing Ailsa. Innis Bree extended her well wishes for Kathryn to pass along to Rama and Delina, and they ended their call with their usual affirmation of friendship. "Goodbye, my forever friend," each said to the other.

Innis Bree punched off the call and went to her bedroom window. The river behind the hotel, the River Tay, she'd learned, glistened in the afternoon light, reflecting her thoughts back to her. They were right, both Ailsa and Kathryn. She knew it and yet had no desire to rein in her frivolous delight. She'd thought she was done with Walter, having cast the deceiver out of her mind like tossing out dirty bath water. Suddenly he was front and center again as she plotted sweet revenge.

That was stupid. It did make her vulnerable. But she didn't care.

The notion that she should care, especially since she'd been so attracted to that Laird Blyth, too, niggled at her mind. Sheep farmer to billionaire. After being so brutally rejected and hurt by her faithless fiancé, not to mention having her entire future obliterated, she supposed she was salving her wounds by taking on every man her age who deigned to cross her path. Seemed like she wanted to take them all on.

She flung herself onto the bed. "Come get me, one and all."

With that, she fell into a deep slumber, dreams of castles and mansions and sheep and Shelties and ... what was it?

Yet another man?

CHAPTER 5

"*Innis Bree*," he whispered, his husky voice laden with wantonness.

She sat up, mesmerized by the sound of the Scottish calling in the same rugged voice she'd heard the night before.

"Me love, come. I've waited so long."

The scent of him was intoxicating, outdoorsy and sexy – heather and woods and animals and manliness. His brawny arm, its Celtic tattoos visible with his shirtsleeves rolled up, stretched out to her, his massive hand there for the taking.

She lifted her hand but couldn't reach him. He stepped out of the darkness, and she gasped.

He was beautiful in the most masculine way possible. Rugged and alluring, red-and-black tartan plaid enwrapping his muscular frame, his body – his very soul – wanted her. She could smell his need for her. She could feel it in her bones. She could sense it in her heart.

And she wanted him, this stranger who had invaded her sleep. The tempting look in his deep lake-blue eyes bid her cleave to him at that very second ...

SHE AWOKE WITH A START. Confused, not remembering where she was, she scanned the room. Ah, yes, the Kenmore Hotel in Scotland. The light at the window informed her she'd slept for about an hour and it was dinnertime. Her stomach growled to verify the fact.

She swung her legs over the side of the bed and shook her head. "What a dream," she rasped. "He seemed so real. Pfft. Like I need another man in my life."

Shaking off the dream, she got up, freshened up, and headed downstairs to grab a bite in the pub. Ailsa had invited her to dinner with her and her mother, but Innis Bree hadn't wanted to intrude, at least not so early in their getting to know each other. She'd suggested another night later. After all, she'd be there for a whole ten days.

The pub was packed with cheerful folks eating, drinking, and spinning yarns. The laughter lifted her mood. She might even imbibe a bit, she decided, something she seldom did except for her weekly Friday happy hour margarita back home. However, "when in Rome" surely applied to Kenmore, too.

There wasn't an empty seat, so she needed to wait. Noticing a frame on the wall with a sketch of Robert Burns and the hand-written 1787 poem Ailsa mentioned, she worked her way over to it and read:

"Admiring Nature in her wildest grace,
These northern scenes with weary feet I trace ..."

Interrupted as a man and his wife left a small booth beside her, she slid into the seat before somebody else grabbed it, wondering if that was very American of her, not caring if others who were standing around might be up for the seat before her. She scanned the patrons. No one seemed to notice.

A roar of laughter went up from the booth next to her, and she looked to see what the ruckus was about. There, to her utter surprise, sat Jeffrey, in the middle of half a dozen men, telling an obviously bawdy story. His spirited gestures and vocal inflection were polar opposites to what he'd been like at lunch that afternoon in his job as valet at Bridgmoor Castle. Even during the tour he'd given Ailsa and her after their host left, he'd been as stiff as a robot. She and Ailsa had joked afterward that he may as well have been wearing the suit of armor they saw because he walked as if he had one on. But here he was, a regular guy telling jokes and drinking beer.

He didn't notice Innis Bree, a good thing as she didn't want to make him feel uncomfortable should he think he had to be more professional around a town visitor. There were other Americans in the pub, too. Looking across the room, she could see a couple who she couldn't hear but who – by simple virtue of their bearing and mannerisms and, yup, white sneakers – were decidedly American. She'd stop and say hello on her way out.

When no server appeared, she realized she needed to go up to the bar to order off the menu posted on a large board atop the shelves of liquor. She didn't want to leave her table. Someone else – maybe another American who would do that kind of thing – would take it. Thankfully, the same nice young woman with the colorful hair who'd served Ailsa and her on the deck that day appeared, apparently having noticed her conundrum. Innis Bree had a hard time following what she said because she spoke so fast but managed to order a sandwich and a glass of beer. When asked what kind of beer, she said, "Whatever is on tap, please."

Innis Bree glanced over at Jeffrey and his cronies having such fun, and a man in the group leaned forward to say something, allowing her to see his face for the first time since she arrived.

"Oh crap. You," she muttered.

As if he'd heard her over the din, he turned his head to glare right at her. Laird Blyth seemed like a new man as he cavorted with his buddies, but his broad smile faded when his eyes fell on her. She couldn't hear him over the ruckus but could tell he asked to be let out of the booth. When he strode her way, her heart forgot how to beat. He stood at the side of her booth looking down at her.

"May I?" he said, gesturing toward the seat across from her.

She shrugged. "Why not?" He probably only wanted to pester her, but she was up for a good sparring match. He'd made it clear before that he didn't like her.

He sat down and placed his beer on the table. The side of the glass said, "Tennent's Lager."

Neither of them spoke as they engaged in a stare-down, like two wrestlers waiting for the ref to blow the whistle to start.

After a bit, he said, "Would you like a bevvy?" He took a sip of his.

"I've ordered one."

"Eh. Right."

They fell back into silence until the server brought her a glass like his. She took a swig and liked it.

"Tennent's," he said, "one hundred percent Scottish, made from homegrown barley and brewed in Glasgow." He held up his glass. "Slàinte mhaith."

"Slainte mhaith," she repeated, having no idea what it meant. She could only hope she hadn't invited him to murder her or something.

They clinked glasses and drank.

"I'm surprised you joined me," she finally got up the nerve to say. "Seeing that you apparently hate me."

"I'm here, am I naw?"

He teased in a way she couldn't interpret. Whether he was making fun of her or wanting to have fun along with her, she couldn't tell.

"I'm curious about your name," she said, deciding to drop, at

54

least for now, the fact he might be mocking her. "Laird is what we'd call lord, right?"

"Aye. 'Tis so."

"Were your ancestors lairds, like lords?"

He chuckled, a hearty sound that relaxed her a bit. His voice again. She wondered if he had any concept of how sexy he sounded. Maybe he wasn't so bad, after all.

"Aye, they were. A laird is a landowner. From what I ken, my ancestors acquired land in the 1500s because they had a long history o' being loyal warriors for the Campbell clan, who ruled the area. The clan was often at battle with the English and other clans. When naw at war, they were farmers who worked the open land together. In the early 1700s, the Blyth at the time, with the family being quite wealthy by then, built the manor house you trespassed in." That hint of a grin she'd seen before materialized. "That Blyth's son inherited it and lost it in the croft system."

"Until you got it back," Innis Bree noted.

"Until I got it back." He nodded. "It went to the English for two hundred years, then fell into ruin. I'll fix that in good time."

"What will you do with it? Live in it?"

He hesitated before answering. "I dinnae ken yet. Time will tell."

Ah, she'd hit a nerve, she could see. She switched gears and went back to her original question. "And your name – Laird?"

"Och. That. After the British stole our land, the Campbell clan leader managed to keep his castle by promising fealty to the British and paying their taxes. They granted him the title o' laird. To do that, he had to break the land into crofts, small farms, each kept by one family."

"So the way of life working together as a clan disintegrated?" Innis Bree was riveted by this story that no doubt impacted her own ancestors, as well as by the fact that this farmer obviously loved the history of his heritage.

"Aye. Many farmers were displaced when they weren't profitable enough, as well as the fact that there were simply too many o' them. That became the 'highland clearances.' They were thrown out o' what had been their family homeland, the clan's homeland, in some cases for centuries. Some died, some vanished, and many, if they could manage passage, went to America."

"We know that my ancestor arrived in America around 1700, very early on, which would've put him before the Jacobite wars and the clearances."

"Better there than here. You've seen the stone fences that divide the land. Crofters lived on a pittance while eking out a living and turning most o' their crops o'er to the laird. Now, finally, to answer your question – the name Laird became popular amongst common folk as a way o' thumbing their noses at the government they saw as their captor, which makes it a perfect name for me." He finished off his beer. "I'm afraid that was a very long-winded way o' telling you how I got my name. I usually dinnae talk so much. I'm afraid my love for a good story got the better o' me. And the Tennent's."

"I love long-winded stories about family history." She finished her beer, too, and they both ordered another.

The conversation rolled more naturally after that. He asked her questions about what she knew of her Scottish family history. The more she drank, the more she had to say. By the time she drained her glass and finished her sandwich, she'd told him about having an ancestor with her same name and about her ancestor who accused a neighbor of being a witch.

"Let me get this straight," he said when she finished her tall tale. "Your eight-times great-grandaunt, the sister o' your eight-times great-grandfather Gillimichell MacIntyre, was named Innis Bree MacIntyre, the same as you. And her father, apparently, believed in witches. Does that frighten you or entertain you?"

Before she had a chance to answer, a sudden quieting of the

room drew their attention to the crowd. The locals all looked toward the door and whatever they saw quelled the chatter. Only the Americans and a few others continued to talk. But even they noticed the change in the atmosphere and shut up, too.

Rory Skeffington stood at the wide interior entrance that connected the pub to the hotel lobby. He scanned the pub like a king surveying his holdings. He spied Innis Bree and paraded over.

"There you are." He smiled at her as he stood by their booth. "The clerk at the hotel desk told me I'd find you here." He nodded at her companion. "Hello, Laird." Feigning confusion, he looked from one to the other and said, "I hope I'm not interrupting anything. Do you mind if I sit down?" Not waiting for an answer, he sat down by Innis Bree.

The other patrons, realizing they weren't going to be able to hear much of what the bigwig had to say, surreptitiously went back to their own lives. Still, the room remained quieter than before, in case they could eavesdrop and get in on something good.

"O' course, you're interrupting, Rory," Laird sniped. "What's so urgent?"

Laird's reply told Innis Bree there was no love lost between these gentlemen. At least, she hoped they'd remain gentlemen during this exchange.

Rory ignored Laird, put his arm on the back of the seat behind Innis Bree, and looked directly at her. "My engagement ended early tonight, and I thought you might want to go for a ride around the loch. It's a beautiful night, and the sky is brimming with stars."

"The sky always has stars, Rory," Laird quipped.

"What do you say?" Rory asked Innis Bree. "We can move tomorrow night's date up to tonight. Not that we have to cancel tomorrow."

"Oh for kristsake. You have a date with this moron?" Laird wasn't good at keeping his opinions in check, glaring at Innis Bree with disgust. "I thought you were smarter than that, being a college professor and all." He stood up, threw some bills on the table for his beer, and stormed off, recapturing the attention of the crowd.

"Wait. Laird!" she called out. But he was gone.

He could be heard outside, whistling and calling, "Come, Maisie." His old truck quickly revved up and streaked off.

The crowd's rapt attention swayed from listening to what went on outdoors back to Innis Bree's table.

"Come on, Innis Bree." Rory got up and held out his hand to take hers.

She didn't take it as she stood up on her own, aware that she'd also refused Laird's hand when he'd rescued her from his mansion during the rain. She looked around the room. Staring eyes all over the place quickly averted in an attempt to pretend they hadn't been watching. She noticed that Jeffrey, Rory's valet, had vanished from his table of cronies. She wondered if he hid under the table to avoid his employer.

"Let's go outside," she said quietly and marched out of the pub door to the outside with the imposing rich guy in her wake.

He went to his Mercedes convertible and opened the passenger door.

She didn't move. "I'm not going for a ride with you, Rory. What you did in there was inexcusably rude. Laird was right about that."

"Were you two actually on a date or something? He's a sheep farmer." His incredulity soared.

"No, it wasn't a date, but we were having an amicable conversation which you interrupted. What if it had been a date? What's wrong with that?"

"He's a sheep farmer." Aghast, Rory repeated himself, gesturing palms up as if it was obvious why she shouldn't be on a date with Laird.

"Yes. So what? We met yesterday and happened to run into

each other here tonight. But that doesn't matter. Date or no date, you were rude. You acted like he wasn't even there."

"I'm sorry, Innis Bree." He ran his hand through his blond hair in distress. "I swear, I didn't mean to be rude. I was so excited to have my meeting end and to be able to see you again."

She gazed into his hypnotizing aqua-blue eyes. He was good – very, very good – at being convincing.

"Are we still on for tomorrow night?" He sounded stricken at the thought of the date being called off.

"I don't know. How about you call me tomorrow and we'll see."

"I need your number." He pulled his phone out of his pocket.

"You know where to find me," she said instead, pointing at the hotel.

They said goodbye, he drove off, and she looked up at the starlit sky. It was indeed a beautiful night for a drive.

Jeffrey appeared at her side so mysteriously she thought he could be in a magic show. Disappear; reappear. What other tricks did he hold up his sleeve?

"Miss MacIntyre, I dinnae work evenings at the castle. You'll be there all alone with him, except for his staff he brings with him from the States. They go to their own wing after dinner and aren't to be seen again until daybreak. I suggest you dinnae go."

"Thank you, Jeffrey. I'll consider it." She peered up at the sky in thought. When she looked down again, Jeffrey the magician had disappeared again.

Innis Bree went to her room, reread some of the copies of documents Ailsa had given her, and fell fast asleep.

"Yer thinking o' going to Bridgmoor Castle, alone, withoot a chaperone, at night, to see the laird. Och me love, why would ye do such a thing? Danger lurks in every corner. Nae, dinnae go. Take me hand, Innis Bree, and come away with me."

She suddenly realized that this specter was more than a mere dream. The ghost of a real man from long ago stood at the foot of her bed. He was a swarthy Scottish rogue who mistakenly thought he knew her. Wearing a tartan kilt and billowy-sleeved shirt, his tussled dark hair fell to his shoulders. His shirt, open half-way down his chest, and that kilt, held by a single belt, begged to be cast off.

"Dinnae go, me love," he repeated, breaking into her trance over the spectacle of him. It occurred to her to close her gaping mouth.

Why the warning about Bridgmoor Castle? His deep voice, infused with sorrow and dread, seeped into her mind like an omen of doom, the tolling of a chapel bell for the death of a loved one.

She did not wake, her slumbering mind tapping into a plane of existence she didn't recognize when awake. It allowed the mysterious man to reach out to her and speak to her so that she could hear and see him. The realization struck that he was always there; she simply didn't know how to find him in her waking hours.

As slowly as a pet testing its new master, he came to the side of the bed. The mattress shifted underneath Innis Bree as he sat down next to her, their bodies touching. He hesitated, his hand suspended in the air. Then he stroked her hair, an intimate gesture that tingled the skin of her scalp. Her fears subsided like a turbulent sea under a charcoal sky that suddenly gives way to smooth waters as daybreak dawns.

"What's your name?" she asked, lazy and content, not bothering to rise from her pillow.

His face lit up. He was entertained by this game. "Ye know me name as well as ye know yer own, eh? I am yer Bruce."

He bent over her, the scent of his raw masculinity taking her breath away as surely as if she'd inhaled the aroma of an intoxicating elixir. As gently as a butterfly, he swept the hair away from her face and kissed her forehead, her cheek, her eyelids, and then, yes, her mouth. The kiss deepened with wild wantonness.

Innis Bree's body melted with desire. She'd never known such a succulent kiss, had never known this was what had been missing in her life that she so desperately needed, the hidden yearning striking out of nowhere.

He lifted his head and traced her lips with a finger. "I am yer Bruce Cieran Blyth. And ye, lassie, are me Innis Bree MacIntyre, are ye naw? Aye, ye ken it as well as I."

He laid down beside her and wrapped her feminine frame in his strong arms. Totally bewitched, she inhaled his heady scent and kissed those splendid lips. Feeling at home for the first time in her life, never did she want to leave this man's safe and loving embrace.

CHAPTER 6

"*A*ilsa, do you believe in ghosts?"

The American and the Scot sat on the hotel deck again, finishing their morning scones and cups of tea. This time, a small fruit bowl had been added for each.

Ailsa swallowed a slice of cantaloupe, poked her fork at her companion, and said, "I'm born and bred in a small town in the highlands o' Scotland with an old kirk, graveyard, and castle nearby. I was raised on stories o' witches and mythical creatures. What do you think?" She chuckled, stabbed another slice of melon, and took a bite.

Innis Bree picked up a strawberry and gestured with it. "Okay. Stupid question." She popped the berry into her mouth and ate it down.

"Why do you ask?"

"I've been having dreams of a Scottish man from long ago – in fact, probably from the era we're researching in the late 1600s and early 1700s. He's so real I can reach out and touch him." She didn't go into detail about the sensuous kiss and embracing. Oddly, she didn't remember anything after that.

"Are they sexy dreams?"

She gulped down her mouthful of tea, surprised by the question. "Why do you ask?"

"Because those are the best kind." The older woman's eyes twinkled with delight.

"Do you have sexy dreams about handsome men from times gone by?"

"O' course. And I dinnae care if they're figments o' my imagination or real ghosts or 'tis simply that I'm verifiably nuts. I'm naw giving them up." Ailsa drank the last of her tea and placed the teacup on its saucer with both hands, nodding adamantly to emphasize her point.

"I see. Well. Huh. Do they have names?"

"Not ones they reveal to me. I name them, though. My favorite is Wild Wyatt."

"Wyatt? That's an old Scottish name?"

"Och, nae, it isna. He's an American cowboy. I dinnae ken how he crept in there. Probably all the cowboy romance novels I read. Have you e'er read Cat Johnson or Mary Leo? *City Girl Seeks Cowboy* or *Cowboy Undone*?"

"I must confess, I have not."

"You must. Anyway, Wild Wyatt might naw be a ghost as much as a wish. Real ghosts, Scottish men and women, have visited me in the night before. Sometimes the men are sexy. The women are usually simply there, as if checking on me to make sure I'm okay. It's always a peaceful feeling when they come. I've ne'er been presented with a frightening ghost."

"My dream ghost wasn't scary once I got used to him. He told me his name is Bruce Cieran Blyth."

Ailsa's eyes widened in surprise. "You dinnae say. A Blyth. We need to look for that name today in the kirk records."

"I wondered the same thing. But then I was thinking maybe I'd simply seen his name, which would explain why it was on my mind."

"As I mentioned yesterday, the Blythes and MacIntyres had to know each other, living here in this village and being under the control o' the Campbells."

"Yeah. This Blyth seemed so real in my sleep, but now it seems silly to think there was a real man by that name a long time ago."

"I say we get a move on and get o'er to the kirk to see what we can find."

On the short walk to the church, Ailsa said, "Ghost men aside, I heard about the dust-up with the real men in your life at the pub last night."

Innis Bree stopped in her tracks, so Ailsa did, too.

"Wait. First of all, 'dust-up'? You got that from American cowboy romance novels, didn't you?"

Ailsa grinned like a Cheshire cat. "O' course."

"Secondly, how did you hear about what happened in the pub?"

"Och, my dear ..." Ailsa playfully punched her arm "... this is a very small town. That happened at what? Seven-thirty? I'd heard about it by seven-thirty-five. The bartender is the son o' one o' my friends. He called her and she called me."

They started walking again, headed for the church.

"I see. Well, at least you didn't hear about it on social media."

"Um, from what I hear, it hit Facebook, Instagram, and TikTok as it happened. People record stuff."

"Oh, crap! Has it been seen very much?"

"Last I knew, there's a poll about whether you should go on a date with the billionaire or reject him because he was rude. I hate to say this, but he's winning."

Innis Bree rolled her eyes in frustration. "Of course, he is. Rory Skeffington has probably never lost at anything in his life."

"So, what're you going to do?"

They reached the steps into the church and stopped as Innis Bree considered the question.

"I don't know. The thing is, I'd love to get inside that castle again. If I don't go to dinner with him, he'll never speak to me again. And I really am curious about him. Maybe he's not as bad as he seems. Mostly, I confess I'm curious about the cellar, the only part left of the original castle. I'm chomping at the bit – I'm sure you've heard that expression in your novels – I'm chomping at the bit to see what's down there."

"I'd love to see that, too. But dinnae go down there alone with him. Take me. And a posse."

"Are you saying I should be afraid of ghosts down there?"

"Nae. I'm saying you should be afraid o' Rory Skeffington down there."

Innis Bree laughed that off as they went into the church. Although warm outside, the thick stone walls rendered the peaceful place of worship cool inside. A small church, it wasn't opulent, instead settling for clean, natural beauty with white walls, dark wood corbels, and a backdrop of wood panels behind the altar. Directly across from the entrance was a glorious stained-glass window in four parts, depicting *Bible* scenes under a brilliant burst of yellow sunlight.

"'I will lift up mine eyes unto the hills,'" Innis Bree read off the glass. "'He leadeth me beside the still waters.' What a beautiful window."

"Aye. It's extraordinary in its beauty, especially for a church this small. Look at all the symbols amongst the figures. The star there. The lantern there." She pointed here and there. "The Mother Mary holding a lily and the Baby Jesus. I love the rainbow o'er here and have always wondered about this pot o' something that appears to be steaming. These are more recent additions to the church, commissioned by families to honor their loved ones. These all would have been plain glass originally." She pointed out another set of stained glass and two with etched glass. "The ancestors we seek wouldn't have seen anything this fancy and expensive."

They looked up at the windows in wonder until their necks bade them stop.

They walked past a black stone font, and Innis Bree ran her fingers across its worn, smooth surface.

"That's from another church that was demolished," Ailsa explained. "It's from the 1600s so it isna the one that would've been used when your ancestors were baptized. And that ..." she said, pointing at an antique chest with bolted strips of metal checkering its wood. "... is the poor box. E'en though parishioners were poor themselves, they gave to those in need. Their offerings were saved in this chest until called for."

"So they had a strong belief in community, helping each other out?"

"Aye. That they did. The whole clan – the clan chief, his family, and his followers – were something like a big family."

They had reached the thick, wood door at the back of the church that led to the basement. Its creaky hinges objected loudly as Ailsa shoved hard to open it. Going down the old stone steps felt like descending into a cave where the temperature remained consistently cool. The smell of musty artifacts and documents permeated the air. With no windows for light, they flipped a switch for the obviously not original electric lights to be greeted by three sad bulbs hanging from the ceiling.

Innis Bree shivered with uneasiness.

"You okay?" Ailsa wanted to know.

"Yes. But it is spooky down here."

"You get used to it. I've worked down here many times on other searches. The boxes are labeled by year," Ailsa explained, pointing to the tables stacked with boxes that filled the dank space, "so we need to find, I'd say, 1650-1700. We'll start there, looking for anything referring to the MacIntyres, Campbells, and now Blythes, too. Remember, howe'er, that anything recorded most likely came from the priest. 'Tis possible that your ancestor being a blacksmith and the Blythes being farmers, they didna keep records themselves. Maybe they didna e'en read or write, although the Scots have always been big on education so that's naw a given. However, if they did, 'tis possible it'll be in Gaelic. I read a wee bit but naw enough to help us. The Campbells would be a different story. They had English tutors for their children, and some e'en went to English university. Their records would've been in the castle, and nobody knows if they're still there. The records, naw the children."

"That's another good reason for me to go to dinner there and look around, especially in that cellar," Innis Bree insisted.

"Och, please. Dinnae be a dobber. There's got to be a better way." Giving up, Ailsa shrugged. "Okay. You ready to get clarted?"

"What's that mean?"

"Covered in mud. There'll be dirt and dust in this cellar. It isna like the maid comes down here to clean the place up. It isna like there's a maid to begin with, eh?"

"I'm ready. I feel like I was born ready for this," Innis Bree said, the historian in her thrilled to get down and dirty with old documents, despite the spooky setting. "Let's get to it."

They cleared a spot on one of the tables, spent half an hour looking for the boxes they needed, and pulled up a couple of rickety chairs to sit down and get to work. Ailsa pulled out a couple of pairs of rubber gloves from her purse for them to wear while handling such aged material. As they sorted through priests' diaries, ledgers, and letters, Innis Bree asked about the "highland clearances" Ailsa had mentioned the day before.

"Laird mentioned something last night that you were talking about." She relayed the story she'd been told.

"Aye. The 'clearances.' That happened later than what we're looking at now. Your direct descendant who went to American around 1700, Gillimichell, would've missed that. Laird's direct ancestors would've stayed here and been in the thick o' it. They ne'er left the area."

"It sounds like a horrible time."

"Indeed. After the Jacobite's lost their final battles, the British absconded their estates. Some Scots managed to go to the English side to become lairds o' their own lands. Most had to relinquish their land and flee the country. In that case, English noblemen or lowland Scots, naw a highlander, who was in good favor with the king would be granted the land. That happened a lot. It was a horrible time, with brother against brother in many cases – those who sided with the English to survive and those who wanted to fight to the death. Scots had a long tradition o' fighting to the death."

"But they'd been undeniably defeated. That must have been hard to take."

"It still is for many. The Campbells, for example, have many branches o' the family, with castles all over Scotland. Not all those branches agreed. They were one o' the most powerful clans, with many loyal followers pledging fealty to them from generation to generation. E'en today, some want to blame the clan leaders who committed treason, as far as they're concerned, for the tragedy o' the clearances. Truth is, it was out o' their control."

"So, some of their own clan members and even their own family members would have seen them as traitors to the clan?"

"Aye. To make it even worse, those clan leaders had to pay so much homage to the British, they had to change the entire work system for their clansmen."

"Laird explained 'crofts' to me."

"So you know how the land was divided up. If a croft wasn't profitable, that farmer was evicted, and someone else was given their croft. That happened to so many, that's why 'tis called the clearances. Some lairds were kind. They paid passage for their people to go to America or Australia to start a new life. But by then, most clan leaders who had become lairds under the English system had little money to spare. Most Scots who emigrated had to pay their own passage. Piss poor, they were."

Innis Bree closed the tattered document she'd been perusing as she put together the pieces of the Scottish immigration story. "So my ancestor, Gillimichell, went to America before any of that. I'd love to know what was going on in his life that made him make such a big change."

"Some went for religious reasons when the Presbyterianism became popular. It was the antithesis o' the Anglicans. Presbyterians believe in a direct connection between a person and God. Anglicans, and Catholics too, believe there must be an intermediary. Their priests, naturally. So that could be it. Or he simply may have left for more opportunity. All we know for sure is that he left and was in Virginia by 1700 and his sister Innis Bree wasna. At least, I can't find her on any ship manifest."

"It's a mystery. One we'll never solve if we don't keep digging."

It was two hours later when Innis Bree came upon a fragile, leather-bound notebook filled with faded, florid writing. Squinting at the first page, she couldn't make out what it said in the dim light. She pulled her phone out of her pocket, turned on the flashlight, and homed in on the handwriting.

"Huh. This one says ... 'W-i ... what's that letter? Oh, 'W-i-t-c ... Holy crap! It says 'Witches 1690-1699'. Ailsa!" She turned to the next page. "It's a priest's record of people who'd been accused of being witches and the people who accused them. Before, you found a church record that said my ancestor John had accused a neighbor of being a witch, but this book is full of them."

Ailsa dropped what she was doing, slid her chair closer, and took a gander at the first few pages. "Holy shite, so it is. It tells us who was accused and who accused but nary a word about what happened after that." Her excitement at having found this telling document became tempered with disappointment that it didn't tell them even more. They didn't know what happened to those who'd been accused of being witches. "Did the priest merely chastise them and let them go? Or were the consequences more dire than that?"

They spent the next half hour pouring over the writing, page after page, until the most dreaded words possible glared up at them. Innis Bree read them aloud, her voice a mere rasping whisper. "Innis Bree MacIntyre. Accused by Duncan Campbell."

"What? Duncan Campbell?" Ailsa was incredulous. "That fud? Nothing but a troublemaker from what I've e'er dug up on him."

"Do you think maybe we can't find her because she was executed for this?"

"Oh my lord, I have nary an idea. Executions would've been up to the clan leader. I ken that early on, in the 1600s, people suspected o' being witches were drowned, what with all this water around us."

A horrible chill came over Innis Bree, freezing her lungs. She couldn't breathe. "I have to go outside." She fled from the basement and ran outside to gulp in air. Hands on hips, she paced until she ended up standing in the graveyard, suddenly feeling overwhelmed by the dead.

"Why did I want to know my family history?" she chastised herself. "Did I really need to know this to get on with my life? Oh, Innis Bree, what happened to you?" Tears welled in her eyes, blurring her vision.

Still, she could see him, misty at first and then coming into focus, leaning against a giant oak tree. Her ghost, Bruce Cieran Blyth. Of course, why wouldn't he be in the boneyard?

He silently beckoned her to come to him, holding out his hands to her. She went to him and placed a hand on the tree to keep from sinking to the ground. He ran a translucent hand down her arm, leaving an electrifying sensation that gave her strength.

"Why are you here?" She asked the question simply, not wanting to scare him away.

"Because yer here."

"Do you ever go to where she lived? Where was that?"

"She? I dinnae ken. I go to the hotel because ye've been a maid and lived there since ye were twelve. I come to the kirk because ye come here to worship our dear Lord Jesus Christ."

"Bruce, listen to me carefully." She kept her voice as gentle as possible in her distress. "I'm not your Innis Bree. I'm her descendent."

"Why do ye say such a hurtful thing, me love? Yer me Innis Bree. I can see it in yer eyes. I can feel it in yer soul. I can touch it in yer body ..."

"Bruce. Look at me. Look at how I'm dressed. Look around you. She's long dead. So are you. And we don't know what happened to her."

"Ye disappeared one night and ne'er came back."

His voice faded away, and she found herself standing there alone, her hand still on the tree. She missed him the second he dissolved away and wondered where he went. Down the hill, the river calmly flowed by. The mountains in the distance, the ancient trees surrounding her – had they seen him, too? If so, they were not disturbed. She supposed that, especially right here near the graveyard, they'd witnessed many a ghost.

She turned back toward the church to find Ailsa sitting on a boulder amidst the tombstones.

"Was that your ghost?" Ailsa asked as she stood up and walked toward Innis Bree.

Innis Bree met her halfway. "Yes. It was Bruce."

"I couldna hear him, but I heard you tell him you weren't his Innis Bree."

"Yes."

"What did he say?"

"Nothing. He left."

"I ken this graveyard well. His grave is right o'er here." Ailsa walked a couple of rows over and pointed at a mottled, moss-covered headstone. "It's hard to read, so get closer and you'll see."

Innis Bree did as suggested and read, "'Bruce Cieran Blyth, beloved father, 1665-1710.' He lived to be forty-five. That's the age of my ghost."

"Nae doubt your ghost is this Bruce. Now read the tombstone beside him."

"'Fenella Blyth, wife of Bruce Blyth, 1665-1755.' Wow. She lived to be ninety. That's rare in those days."

Ailsa cocked her head to study the headstones. "I've always found it curious that his says naught about being a husband and hers says naught about being a mother. 'Tis as if they weren't on the same page in life."

"Yeah, that's weird. Huh." Innis Bree had no idea what to make of that but suspected there was a story to be told there, one they would probably never know.

"Well, I say we've had an astonishing morning and need to chow down to fortify ourselves for the afternoon."

Innis Bree was relieved and delighted that Ailsa wasn't fazed by the ghost. They headed for the pub and some much-needed lunch.

When they returned to the church basement, they found something that sent them into a tizzy, something that flummoxed Innis Bree and sent Ailsa into a fit of laughter.

CHAPTER 7

"*L*ook at this!" Ailsa shouted. "Holy shite. Och, sorry." She crossed herself.

Innis Bree moved her chair to get closer. "What are you sorry about?"

"Swearing in the kirk. Although I've heard worse in this place. Okay. Right here." She slid over a tattered book and pointed to a spot on a yellowed page.

Innis Bree struggled with the penmanship but managed to figure it out. "'July 27, 1690, betrothal blessed for Innis Bree MacIntyre and Bruce Cieran Blyth.' What? No. My namesake was officially engaged to my ghost? No wonder he thinks I'm her. Laird must be related to him."

Ailsa broke into laughter. "Aye. I know the Blyth family tree well, like I know most o' them from this village. Bruce was Laird's seven-times great-grandfather. Seeing that Innis Bree is your eight-times great-grandaunt, and they were betrothed but didn't marry, it looks like you and Laird are here to battle out whatever happened between the two o' them."

"This is unbelievable. The one person in Kenmore who hates

me, and I'm not too fond of him, either ..." she left out the part about being so physically attracted to him she wanted to jump his bones "... and our ancestors apparently were in love. And it somehow ended badly."

"Perhaps e'en tragically. We have to find out the end o' this love story, eh?"

"Apparently, whatever happened wasn't good. Bruce the ghost says she disappeared."

"We know her parents and brother, our Gillimichell, went to America a few years later. They died and are buried in what is West Virginia today, although it was Virginia Colony back then. But Innis Bree is naw in the American records with her family and naw in any marriage records anywhere in Scotland that I can find. We see that Bruce married. So what happened to your poor Innis Bree?"

Hard as they tried, they found nothing that provided a clue. The rest of the afternoon produced nothing helpful, other than the realization they probably needed to visit the Edinburgh Central Library's National Archives, where they might find more if they got lucky. Ailsa called to arrange their visit. The result was a suggestion they come the next afternoon when it probably wouldn't be too busy. They'd drive into Pitlochry mid-morning and take the train into the city. It was only an hour and a half drive from Kenmore to Edinburgh, but Ailsa hated driving in the city and Innis Bree wasn't about to try to drive on what was the wrong side of the road for her. The two-hour train ride would be less stress for both of them.

Innis Bree went back to her hotel room for a late-afternoon nap to be greeted by a dozen red roses in a toney crystal vase. The accompanying card may have been schmaltzy, but it made her smile.

My dearest Innis Bree,

My humble apologies for my rudeness last night. Please have dinner with me at my castle tonight to let me make it up to you. Your coach will await at seven o'clock.

Your Prince Charming,

R.

She wondered where someone would get flowers like this in Kenmore, as she hadn't seen a flower shop. She reckoned there might be a garden on his vast estate, although she doubted he'd gone out to pick them himself.

Would she go? She hadn't decided yet. In fact, she'd been so excited about her ancestry quest, she hadn't thought about this all day.

She opened her window to the warm summer air and relished the sound of the gurgling river below. The scent of the roses filled the room. She laid down on her bed and pulled the colorful, hand-sewn quilt over her.

He came to her again, her ghost Bruce. As gently and patiently as if she were a child, he bundled her into his arms to keep her safe as she slept.

~

SHE OPENED her eyes to see 6:00 p.m. glaring at her from her phone.

"Damn. I slept for two hours."

A yawn struck, telling her to sleep longer. But a knock came at the door, forcing her to get up and answer it.

"Miss MacIntyre," the teenaged boy greeted her with a bop of his curly-top head. "This is for you." He handed her a beautifully wrapped box, not very deep and about a foot square, with a card tucked underneath the fluffy gold bow.

"Thank you." She took the gift, put a finger up for him to wait, pulled two pound notes out of her jeans pocket, and handed them to him.

"Thanks," he said with a smile that displayed shiny braces.

Innis Bree shut the door after watching him joyfully bound away. Placing the box on the bed, she plucked out the card and opened it.

My Sweet American Princess,
Your silver coach will arrive at seven o'clock this evening.
I shall await with bated breath.
Yours in body, heart, and soul,
PCR

"PCR? What on earth? Oh. I get it. Prince Charming Rory. Geez."

She tossed down the card and carefully slid the gold ribbon and bow off the box, unwrapped the gold foil paper, and opened it. A dozen plump, bite-sized chocolate hearts, which she guessed to be freshly handmade by his cook, stared up at her. She lifted the box to take a whiff. Surely it would be a sin to resist the hard work of a master who could produce this kind of bliss. She popped one into her mouth. And another. Even numbers had always seemed like bad luck, so she ate a third.

"No! No more. I'll spoil my dinner." She slammed the box closed and set it on the bedside table. "Dinner. What am I going to do about that?"

She hadn't decided yet if she wanted to except the invitation. If she did, she'd have to wear her second pair of jeans, as they were clean, and a blouse. She'd brought no dress-up clothes.

Another knock came at the door. She opened it, expecting the teenager. To her surprise, the desk clerk held a larger box. It had the same gold wrapping, leaving no question as to its sender. She took it, thanked the woman, and offered a tip that was refused with a swish of the hand.

By the sheer weight of the package, Innis Bree suspected what lay within, and she was right. After ripping the paper off this time, she held up a shimmery summer dress in sultry deep red, mid-calf length with spaghetti straps. If she chose to accept it, it would be the loveliest item of clothing she'd ever owned and undoubtedly the most expensive, as well. She held it up to her body and twirled around, holding out the skirt on one side. The full-length mirror presented her with a vision of pure glamour.

Carefully, she laid it down on the bed and read the card.

Lovely PIB,

"PIB? Princess Innis Bree? Is this guy for real?"

The fairy godmother no doubt has not had time to create your gown for this evening, so I've taken the liberty of helping her out. A little birdie whispered your size, so I expect it will slip on like a glove.

Your coach will arrive soon, my dear. My heart quickens with eagerness as I await your presence.

Yours,

PCR

Something else lay in the box. Pushing golden tissue paper aside, she took out a pair of gold, strappy sandals. Just in case there was gold jewelry or something at the bottom of the box, she pulled out each piece of tissue. Nothing more, thankfully. She'd always had a hard time accepting gifts. This was over the top.

Walter and his way of nudging that turned into pushing flashed through her mind. Was this the same thing? Was she a push-over?

But the more she fondled the slinky fabric of the dress, the more she wanted to accept this present. She wanted to be girly-girl for an evening. She wanted to feel beautiful. She wanted to know that someone wanted her.

Being dumped by Walter, she finally admitted to herself, had done a real number on her self-esteem. What better pick-me-up could there possibly be than a date with a billionaire who owned a castle and handed out extravagant gifts wanting to sweep her off her feet? None, she swiftly decided. There was nothing better. This was exactly what she needed.

"Walter be damned! I'll go and have the time of my life. And I won't let Rory Skeffington push me into anything I don't want to do."

There wasn't much time to get ready. She flurried around her room and by seven o'clock was walking down the wide, carpeted hotel stairs looking like a million bucks. Or a billion bucks, considering the source of her attire. Rory stood there waiting for her at the bottom of the stairs, unable to take his eyes off her. They didn't speak as he took her hand and kissed the back of it like a seventeenth century nobleman and escorted her to his silver Mercedes.

It took five minutes to reach the castle, where an evening like nothing she ever could have drummed up in her wildest imagination awaited.

Laird Blyth and his crony Jeffrey Swain laid on their bellies in the heather on a hill overlooking Bridgmoor Castle. Laird's Sheltie Maisy laid at her master's side. Each man leaned on his elbows to peer through a pair of military-grade binoculars they'd inherited from serving in the Highlanders Battalion of the Scottish Army. They'd done reconnaissance here three times before and had already decided that the fourth time would be their last. When they made that commitment, they had no idea that Innis Bree MacIntyre would be their final target. Or rather, they feared, Rory Skeffington's target.

"Jay-sus, mate," Jeffrey cursed, "she's bonnier than any o' those movie stars and models he brings. She's a bobby dazzler!"

"I can see that with my own eyes, you ken." Laird felt cranky, seeing the woman he coveted being squired by a man with the kind of wealth he'd never know.

"She didna strike me as the type to fancy a lavvy heid like him, eh? I'm surprised she came."

"Aye, me, too. I guess I had her all wrong. I thought she was a canny lass. But nae."

"You're scunnered, eh?"

They watched as the couple got out of the Mercedes and went up the front steps of the castle, her arm wrapped around his. Laird stared, transfixed by the transformation in Innis Bree. Her natural beauty was stunning enough, which made him hate to admit that with that fancy dress and her hair piled on top of her head with a rose tucked into it, not to mention the red lipstick – gawd, what that red lipstick could do to a man – she was the most alluring creature he'd ever witnessed.

He squashed his wanton desires as best he could. Their mission wasn't about his own lust. It was about making certain the big-shot American interloper wasn't abusing women. There had been suspicions ever since Rory Skeffington bought the castle a year earlier, claiming to be an environmentalist who cared about saving the land, a green laird as they were unaffectionately called here, but who'd never shown a wee whit of interest in the land. Consequently, gossip had quickly turned to rampant speculations about what might be going on in the castle. He flew in on his private jet every six weeks, a different dame in tow each time. They would disappear into the castle for three or four days and come out to fly away again. Seldom did they come into town, as the one-thousand-acre castle grounds even had its own airstrip. Skeffington brought American staff who came and went with him. They were like ghosts coming and going in the night.

Jeffrey had been hired six months earlier to provide security for the place in between the owner's visits and to serve as valet when Skeffington was in residence. The Scot immediately became suspicious when he couldn't access the cellar, having been left without a key. He's confined this to Laird, making him wonder, too, what went on down there, if anything at all. It was, after all, a very old building. It was possible the key had been lost long ago, and Skeffington had no interest in exploring an undoubtedly moldy, dank cellar. The owner wasn't, by any account, interested in the history of the place.

"So why did he bother buying it if he isna interested in its history?" Laird had asked when Jeffrey first shared his concerns months earlier. The two men had been best mates since primary school, having shared four years in the Army with fighting in Iraq, to boot.

"I've nae idea," Jeffrey had answered. "I'm there during the day when everything seems perfectly normal, except the women are often – how can I say this politely? They're dunderheids."

"That wasn't very polite," Laird had snickered.

"Well, aye. He talks oot o' his fanny flaps. It's hard to ken how those women believe anything that comes outta his mouth. But they do."

That first part had made Laird laugh. It also made him share Jeffrey's concern that women might be mistreated or led astray in that castle. One evening while in their cups, they agreed to spy on the place a few times to make sure their town and their land wasn't being besmirched by a reprobate. Mostly, though, they wanted to make sure that, dunderheids or not, women were safe there.

Jeffrey put down his binoculars and stood up. The couple had gone inside and closed the door. "How about we go get a pint or two and come back later. They're likely to be in there for a while."

"We don't need to come back," Laird relented as he lowered his binoculars and got up, too. "She's a grown-up woman and can do whate'er she wants. It isna like we've e'er seen a lassie come out o' there with so much as a bruise or bump or scratch. When they're leaving, they always look happy or tired but ne'er abused. And they all look auld enough. She's probably thirty or so."

"You're sure, mate? You dinnae wanna come back?"

"I'm sure. Let's go to the pub. Come, Maisie. Time for a bevvy, eh?"

Maisy hesitated, clearly wanting to stay near the castle. Or near Innis Bree, Laird surmised. Could a dog really know who that had been from this distance? She'd immediately taken to the American woman when they first met.

"Come on, love," Laird coaxed.

The dog let out a whimper before coming to his side.

As they turned to go, Jeffrey glanced at the imposing stone structure once more, looming like a haunted castle in the moonlight as if right out of Shakespeare's *MacBeth*. "I do wonder what's in that cellar," he opined. "I hope 'tis nothing, and I'm merely an auld dunderheid myself for fussing about it."

Laird took a last look and wondered about that himself. "Well, mate, the truth is 'tis none o' our business." He clapped his friend on the shoulder, and they abandoned their spy mission. The short trek into the village took them directly to their awaiting pub.

The men went inside, and Maisie took up her usual position outside the pub door. This time, however, she laid down facing the castle, her eyes wide and her mind alert.

CHAPTER 8

A prism of candlelight reflected off her beveled Waterford crystal wineglass as Innis Bree sipped the 1995 Château Pétrus Bordeaux, causing a kaleidoscope of pinks, lavenders, and blues to illuminate her radiant face. She set down her glass, and soft shadows from the candle on the table returned to her features. Rory Skeffington's besotted stare empowered her as she discovered she had the ability to cast this kind of spell over a man, especially such a handsome, powerful man.

She smiled at him coquettishly, dipping her chin and looking up through hooded eyes, her long eyelashes casting feathery shadows on her cheeks. He lifted his glass, and they toasted without words.

The candlelit dinner had been set up at an intimate table in the vast ballroom. Crystal chandeliers giving off low light warmed the cavernous space while soft music coming from hidden speakers set a cozy mood. Although the shiny wood dance floor stretched the length of the room, a thick pink and baby blue Persian carpet had been placed on this end to soften the space. Candles on tall stands circled the entire room, with a multitude of candles nearby, reflecting off the mottled mirrors that covered one long wall. The view of Loch Tay out the massive windows, with moonlight trickling across the water, completed the enchantment.

However, by the time they finished their salad and the main entrée arrived – filet mignon with stuffed mushrooms – Innis Bree had already tired of the game of playing a vapid flirt, as well as the pretentiousness of first-date chatter. Mesmerized when they first got there, the novelty had worn off. She wanted something more, something she couldn't quite describe. Something more … real.

She set down her glass and dove in. "I have a confession."

"Oh, pray tell. I love confessions." He winked at her over the rim of his wineglass as he took a sip. The candlelight accentuated his chiseled features and made his vivid eyes sparkle.

"At first, the only reason I even considered coming here this evening was so I could be inside the castle again. Historically, it's a fascinating place. Jeffrey gave us a nice tour yesterday, but there's a lot we didn't see. He told us how all records and books were sold to the National Library long before you came along. But I wonder if anything is hidden anywhere, like in the cellar. Have you ever been down there?"

"Oh, yes. Many times. In fact, it's my favorite part of the castle. I can take you there if that kind of thing appeals to you."

"What's down there?"

"It's a …" he paused "… dungeon. My dungeon."

"Truly?"

"Yes, truly. Accoutrements and torture devices galore. I'm the prince who can show my princess the workings of a real castle dungeon."

"Oh, I can't wait."

"I wasn't sure you'd like that kind of thing."

"Oh, I do. I assure you."

"I'm happy to hear that."

The hesitation in his voice made her pause, but she dismissed it as a misread signal on her part. Surely, he didn't think she'd be afraid of a castle dungeon. She was a historian, after all, and those kinds of things were common throughout history.

"Ah, there's more to my confession," she went on. "You see, I admit that today I was thoroughly flattered by your attention, the gifts, and all of this. You're good at this, and you know it, the prince and princess at the castle thing." She swept her hand around the room. "I wonder what this is all about. You don't even know me. And you certainly don't expect this to be a long-term thing. I suspect that isn't on your mind, no matter who the woman might be sitting here across from you. What's going on?"

He cocked his head and studied her. The smile that slowly came over his face became spectacular. "I love your candor. I love it that you aren't afraid to question me. And I love it that you're one of the prettiest women I've ever had the pleasure of sharing a meal with. Oh, I know, that pretty part doesn't amount to much in the long run. But just so you know, you are. That aside, this is my way of getting to know you better. You are right, though ..." he circled the rim of his glass with a finger "... that I'm not thinking long term. I never think long term unless I'm in my office talking investments and financial gain." He shrugged unapologetically. He wasn't ashamed of who he was.

"I can appreciate that." Innis Bree placed a hand on the table. He reached for it, and they held hands. "You're a grown man who knows what he wants and doesn't want, and you don't want commitment. At least you're honest about it."

"I'm glad you understand. Many – many! – do not."

"So we don't have to worry about going steady," she teased, pulling her hand out of his, "or any of that stuff."

She relaxed. Now she could enjoy pretending to be a princess for one enchanted evening because there were no expectations. And without commitment, there certainly wouldn't be any sex. It would be a Disney movie played out for real. Flirting and romance and all that, but no hanky-panky.

A pesky thought, however, flitted across her mind. Maybe in real life there was more. Did she want more? She didn't know yet.

They finished their meal, and the server asked if they'd like their crème brûlée now or later. Rory raised a palm to Innis Bree, inviting her to answer.

"Later, please, after we've walked around a bit. Thank you."

The server disappeared. Rory stood and put out a hand. She took it and stood up beside him, gazing up into his eyes. A smooth cello played in the background, and without a word they stepped away from the carpet, he took her in his arms, and they waltzed around the ballroom.

Innis Bree felt like Cinderella at the ball. She wondered if that fairy tale character felt what she felt right now. If so, it never could have been written into a children's story. The heat between his body and hers radiated with need. He pulled her closer; she became lost in his embrace. As the song ended, their kiss came as naturally as if they'd known each other for a lifetime.

They stepped apart with faces flushed and hearts aflutter as they stared into each other's eyes.

"Come. I want to show you what you've been wanting to see." His voice seared with lust. "Come with me to my dungeon."

LAIRD LAID in his spot in the heather, binoculars in place. Maisie dutifully laid next to him on her belly, two front paws neatly side by side, pointing toward the castle.

They'd been in there for two hours, the Americans, Innis Bree MacIntyre and Rory Skeffington. Laird knew that neither of those two adults were any of his business. Yet he found himself belly down on the ground, spying on them again.

He'd stayed at the pub for an hour, excused himself, and come back to this spot like a buck to its rutting circle. He shoved himself up to sit on his haunches. "I need to leave, eh, lassie?" He ran a hand through Maisie's fur. "I ken this is madness but, feck, I cannae make myself go. Pardon my language." He raised his binoculars again.

Nothing.

The castle sat there like a sleeping giant, the dark of night eerily cloaking its breadth.

Laird settled in again. "Nae. I cannae go and leave her there."

He pulled a pack of Kensitas Club filterless cigarettes out of the breast pocket of his shirt, shook it until one of the two remaining white sticks popped up, snagged it in his lips, and replaced the pack. He rummaged in his jeans pocket, came up with a pack of matches, and lit up.

"Damned baccy." He exhaled a long stream of smoke as he cursed the habit. "Nae more. I gave it up for fifteen years. I'll do it again."

In the meantime, he enjoyed his gasper, inhaling deeply and exhaling with pleasure. He'd been hooked as a teen, gave it up, then started again two weeks ago. It was evident to everyone who knew him why. His divorce became finalized then. Although his wife left a year earlier, she'd wanted him to sell the sheep farm, including the animals, land, and old mansion, and give her half the money. They wrangled in court for eleven months until the judge eventually sided with Laird, who'd bought the farm prior to meeting her. Besides, she'd left him and was already "in domestic cohabitation," as the divorce suit stated, with the bastart actor in London.

Laird had met his ex while he was in the Army, and he'd imagined a happy home-life with bairns, dogs, and, aye, sheep. Alas, that turned out to be a twisted fairytale destined for an unhappy ending.

He finished his smoke, stamped out the butt, put that in his pocket, too, not wanting to leave any evidence of his stakeout, and raised his binoculars again.

Still nothing.

"What goes on in that bloody place?"

No one and nothing answered him.

He leaned against a boulder, almost dozed, and shook his head to clear the cobwebs. Vigilant. He needed to be more watchful. The castle looked even more forlorn now, as if sagging with the weight of its secrets.

He went back to spying. Maisie silently stayed at his side. Neither was about to give up on Innis Bree MacIntyre.

Innis Bree could have been blindfolded and still would have known from the musty smell alone that they were entering an ancient, dark, sequestered part of the castle. The narrow, spiraling, stone steps encased in encroaching walls on both sides caused a bout of claustrophobia to wave over her. She shook it off, not about to miss out on this once-in-a-lifetime chance to be inside an authentic, historic castle dungeon. Who knew what kinds of torture may have ensued in that very place? Not that she advocated for torture but being educated about it informed her knowledge of the cultural practices and belief systems of the people in the era in which it was used.

Rory led the way, the low lights he'd had installed offering meager guidance on the uneven steps. He stopped and reached back to touch her arm. "Are you okay? Here." He took her hand. "Put your hand on my shoulder."

She did as instructed, which helped keep her balance with him being in front of her. She ran her other hand along the stone wall, wondering how many hands over how many centuries had touched that very same wall. And how many had done so in agony, knowing they were descending into hell, never to return.

At the bottom of the steps, they came upon a short hallway with a heavy wood door at the end. A small window with black bars across it and a bulky rusted bolt looked almost surreal to Innis Bree, like fictional movie props. Rory took a large antique key out of his pocket, like in a horror movie, and unlocked the door. It opened with a creak that would've made Tim Burton proud.

Rory Skeffington seemed quite proud, too, shoving the bulky door open and taking her hand to guide her over the threshold. "Come in, my princess."

She stepped inside and felt queasy, as if her life was about to take a drastic turn. Again, she thought of the prisoners who felt that and so much more, knowing a horrendous fate that included unspeakable pain awaited them.

He stepped a few feet away, leaving her in the dark by herself. She struggled to breathe. He used his flashlight to find a box on a table, took out a lighter, and proceeded to light candles scattered about the space.

Little by little, light illuminated the dungeon, and Innis Bree felt better. She could see a large room with a low ceiling. Every surface – above, around, and below – was constructed of heavy stone. No prisoner would ever have found a way out of this tomb. As more candles lit up, she could see the outline of some kind of odd-shaped chair or something, probably misshapen after years of wear. In some places, chains hung from the ceiling and protruded from the walls, more indication that prisoners were not treated humanely. One wall held pegs, perhaps as many as twenty, with all manner of torture equipment hanging on them. Once she got her bearings, she'd investigate more closely. From where she stood, she could see ropes and spiked collars and whips and ...

Wait.

Centuries-old leather would be cracked and worn, even disintegrated. These looked … new.

She spun around to be confronted with a bare-chested Rory sitting on, of all things, a four-poster bed with filmy black gauze hanging from the posts and red satin covering the plump mattress and fat pillows. Certainly, no prisoner had ever had a bed – especially *that* bed – to sleep on.

"What in hell?" she yelled. "What are you doing? What is this?" She spun around to take it all in, and it hit like a bomb. "Ohmygod, I'm in one of those BD-something-something places! I don't even know what that stands for. Why didn't you tell me?"

"What are you talking about?" He jumped up and grabbed for his shirt. "I told you it was a dungeon with all the accoutrements we could ever want. How could you have misunderstood that?" In his hurry to button his shirt, he had it all askew.

"I … I …" She backed away from him and stumbled into a wall strung with leather masks, corsets, garter belts, and more. In her frenzy, her hand became tangled in a black leather shackle. As if tinged by fire, she yelped and struggled to release her hand, inadvertently swiping the hanging items and sending them flying across the floor. A whip wrapped itself around her arm like a slithering snake. Having lost her balance and frantic to get out of there, she stumbled as she tried to dislodge the thing. Frustrated that it clung to her arm, she screamed. Finally, it came free. She started to toss it aside, thought better of it, and threatened him with it as if she knew how to use it.

He reached out to her. "Innis Bree, put that down. We'll leave. Come."

She cracked the whip. He jumped, stumbling into a table. It tumbled over. Sex toys and condoms crashed to the floor.

She sobbed, "Get me out of here!"

Rory went to the door and heaved it aside. "It's all right. We'll go right now." He grabbed his flashlight to light the way but couldn't keep up with her as she careened up the stairs.

Back in the main part of the castle, she fled across marble floors until reaching the entrance. Yanking the front door open so violently she nearly fell, she rushed outside and down the steps to the gravel driveway. There, she bent over to put her hands on her knees and breathe.

He jogged up behind her and stopped a few yards away. "Innis Bree, I'm sorry. I had no idea you didn't understand what I was saying. We've been playing a prince and princess game all evening. Everybody knows a *dungeon* is a sex dungeon. It's okay. I won't touch you. I promise. Let me drive you back to the hotel."

Taking one more deep breath, she straightened her spine and menacingly held up the whip. "Not *everybody* knows that you numbskull. Never tell a historian you're taking her to a castle's dungeon when it's a 'sex dungeon.'" She mocked him with air quotes. "She expects an immersive history lesson, not sex play. And, by the way, I was hoping for a look throughout the whole cellar, searching for a hidden treasure chest or secret books or something. Not sex toys." She reeled around and headed for the village.

"Wait!"

She spun back, hands defiantly on hips, whip dangling at her side. "What?"

His voice took on a teasing tone. "Have you ever considered the possibility that you watch too many movies? A treasure chest in the cellar? Really? I mean, maybe a hidden body. But treasure?"

"Oh!" She lashed the whip in his direction. "Leave me alone."

"Innis Bree, come on," he pled.

She waved him off and escaped like Cinderella at midnight. Except in this fairy tale, she didn't expect him to show up tomorrow with that stupid shoe.

∽

"FECK!" Laird swore as he stared through his binoculars.

Maisy whimpered.

"Sorry, love. I ken you hate my cursing. But I cannae hear what they're saying. Shite. Och, sorry again."

A breeze had kicked up, and although normally he might have been able to hear yelling from this far away, in the wind he could not. Standing at the ready lest he needed to run down there should things get violent, he watched their every move. Only their wild gestures told the tale, and a compelling tale it was.

"She's furious with him. It looks like he tried to put the moves on her, and she wasna having it. That's good, eh, lassie?"

Maisie snipped agreement.

"What is she carrying? I cannot quite see it. Holy shite! 'Tis a whip, and she snapped it at him!" He watched intently, realizing something. "Maisie, lass, I thought I might need to save her. 'Tis sure she can save herself." He shook his head in wonder.

He continued to watch as Rory Skeffington, his shirt buttoned crookedly, followed Innis Bree to the castle gate where he pressed numbers on a keypad to open it up and let her out. The wind whipped that silky dress around her legs; her hair had become undone and fell in random curls about her neck; a strap on one of her sandals broke and she tore the thing off and cast it into the gorse. Outside the gate, she tossed the whip away, too. Skeffington left her alone as she walked, with one shod foot, the two blocks to the hotel. The rejected man scratched his head in apparent disbelief, picked up the whip, went inside the gate and closed it, and plodded back to his domain, a long way for someone Laird had never seen walk farther than the distance between his car and the pub.

Laird had crouched down again in case his nemesis looked around once the woman was gone. He didn't stand up until the

American interloper disappeared behind his fancy castle door, and Innis Bree would be safe in the hotel. He pulled his pack of cigarettes out of his pocket, took out the last one, and crushed the package. He put the crushed ball into his pocket, lit up, took a long draw, and vowed to himself he'd never buy another pack.

"Maybe he's finally got his comeuppance, eh?" He chuckled and left his smoke dangling from his lips as he scratched behind Maisie's ears with both hands. "Leave it to our Innis Bree to do it." He removed the stick and blew a smoke circle as he studied the stars in the sky. "Huh. 'Our Innis Bree.' Nae. She isna. 'Tis daft o' me to say so. She might be your friend, but she hates my e'er-lovin' guts. Besides, what do I want with an American lass anyway? We have absolutely nothing in common." He finished his cigarette, stomped out the butt, and this time defiantly decided to leave it right there. "Let them find my DNA if they want."

Maisie turned circles and galloped down the footpath through the gorse, headed for the village. They slipped through their hole in the fence, hidden by brush. Once they were off castle property they went back to the road, Maisie sniffing as she followed the scent of her new friend. When they reached the truck, the dog bopped her head toward the hotel door.

"Nae, lassie, we must go home."

The pooch reluctantly jumped in the truck, her head hung low for missing Innis Bree.

CHAPTER 9

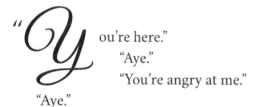 ou're here."

"Aye."

"You're angry at me."

"Aye."

Innis Bree studied Bruce as he looked out the window. He wore the same red-and-black wool kilt, billowy-sleeved shirt rolled up at the sleeves, and leather vest as before. With his wavy russet hair, god-like build, and that outfit, he was the epitome of a Scottish highlander stud.

"You were quite the ladies' man, weren't you?"

He faced her with a sly grin. "What do ye mean 'were'? Aye, ye ken well enough the lassies are attracted to me. But ye also ken I only have eyes fer thou, me Innis Bree."

She mulled over how to proceed. This ghost wasn't about to accept the fact he was dead. She supposed that news was quite a shock to a soul who refused to leave the earth, so decided to try to be understanding and take it slowly.

She got out of bed and walked around him to close the window against an arm of Arctic air that had reached down to seize Scotland. They stood side by side, neither looking at the other.

"You're angry because you saw me leave with a man this evening. Right?"

"Aye." With belabored footfall, he strode to the one easy chair in the room and fell into it. Finally, his gaze fell on her.

Innis Bree crossed the room and sat on the end of the bed, facing him, his beauty almost inconceivable to her. Not only his physical presence but the endearing aura of his beleaguered heart and soul pulsated to draw her to him. Softly, she said, "Bruce, do you know why I talk and dress and behave differently than before?"

His features fell with despair, his voice a melancholy rasp. "I've been pondering that very thing. I think mayhaps I've been ill and nae in me right mind, asleep fer a long time. Ye have been taken by fereigners and taught these strange ways. Ye dress in unfittin' lad's clothes during the day, and tonight ye dressed like a hurdie and left with that minted fop. Tell me, has someone forced ye into being a hoore, me love? Ye kin tell me. I'll slay them fer ye, that ye ken. Off with their heids if they've done this to ye."

"No, Bruce. No one needs to lose their head."

"Dinnae be afraid, lassie. Ye can tell me. Whatever it is, it cannae destroy our love. Nothing can destroy the rapture o' our souls."

His sincerity and urgency broke Innis Bree's heart. She knew she must make him understand. Yet, as if hypnotized by his yearning, she wanted to let herself dissolve into the comfort of his love. She wanted to be his Innis Bree.

Yet she knew she could not.

"Bruce, dear sweet Bruce, I have not been kidnapped. I am not a whore. More than three hundred years have passed since your Innis Bree was here. She died long ago. I told you before, and it is true, that I am her descendent. She was my aunt many generations ago."

"Ye speak gibberish. If me Innis Bree is three-hundred-years deid, then I would be, too."

"Yes, Bruce. Yes."

He vanished into the night.

THE MUTED GOLD of the early morning gloaming outside her window soothed Innis Bree. She reached over to see if Bruce was still there and her hand landed on a cold patch of sheet. She'd gone to bed disturbed by her fruitless talk with him, only to fall into his ethereal embrace as she slept. Allowing herself to be his Innis Bree for a night brought her peace and good rest. There had been no sex – at least none she remembered – only the deep comfort of feeling loved.

She wiggled her fingers and toes and decided to snuggle back into her covers. Half a minute later, however, her eyes flew open. Her phone told her it was six-thirty. A busy day lay ahead, starting with an eight-thirty meeting with Ailsa, earlier than usual, for their breakfast on the hotel deck. They wanted to leave for the Pitlochry station no later than ten to be in the city before one. That would give them a couple of hours to visit the Edinburgh Castle, which Ailsa insisted she'd love, before getting to the National Records building by three.

Before all that, however, there was something she must do.

The bicycle the hotel clerk offered looked older than Innis Bree herself, but it worked well enough. With a shabby basket on the handlebars and back pedaling for brakes, she found it charming. She turned onto the gravel road that led to Laird Blyth's dilapidated mansion and saw a wooden sign, "Blyth Lane." The day he gave her a ride in his truck, when he found her in his mansion, it'd been raining so hard she hadn't been able to see what lay along the route. Today, with the morning sun in a clear sky, she could see it all.

Closest to the village was a white farmhouse that looked to be about thirty or forty years old. Not ancient. Two giant oak trees shaded the front lawn, with a variety of flowers in beds and window boxes. She got a glimpse of a vegetable garden. It was a cozy setting.

A large stone barn came next, set back in a field. There was a patch of stone fences, cutting the land into squares that sprawled out all the way to the hills.

A cottage sat in front of the fences with a dirt lane leading to it from the gravel one she was on. What had once undoubtedly been a thatched roof had been replaced with metal, but the stone structure with small windows was old. As a croft, it would be from the 1700s.

She pedaled along, enjoying the morning. When she crested a hill and came upon a pasture of sheep with the mansion in the near distance, she stopped and got off the bike. It was one of the most perfectly serene scenes she'd ever witnessed. Blue wild-flowers grew along the lane, and she wondered if it was against the law to pick wildflowers here like it was back home.

"I guess I'll find out. Scottish jail can't be any worse than a faculty meeting." She shook her head at herself and picked a hand-ful, placing them in the basket on the bike. She raked her fingers through her loose hair to shove it away from her face and placed a posey over an ear. It made her smile.

She hopped on the bike and headed for the manor house.

He was there, his back to her, as he worked on the collapsed section of the house. His truck was parked to the side. Maisie saw Innis Bree from afar and popped up from where she'd been lying down. In a tizzy, she looked up at her master imploringly as her body quaked and her tail flailed. She looked at Innis Bree. Back at her master. Her wagging quickened as she did a little dance with her front paws. Laird gestured to her with an upraised palm, and Maisie bounded out to their guest, barking with glee. The dog sat, apparently having been taught that was how to greet people, even though her body still quivered with joy.

"Hi, Maisie. How are you, girl? Oops. I guess it's lassie here, isn't it?" Innis Bree parked the bicycle at the side of the lane and squatted down to pet her new friend.

Maisie responded with a raised paw to indicate she wanted to be petted on the ruff under her chin. Innis Bree couldn't deny the request. After a minute, both females walked the remainder of the distance to the house.

He hadn't stopped working, picking up stones from where a wall had long ago fallen and heaving them into a pile. Even though it was only about eight o'clock, he'd obviously been working for a good while. The size of the pile, the dirt on his work gloves, and the sweat on his tee shirt were testaments to that. The shirt clung to his back, outlining his muscular frame.

"Hello, Innis Bree," he said without looking at her, instead continuing with his task.

"How'd you know it was me?"

"Maisie hasn't been that excited about anybody in a good long while. It had to be you." He finally turned around to face her, rock in hand, which he threw with more force than he had the others. "To what do I owe the honor o' your visit to my fallen down manse?" His tone was anything but welcoming.

"Cranky this morning, aren't you?"

He used his forearm to wipe sweat off his forehead. "Truth is, Miss MacIntyre, I'm *cranky* every morning. Now, why are you here?" He removed his work gloves, tossed them aside, and spread his arms out in exasperation.

She liked the way his biceps bulged with the gesture but shook it off. She had no time for such foolishness.

"I came to tell you something. I didn't know for sure you'd be here. But if you were, and you are, I wanted to tell you that you were right."

"Pray tell, what am I right about?" He took a few steps closer, fists on hips.

Something told her he wasn't purely mocking her but also entertaining himself by being difficult.

"I shouldn't have gone out with Rory Skeffington. It was a mistake."

"You dinnae say. And what made it such a mistake?"

"Well … well …" Tears sprung to her eyes, and she hated herself for it.

"Och nae. Dinnae go crying now." He gestured broadly, flummoxed. "It cannae have been that bad."

She thought him smarmy. Maybe her date with Rory Skeffington had been wretched. What made him think it wasn't?

"He has, well, he has this room in the cellar of the castle."

He squinted and slowly nodded once. "I see. Perhaps we'd best sit." He motioned toward a low stone wall that seemed solid enough.

As soon as they sat, Maisie laid down at her feet, sensing the distress and giving comfort.

"Innis Bree," Laird said, his voice softening with concern while his jaw clenched with potential anger, "he didn't force himself on you, did he?"

"No, it's not that. I ran away when he, you know, put on the moves. You see, he has one of those BD-something-something rooms that are in erotic books and movies," she confided, her voice faltering, "I guess."

"Eh? You guess? Ah, I ken. You dinnae watch erotic movies or read those books. So, the room had equipment in it, like ropes and such?"

"Yes."

"I see." He hesitated, visibly contemplating what to say next. "Do you want to ken, to know, what that's all about?"

"I'm not totally stupid. It's pretty obvious. I've heard of it but never paid any attention. It's not my kind of thing. I don't remember exactly what it's called."

"'Tis BDSM, although sometimes 'tis called other things, too. Do you know what BDSM stands for?"

"Maybe 'binding,' 'dominating' ..." she shook her head "... and I don't know, and I don't know."

He leaned away from her in mock wonder. "Innis Bree MacIntyre, you might be the only living being o'er eighteen who doesna know this. I take that back. With today's social media, the only living being o'er fifteen. 'Tis bondage, so you were close on that one. Discipline or domination, so you got that one. The S is sadism, and the M is masochism."

"How do you know all this stuff?" She popped up off the wall, throwing him a leer of disgust. "Do you have one of those rooms?"

He chuckled, leaned his elbows on his knees, and rubbed his stubbly chin. "Nae. I dinnae. I do read books and watch movies, though. 'Tis in his cellar, you say?"

"That's what got us into trouble." She paced back and forth, still trying to put it all together. "He said he'd show me the dungeon, and I was excited because I thought I'd be seeing a historical torture chamber."

"Wait, wait, wait. He sent you all those gifts and dolled you up in that red dress and squired you ..." he sat up and pointed in that direction "... to his castle in the dark o' night and you thought he wanted to take you on a historical tour? Excuse me for asking, but are you daft?"

She stopped pacing and confronted him. "How do you know about the gifts and red dress? Did you see me?"

"Och, please. Everyone in the pub saw you come down the

stairs and leave with him. Didna you see all the necks craning to get a gander?"

She hated to admit she'd been so enchanted by Rory she hadn't noticed other people noticing her. "You were in the pub."

"Nae. I came in later and heard all about it. You haven't answered my question. After all that, did you really think he wouldna try to – I dinnae ken how to say this politely – try to shag you?"

"I've never heard 'shag' before, but I can guess what it means. The answer is sure, I thought he might try, but I didn't expect it to get that far because I would say no." She gestured nervously as she tried to express emotions she couldn't quite identify. "It's just that I wanted to feel like a princess for once in my life. Special, you know?"

"I cannae say that I do. I've ne'er wanted to be a princess. You managed to get away from him, aye?"

"Yeah. I admit that when he realized I didn't understand, he immediately offered to take me upstairs. I guess he was okay about it. But I was mad that he hadn't told me what was down there."

"Are you sure he didna tell you and maybe you misunderstood?"

That baffled her. She hadn't thought of that. "I don't know. Maybe."

"Would you like me to talk to him?"

"No! If I decide he needs talking to, I'll do it myself."

He nodded, amused. "Aye, I'm sure you will."

"It was okay in the end. I left and walked to the hotel by myself."

He paused before saying, "So I heard. You came back early, alone."

"Oh, Laird, my life is shit." She felt herself spiraling out of control, falling into a pit of self-pity. A part of her brain knew this was TMI territory, but another part took over and she couldn't stop herself. "Deep doo-doo shit."

"Now you're talking about the Walter who buggered off on your trip?"

"O-o-ooh, it's worse than that. This wasn't a mere 'trip'. This, right now, is supposed to be my honeymoon. I'm on my honeymoon all by myself. How pathetic is that?"

"Ah, quite so. A honeymoon all by yourself isna quite a honeymoon, is it?"

"Hardly. And that wasn't even the beginning. First, I was fired. I worked my butt off for nine years, working crappy restaurant jobs while I was in college. Server, dishwasher, busser, you name it, I did it. All that so I could earn a doctorate degree in history and teach college. It's all I've ever wanted to do. I love teaching. I love my students and my colleagues. Although I confess, I hate the boring faculty meetings. All those years, all that work …for what? Nothing. My dean hated me as much as I hated her, and she fired my ass."

He stretched his neck to feign looking behind her. "'Tis still there, I must say."

She ignored the remark, not knowing what to make of it. "I have enough money saved for one year. After that, if I don't find a new job, I'll be out on the street."

"You dinnae say. I'm going to venture a guess you won't become a streetwalker, eh?"

"Oh hardy har har. No. Of course not. Walter and I had been looking at houses. We talked about starting a family. I had neat little pictures in my head of what my life was going to look like from now until happily-forever-after." She'd worked herself into a frenzy, stuck in the muck that made up her life. "Now the pictures are all gone. My future is a total blank."

Considering her plight, Laird took his time responding, eventually suggesting, "Maybe that means you can fill in the blank any way you want."

Too steeped in her wallowing to take that in, she volleyed with, "I thought that was what I wanted. We were supposed to get married last Saturday. On our honeymoon here we were going to visit a Scottish ancestor town for each of us." Her eyes fell on the sheep in yonder pasture, and she paused, lost in misery. "Instead, he threw me out like yesterday's sushi."

"Ouch."

"Ouch indeed. My wedding dress is ripped up on the floor of my apartment. Walter might have ruined my life, but I refused to let him ruin this once-in-a-lifetime trip I've been dreaming about for years." Deflated, her energy zapped and her ire useless, she sighed as her body sagged with remorse.

"Walter sounds like a flaming bastart."

"I hate men. No offense intended."

"None taken. I've hated women e'er since my divorce."

She stopped pacing and glared at him. "Ohmygawd, I can't believe I told you all that. I dumped it all right on you. I'm so sorry." Flustered, she spun around to leave. "That's not why I came here," she threw over her shoulder as she headed for her bike. "I just wanted you to know you were right about Rory Skeffington."

He scurried to catch up and took her arm to stop her. She turned to come face-to-face with Laird Bartholomew Blyth. The surprise of his nearness shook her to her core. A few inches taller than she, it struck her that they'd be perfect dance partners, creating an urge to take his hand in hers, place her other hand on his shoulder, and sway to imaginary music.

"It's okay," he insisted. "You hate men. I hate women. We're quite a pair, eh?"

"Quite."

Those lake-blue eyes of his – she couldn't help but swim in

them. And the scent of him was familiar. Could it possibly be the same fresh air and heather and manly scent as her ghost?

His hand slid off her arm and inched around her waist. Closer and closer they came, their bodies gravitating to one another of their own accord, detached from conscious thought. In one another's arms, they moved together until her breasts grazed his chest.

"Innis Bree," he rasped, weaving a hand into her hair, grabbing hold, and ravishing her with a kiss so all-consuming she thought she might faint from the sheer bliss of it.

He let go and backed away, throwing his hands up as if she held him at gunpoint and threatened arrest. The sudden detachment left her feeling bereft with abandonment.

"Shite. I'm so sorry," he lamented, placing his hands on his head and backing farther away. "I shouldna have done that. You're vulnerable right now. I'm a moron. We cannae do this."

"Oh. Oh, of course not," she stammered. "Of course not." She stumbled backwards, then ran for her bike to flee. She picked up the bike but dropped it in the middle of the lane. In the second it took her to turn around, Laird had bounded up behind her.

A horn honked up the lane, diverting their attention. They stepped apart, embarrassed and clumsy. Laird's sister's red Citroën barreled toward them and stopped. A cheerful red-haired woman hopped out of the driver's side, and a large man stumbled out of the passenger side, a cast-like boot on his foot.

"Hi! I'm Jenny, Laird's sister." The energetic woman bounded up to them. "Your Innis Bree MacIntyre. I've been wanting to meet you." She extended a hearty handshake. "This is Clyde the hobbler," she chuckled.

Laird had gone to the car and helped Clyde get out a pair of crutches. The jolly man hobbled up and shook hands as well.

"So glad to make your acquaintance. Jenny's been champing at the bit to talk to you."

"Aye," Jenny picked up. "I hear you're working with Ailsa on your family history. That's wonderful. With this being such a small village, I'm sure you'll find some kind o' connection between our families long ago. When I saw you go by, I figured you were taking a nice morning ride, perhaps without knowing who'd be out here."

"Truth is," Clyde interrupted, "she was so afraid her dear brother here would be a crabbit to you when you accidentally came upon him, she wanted to intervene."

Jenny clapped her husband's shoulder with the back of her hand. "That was a secret."

"Sorry, love." Clyde smirked, not sorry at all.

Jenny tunked her head sideways toward Laird. "He can be a beast at times, but I assure you he's a good bloke at heart."

Innis Bree's emotions reeled. It hadn't been his heart she'd been homing in on. It was all that other stuff on the outside, those deep blue eyes, that unruly dark hair, the square jaw, the tempting mouth, his body … oh mercy, his body. She'd been aching for him to turn into a beast. She strained to pull it together and act like a normal human being rather than a sex-craved idiot who had no business being attracted to a man who had nothing to do with her life.

"I'm glad to meet you," she said as casually as possible. "As for family connections, Ailsa and I have already found a connection between our families. In the late 1600s, according to church records, an Innis Bree MacIntyre, my name, was 'betrothed' to one Bruce Cieran Blyth. But we don't see that they ever married."

"You dinnae say," Jenny marveled. "How interesting. Will you let us know if you find out more?"

"Yes, I'd be glad to. Which reminds me, I have an appointment with Ailsa right about now. We're going to Edinburgh this afternoon to see what we can find in the archives. We're working on tracking down that Innis Bree."

"I daresay Bruce is in the graveyard right here at the kirk," Jenny said.

Innis Bree wasn't about to go into how she knew that all too well, as she'd seen his ghost right there.

"He's our many times great-grandfather," Jenny continued. "Laird, you have the family Bibles. You can look it up. Be nice to the American lady and help her out."

Laird raised his eyebrows at his sister while Innis Bree's knees went weak with a quick image of how she'd wanted him to "help her out" only minutes before.

"Well, I'd best be going," she said. "It's great to meet you. Thanks." Another part of her brain screamed, *You ruined my life!* Of course, she didn't know if that was true. Would he have kissed her again if they hadn't been interrupted? Nah, surely not. He'd only felt sorry for her, probably, that first time.

Dejected and confused, she got on her bike, waved, and rode away.

Maisie trotted along behind her, barking displeasure at her leaving. She wondered if Laird felt displeasure at her leaving. Or was he glad to be rid of her?

CHAPTER 10

"I'm so sorry I'm late." Innis Bree rushed to take the chair that awaited her at the table where Ailsa sat on the deck of the hotel. She took a big gulp of the water that had been placed at her spot. Her usual glass of orange juice awaited, too. A teapot in a cute cozy also sat on the table.

Ailsa took her in and said, "Huh. You look different. What is it?" She rummaged around in her tote bag to come up with bright-pink-framed glasses and put them on to investigate.

"What do you mean? It's only me, same jeans, same tee shirt, same ponytail I wear every day." She'd thrown her hair into the ponytail only minutes before and hadn't checked in a mirror to see if was askew. She took a long swig of her juice to pretend to be normal.

"Nae, that's naw it. There's something different. Ah, I see!" Ailsa lowered her voice to a whisper. "You fancy a man right here in Kenmore." She rubbed her hands together in delight, her bracelets singing their usual merry tune.

"What? Don't be ridicu … Oh good heavens, how could you tell? And it certainly isn't love. It can't be. It's a simple school-girl infatuation. And he hates my guts." Innis Bree gave up being coy. That would never work with Ailsa.

The teenaged server with the colorful stripy hair appeared with a basket of baked goods, set it down, and examined her. "You look different. What is it?"

"Um, no, it's the same old me."

The girl frowned and shook her head. "Nae. That's naw it." She sauntered away.

"I'm surprised," Ailsa said, "but pleased if you are. Are you pleased to have this attraction?"

"I honestly don't know. I mean, it's foolish, isn't it? I am, after all, on my honeymoon," she chaffed.

"Pfft. Thank the Lord that honeymoon ne'er took place, not with your fiancé's willy-nilly inanity. Did you love him, Innis Bree? I mean truly love him, as in a soulmate?"

"I ... I don't know. Truthfully, I've started to fear I was in love with the idea of having stability and a family more than I was in love with him. I can never let that happen again."

"There's nothing wrong with wanting those things, as long as they're accompanied by deep love for each other."

"Ailsa, you never talk about your love life."

"True. I don't, not usually. But everyone around here knows my story, so I may as well tell you, too. I've been a widow for forty-eight years. That's right. My husband died in an accident in the foundry where he worked when he was only thirty. I was twenty-six and pregnant with our daughter. I raised her alone. She's a nurse in Glasgow with a lovely family. I have three grandbairns and two great-grandbairns." She beamed, proud of her brood.

"You never wanted to marry again?"

"Nae. I wasn't against it, mind you. I'm still naw against it. The right man simply hasn't come along yet. I'm fore'er hopeful."

"Hope is the will to love. I read that somewhere once."

"Really? That's right. There isn't merely a hope you'll find love.

Hope is love in disguise. The desire to love, the will to love, the need to love. One must believe in love and be able to love in order to hope. Och, I'm getting all philosophical here. Let's get back to you. You say 'tis an infatuation you feel. Might it be more? I ken many people would say you cannae ken that in a few days. I disagree. I think you can if you're naw fooling yourself for some needy reason."

"That's what I'm not sure about. I'm probably as needy as anybody could get." She decided to forego mentioning that she'd spent the night with a man, albeit a ghost. Besides, they'd only slept in each other's arms, at least as far as she remembered. "I admit, I'm lonely. I thought I'd be married by now. It isn't easy being fired from your work and being left almost at the altar within days of each other."

"I'm so sorry that happened to you. It's wise to be careful about fancying Laird."

"Laird? How did you know? I had a date with Rory last night. I assumed you assumed it was him."

"Och nae, love. Everyone saw you come home early. It looked like you'd been running. Nobody took him seriously. When I heard you'd taken a bike out this morning, I figured there was only one place you would go."

"Geez. Am I really that transparent?" Innis Bree pointed at herself with a piece of scone in hand then popped it in her mouth. "I may as well shout it from every social media platform out there."

'Oh, that's already done, I fear. The tourist who posted the showdown between Rory and Laird in the pub? They ended up with a 50-50 response as to who people thought you should pick. When you came back early, the Rory camp was mightily disappointed."

"Oh, good lord. I hope my friends back home didn't see that."

"How about Walter?"

Innis Bree hadn't considered that. "Walter. Huh. Having him

see two handsome men bickering over me – well, actually they hate each other, and it wasn't so much about me, but people wouldn't know that. It must've looked like a fight over me. That would show Walter a thing or two." She happily poured herself a cup of tea.

Ailsa tittered, and the mood lightened as they ate their breakfast. "Tell me, what happened on your date with Rory? Why did you run away from him?"

For the second time that morning, Innis Bree told her tale. The retelling somehow made it less traumatic, and she could see that perhaps she'd played a part in the misunderstanding. Ailsa didn't say much as she nodded reassuringly.

When they'd finished eating and sipped the last of their tea, Ailsa said, "We have an hour before we need to leave for the train station. There's something I want to do. You must come with me."

"What is it?"

"You'll see."

Five minutes later, Innis Bree found herself crawling through a hole in the fence that supposedly kept Bridgmoor Castle private.

"Everybody in town kens how to get in there," Ailsa explained. "It's hidden by brush but easy enough. The various owners o' the castle since the '90s have all been vacationers who are seldom in residence. When they're gone, townfolk like to hike the property. It's such a beautiful place."

Innis Bree had to hustle to keep up with the older woman as Ailsa led the way, marching down a hill of heather and right up to the grand entrance to the castle. She pounded on the door like an angry invader.

Jeffrey opened the door a crack, saw who it was, and opened it wide. "Hello, ladies. Are you here to speak to Mr. Skeffington?"

"Jeffrey, love," Ailsa groaned, "you don't have to be that hoity-toity with us. Give it up."

Jeffrey's face relaxed as he whispered. "I know, Miss Ailsa, but he likes it this way. I'll get fired, I fear, if I dinnae play his game."

"Well ..." Ailsa placed the back of her hand on his chest to move him aside and stepped in "... speaking of games. Please get 'Mr. Skeffington' for us, will you, love?"

"Aye." Jeffrey motioned for Innis Bree to enter, too, then took them into the parlor to wait.

Although he'd invited them to be seated on French-style chairs in shiny blue brocade, as soon as he left, they got up to roam around the room. Innis Bree checked out the architecture, bold crown molding, mullioned windows, the chandelier medallion, and parquet floor. Ailsa was more interested in the lush upholstery fabrics and Persian carpets. It took a full fifteen minutes for Rory Skeffington to appear, leaving Innis Bree to wonder if he'd been down in his cellar playing around.

"Ladies." He nodded and half bowed. "To what do I owe the pleasure of this unexpected visit?" He looked at Ailsa, avoiding Innis Bree.

"Sit down, Rory," Ailsa demanded. "We need to talk."

Innis Bree wasn't sure what was coming, but she had a good idea that Rory Skeffington was about to get the scolding of his life. She couldn't wait.

LAIRD CONTINUED his work of clearing debris from the open section of the mansion, which revealed what lay beneath fallen stones, leaves, and dust. The three-hundred-year-old craftsman-ship on the marble and wood floors was spectacular. Surprisingly, they were mostly intact. Interior walls in that half of the house were gone, however, wooden stubs remained to delineate where rooms had once been. The outer stone walls and chimney survived, looming upward without much support. His degree in architectural engineering and experience rebuilding war-torn structures in Iraq while in the Army made this project an easy task.

He'd ordered steel beams that he'd install to support the walls from the inside to assure the building's safety. Once they were in place, Clyde was going to help him install oak rafters that would buttress across the area like those on the ceiling of the kirk. That would provide stability and a striking architectural element as well. The space would remain open-air with no covering of ceiling and roof. A fireplace the size of his truck sat on the wall that joined the half of the house that remained solid. Many nights since he'd finally managed to buy the manse a year earlier, he'd lit a fire and sat in a camp chair right there, drinking Aberfeldy Scotch Whisky, the glorious open sky above.

His emotions roiled. Pushing himself, he worked like a demon possessed.

"Damn, lassie, what have I done?"

Maisie lifted her head off her paws and panted in anticipation.

"I've nae business having anything to do with Miss Innis Bree MacIntyre, do I?" He stopped working and kicked some fallen brush out of his way. "Our lives are four thousand miles apart, eh? She did seem attracted to me right at the end there. Do you think? Pfft. Leave it to Jenny and Clyde to save my arse. I was about to grab her for another kiss. I woulda made a total eejit out o' myself. I need to keep my hands off. Besides, I hate women, right?"

He went back to work until Maisie drew his attention when she whimpered.

"What? Are you calling me a lying bastart? You dinnae believe a word I'm saying, do you?"

Maisie snarked.

"Aye. Neither do I, lassie. Neither do I."

"WE'LL START WITH YOU, Innis Bree." Ailsa pointed at her, causing the young woman to wince.

"Me?"

"Aye, love, you. How old are you?"

"Why, I'm thirty-two."

"And you claim to ne'er have heard of BDSM before?"

"Well, of course, I've heard of it in a rather oblique way. I know in theory what it means, but I've never been interested in the details."

"Och, theory. Therein lies the problem. I'm naw in any way suggesting you need to be interested in it. Or do it. What I am suggesting is that you need to get your head out o' your textbooks and theories and the past and pay at bit o' attention to what's going on in the world around you today."

Bolstered by that, Rory chimed in. "Haven't you ever read *Fifty Shades of Grey?*"

"Heavens no." Innis Bree felt as if she was being interrogated by two bad cops.

Ailsa held up a hand to silence Rory and turned her attention back to Innis Bree. "I'm naw suggesting you read that or any other such novel unless you want to. I'm saying it may have been clearer what Rory was up to if you'd had your head out o' the past. You wanted to see a historic castle. He wanted to have kinky sex. From what you told me, you should at least have been suspicious and clarified with him before going into a cellar, o' all places."

"I, I, well, it didn't occur to me."

"I'm saying it should have. You're a grown woman. You're naw a high school virgin."

"It wouldn't surprise me if she was," Rory interrupted, rolling his eyes.

"Shht. Quiet, Rory. You'll get a turn. Innis Bree, at the very least, it should have been obvious he wanted to have sex with you. After all, it was obvious to everyone else in the village."

Innis Bree blushed, crossed her arms over her chest, and sunk into her chair to pout like a kid.

"And you." Ailsa turned her attention to Rory, who flinched. "Has anyone e'er told you you're quite a shite?"

"You can't talk to me that way in my own home." He bristled with indignation.

"I just did. Answer the question, please. Has anyone e'er told you..."

"Okay, okay. If you must know, yes. There. Satisfied?"

"Women you've dated?"

"No. Never. Only, well, only one woman."

Ailsa glared at him for more.

"Okay, okay, okay. My mother. Every time I visit her, which is why I don't visit her."

"I see. So this concept isn't totally new to you. Keep that in mind. Now, for the matter at hand, you told Innis Bree you had a 'dungeon,' correct?"

"Yes, I did," he insisted defensively.

"You did naw say 'sex dungeon.'"

"I don't know. I guess not. But everyone knows what a dungeon is these days." He became belligerent, his face reddening like a child whose favorite toy has been taken away.

"Nae, Rory, 'everyone' does not know that, as you have now learned. I want you to make a promise to me. If you do that, I promise not to make any trouble for you here in Scotland."

"What kind of trouble? There's nothing you can do. I've not broken any laws. The women I bring here are of age. I make certain of that. They consent to everything we do."

Ailsa considered that. "Why did you buy this castle?"

He shrugged. "For the cellar. For the game playing. Prince and princess. Women love that crap. What better way to play the game than to fly American women over here on my jet, bring them to my castle, and, and ..." he fumbled for an appropriate word "...

frolic in a real dungeon? Most women are head over heels – no pun intended – for the whole thing."

"Do you make it clear to them from the beginning that the sex dungeon is included in this game?"

"Yes. Of course. At least I thought I'd always been clear. And if anyone ever wanted out, which they never do, I would never force them."

"Innis Bree, he didn't force you, did he?"

"No," she admitted with a pitiful sigh.

"So we have a very turgid misunderstanding here. Now, to answer your question, Rory, about naw doing anything wrong, legally you have naw. Morally and ethically, you have. The deal I want to make is this: you must tell every woman you date what your end goal is right up front. You must say it clearly, spelling it out so there will be nae misunderstandings. Naw 'I have a dungeon,' but 'I have a sex dungeon and am into BDSM. That's bondage, dominance, sadism, and masochism.' Or howe'er you would describe it clearly. 'If you don't want to participate in that, no hard feelings, but I'm not interested in dating you.' Got that?"

The bridge of his nose crinkled with a frown. "Part of the fun is the surprise."

"Nae surprises. That's not the ethical way to do it."

"What could you possibly do to me if I don't agree to your deal?"

"Och, Rory, you have no idea how miserable I can make your life here in Scotland. I'm an auld bird with lots of friends in high places. Who knows? You might get speeding tickets. Your airstrip might naw be up to standards, and you'll lose clearance to fly here. Your passport might be questionable and could be taken away."

He stared at the elder woman, unsure of her ability to pull that off. Finally, he said, "First of all, Ailsa, I agree about telling women my goal up front. Since last night, I'd already come to that conclusion on my own. The last thing on earth I need is to have my time eaten up by some ridiculous court case if some woman tries to sue me. We live in litigious times, that's always a possibility. Secondly, I've decided to sell the castle. It was great fun at first, the novelty of coming to an authentic castle to play a fun version of the prince and princess fantasy. But I'm tired of the time it takes to get here. I can build a dungeon – pardon me, a 'sex dungeon', to be clear – at home. So, I'll be out of your little village in no time."

"Good! Isn't that marvelous, Innis Bree?" Ailsa popped up out of her seat.

"Ah huh. Marvelous." She stood up, too, so Rory did, as well.

"Wait," Ailsa said, plopping back down. Innis Bree and Rory followed like lemmings. "One more thing. Well, two things, really. How did you get those beautiful clothes to Innis Bree so fast? And may we see the cellar? After all, it was a desire to see it that caused all this trouble to begin with."

Rory studied her before breaking into laughter. "You 'old bird,' as you call yourself. You're curious about a sex dungeon, aren't you?"

"I'm guessing it's my only chance in this lifetime to see one."

"Okay, follow me. We'll start with the clothes."

He summoned Jeffrey who joined them as they went upstairs, down a long hallway, and into a room that had been locked. Rory pulled a ring of keys out of his pocket to open it. Jeffrey had never seen the room before and was as dumbfounded as the women.

At least two dozen dresses, red on one rack, black on one, and blue on another, all in the same style in sizes four to fourteen, hung there as if in an upscale boutique. Shelves full of shoe boxes lined one wall. A standing case with glass doors stood against another wall with flashy jewelry inside. A long table held boxes and wrapping supplies, the gold paper and ribbons familiar to Innis Bree.

"I like to be prepared," Rory explained, quite proud of himself.

Innis Bree fingered one of the red dresses. "They're all the same. You simply pulled out what you guessed to be my size. It wasn't something special you did for me and me alone."

He shrugged. "I admit, that's how it works."

"They're beautiful." Mesmerized, Ailsa ran a hand down a blue sequined gown.

"Let's see." Rory took down the one she ogled. "You're small. These are American sizes. Eight perhaps?" He held it up to her. "Yes, perfect. It matches your eyes. Here …" he shoved it into her hands "…take it."

"Och my! Nae. I cannae." She hung it up.

"Why not?"

"Thank you for the offer, but where is it you think I'd be wearing something that grand?"

He shrugged. "You never know. Better ready than sorry."

He didn't force the issue, and they left the upstairs to examine the cellar. This time, Innis Bree got the kind of tour she'd been hoping for in the first place.

As they started to descend the stairs, Rory flicked a switch and turned a rheostat knob. Bright light shone.

"Wait!" she quipped. "You had good lighting here all the time. You rat."

The journey down the narrow, spiraled stairs was much easier in the light. When they reached the sex dungeon, Rory used his antique key to unlock the door. Inside, he flicked another switch that brightly illuminated the room.

The two guests, Innis Bree and Ailsa, and Jeffrey silently roamed around the space, bug-eyed and not touching anything as if fearing contamination. Their host leaned up against a table, arms folded, bored.

Innis Bree pointed at something hanging amongst other items on pegs. "Look at these, Ailsa."

Ailsa went over, examined it, and said, "They're beautiful. What wonderful craftsmanship."

That caught Rory's attention, and he came to see what they were talking about. "Ah. The chaps. Exquisite tooled leather from a master saddlemaker in Texas."

"She likes American cowboy romance novels." Innis Bree nudged her friend.

"The whip matches, I see." Ailsa pointed out the whip hanging next to the chaps.

"Yes, the whip our friend here tried to lash me with." He'd taken on a teasing tone as he motioned toward Innis Bree.

She ignored him and surveyed the room some more, coming up with a conclusion. "These pegs you use are really old. Your new chains are attached to rusted metal rings embedded in the walls. This indeed would've been a torture chamber before you made it a, you know, what you made it. Were there any old devices left here when you bought the castle?"

"No. It'd been cleaned out, like most of the rest of the place except for the foyer."

"There must be other rooms down here," Jeffrey noted, looking around.

"Right this way." Rory led them down the hall to a short, heavy door Innis Bree hadn't noticed the night before in the dim light. They had to duck down to get through. Their host turned on more lights, and a long, narrow hallway emerged from the dark. He didn't walk far before stopping. "There are a number of smaller rooms down here. I have no idea what they were for. I only had lights installed in the larger one at the end. I thought maybe I'd make it a sexy, spooky bedroom. It ended up creeping me out, and I never did it."

"Creepy, indeed." Ailsa shook her head. "Get a grip, Rory."

He led them down the hall, and with each step Innis Bree found herself becoming more and more unable to breathe, claustrophobia overwhelming her. The walls moved in, the ceiling inched down, and the floor rumbled under her feet. Refusing to let it get the better of her, she soldiered on without a word until she had to gasp for air.

Jeffrey came to her aid, protectively wrapping an arm around her shoulders. "We'd better go," he insisted.

"No. No. I'll be okay." An incomprehensible need to see that room overtook her fear. It wasn't a matter of wanting to see it anymore. A powerful urge made it necessary.

Ailsa patted her arm, Jeffrey let go but stayed close, and they made it to the end of the hall. Even Rory looked pale and peaked, uneasy about what lay behind that door.

"Rory," Innis Bree whispered, "do you think there are ghosts down here?"

Rory visibly shivered. "Yes. Especially in here."

Once again, his magic key unlocked the door. It creaked open, and they stepped inside. An impossible whoosh of air struck. They flinched with surprise. Innis Bree and Ailsa yelped and clung to each other. Getting their bearings once the lights were on, they could see it was a medium-sized room with no access to anything outside its walls. No one asked where the gust had come from. No one dared.

They circled around to discover hundreds of crude images and crooked letters carved into the stone walls. Gobsmacked, the women tenderly ran their fingers over the etchings in the stone, without words, sharing the knowledge that people had suffered interminably here.

An urge to cry struck Innis Bree. She choked it back. She needed to stay alert for some reason she couldn't grasp. Her foot faltered on the uneven dirt floor, and she reached out to the wall to steady herself, her hand landing on a carved Celtic cross. Someone imprisoned here had managed to maintain a belief in God. The presence of the people who had endured excruciating pain here was so acute, she felt their urgent breath upon her neck and quivered with a mix of fear and sorrow.

"This has to be where prisoners were kept when naw being tortured and killed in the other room," Jeffrey said. "They had time to do all this while going mad."

"You can see why I decided not to use this room," Rory said. "It creeps me out. Let's go."

They left the cellar, Rory in the lead and Jeffrey last in his desire to protect the women. Once emerged from the morbid depths, Rory asked if there was anything else his guests would like to see. Both women agreed they'd had enough for one day.

As they walked out the front door, Ailsa turned to their host. "Thank you for listening to me today, Rory. And thank you for the tour. I have only one suggestion left for you."

Rory, having warmed to them considerably, asked, "What might that be?"

"Go visit your mother, love. Listen to what she tells you. She's right. Bye!" She waved with a jangle of her bracelets. Having refused a ride, she and Innis Bree walked down the driveway, trekked across the yard, climbed through the hole in the fence, which it turned out Rory knew all about, and returned to the sanity of the village.

Once there, Innis Bree asked, "Ailsa, could you really do all those things you threatened to do, like have his passport taken away?"

"Och heavens, nae. That was a crock o' shite. I think he only half believed it himself."

"So maybe he won't do as you asked, making it more clear to women what he wants."

"Aye, he will. Naw because he fears an auld bird like me, but because now it's occurred to him to fear a lawsuit. That will involve time and money, and money is all that matters to Mr. Rory Skeffington."

CHAPTER 11

*A*ilsa drove them to the Pitlochry station where they caught a train to Edinburgh. They grabbed lunch in the dining car during the two-hour ride that stopped in historical small towns along the way.

When their train arrived at Waverly Station in the center of the city, Innis Bree was enthralled by the beauty of the enormous nineteenth-century building. As they walked toward the exit, Ailsa guided her with a hand on her arm so she wouldn't trip from looking up to take in the massive skylights, especially the ornate glass cupola in the center of the terminal ceiling.

"This place is magnificent!" she marveled.

"Aye, 'Tis at that." Ailsa agreed.

Once on the street, they walked a couple of blocks before turning down High Street, famous as The Royal Mile, the stretch between Edinburgh Castle and the Palace of Holyroodhouse, which put them in the part of the city known as Old Town. With evocative medieval cobblestone streets and stone buildings, the past soared around them, immersing Innis Bree in the richness of

Edinburgh's history. She could only imagine the secrets from the past that were safely hidden, never to be disclosed, down the narrow lanes and dark alleyways off the main street.

The castle on the hill came into sight, its fortress-like presence towering above the city.

"Look at that!" Innis Bree pointed. "Wow! It's so beautiful."

"Aye. You've undoubtedly read about it. Built in the eleventh century by King David the First, 'tis o'er nine hundred years old. Some o' the original parts o' the structure are still standing, like the chapel he built for his mother, Queen Margaret. Mary Queen of Scots once lived here, too. 'Twas used as a royal residence and a military base for centuries."

They ventured up the hill to tour the castle. The crown room with Scotland's crown jewels and the great hall that was once used for banquets and other special events left lasting impressions on their American visitor. But it was St. Margaret's Chapel that stole Innis Bree's heart. The spirit of the devout queen from nine hundred years earlier who'd said her daily prayers there was still present in the tiny room with its simple altar.

After a couple of hours, they left for the National Records of Scotland, which was back where they'd come from on the other side of Waverly Station. They grabbed a taxi, having tired of being on their feet. On the way, Ailsa told Innis Bree that the funds for the original records building on the site came from Jacobite estates absconded after the last uprising in 1746.

The place was enormous. Innis Bree had no idea how they kept track of the hundreds of years of official and unofficial items stored within. A docent escorted them to a room for "private and corporate bodies" so they could search for personal records like diaries and letters from the Kenmore area that had been donated.

"You speak Gaelic, I presume?" the young man asked as they entered the large room filled with shelves containing stacks and boxes. "Anything more than a couple hundred years old may not be in English. Even more recent items might be written in Gaelic."

"I speak a little," Ailsa answered. "Is there someone who can help us out?"

"Certainly. *Mi*. Me. I'm the archivist who can help you."

He led them to items from the Kenmore area, gave them each a pair of rubber gloves so the oil from their skin wouldn't damage the delicate old documents, and they carefully dug in. They would see something that might be interesting, he would take it to a table, and they'd go through it. Most were ledgers of Campbell estate accounts. The amounts were surprising. They'd been a wealthy clan in times gone by.

It took ninety minutes to find a box that held letters to and from people who'd lived in Bridgmoor Castle. Excited at the fabulous find, they scoured the pages for dates, and Innis Bree came up with a stack that had been written at the right timeframe for their search. Although written in Gaelic, she'd been able to recognize the names and the date, 1690.

The archivist shook his head. "There are a dozen long letters here. We close in twenty minutes. We don't have time to go through all of them. Can you come back tomorrow?"

"Can we take photos?" Ailsa asked.

"Aye, without a flash. The light in here is good enough that your photos should be fine."

They went to work, each woman clicking away to beat the clock. They finished only a few minutes before they had to get out. Thanking the archivist as they went, they left the building, excited about what they might find once the letters were interpreted.

"Come have dinner with Mam and me tonight," Ailsa insisted. "Her Gaelic is excellent. Much better than mine. She grew up with it. She'll be able to bring back words from three hundred years ago."

Innis Bree shuddered with anticipation for what secrets might lay within the very phones they held in their hands. But before catching the train, she wanted to pop into a dress shop. Tired of wearing what Bruce called her "lad's clothes," she wanted a summer dress. Fortunately, they found the perfect shop right away and she bought a dress, shrug, and strappy sandals.

On the train ride home, they marveled at the documents, most of which they couldn't read because they were in Gaelic, on their phones. Even though it would be late, they couldn't wait to get home to Ailsa's mam, Garia, who would be able to read them.

"THIS ONE." Garia, Ailsa's ninety-four-year-old mother, spoke with reverence, her aged voice with its distinct Scottish flare clear and crisp. Ailsa had sent the photos of the letters from her phone to her printer so her mother held sheafs of paper, lifting one page out of the stack and setting the rest down on the side table.

Ailsa and Innis Bree had pulled chairs up close to the fire, facing the old woman. A gentle rain tapped at the windows. It had become a perfect evening for a highlander ghost story from a mysterious time gone by.

The moment they stepped into the small, lovely home on the other side of River Tay, Innis Bree fell in love with Garia Adair – Adair being Ailsa's maiden name. This part of the village wasn't as old and historic as that along the main street where the hotel was, but it held a charm all its own. The house was warm and cozy, delightfully lived in with cushy furniture, shelves bursting with books, and a wood-burning fireplace. A calico cat snoozed by the fire. White lace curtains and a flat-screen television married old and new in the living room. "A May-December romance," Innis Bree said of the space, which made her hosts laugh.

Silently reading, translating in her mind, Garia was a story unto herself. Although wheelchair bound, she sat up straight and strong, her long white hair gathered into a braided bun on top of her head, her crowning glory. A plaid wool wrap covered her shoulders. Innis Bree homed in on Garia's face as they waited for her to tell them what the Gaelic letter said, and in those features, Innis Bree witnessed an existence of immense joy and sorrow, a common yet extraordinary life. All those experiences had turned into a maze of laugh-lines and grief-lines that caught the glimmers of the flames, making her lived beauty hauntingly mesmerizing. Innis Bree couldn't take her eyes off intriguing Garia.

"Ah," the old woman uttered as she adjusted her glasses, "I have it now. 'Tis a letter that was ne'er sent, written by Tess Campbell, who was the sister o' Duncan Campbell. They were the bairns o' Clovis Campbell, the clan chief. They lived in the castle."

All eyes fell onto the piece of paper with its florid writing that she held in her hand.

"'*M' ulaidh ort!*' That means 'me dear' and is quite romantic. So this may have been written to a male friend. Here's the translation. 'How I wish ye were here to advise me family during this trying time. Me brother Duncan has lost his mind and is doing us in with his proclamations o' love fer a common village girl, Innis. Silly name fer a girl, better suited fer a man.'"

Garia and Ailsa glanced up at Innis Bree, who shrugged.

"Do you know that Innis is more commonly a male name in Scotland?" Ailsa asked.

"No. I had no idea."

"It's used for girls, too, but naw as often," her friend assured her.

Garia returned to the letter. "'At least this Innis has common good sense, as she rejects his advances in favor o' those o' the son o' me faither's second, a Blyth. Still, Duncan's wife is between and betwixt.'" Garia scoffed. "He was married, the bastart." She straightened the page and continued. "'Faither is threatening to send Duncan to America. His wife refuses to go, saying she won't live amongst bloody back-woods barbarians.' Och, sorry, Innis Bree."

"That's okay. I know people from other places have thought that about Americans for a long time. Many still do, with good reason, I suppose."

Garia nodded and read, "'I must hurry, as Faither is coming and insists I write in the English our wretchedly boring tutor taught us. Godspeed and arrabest, Tess.'"

"I'll look up Duncan Campbell to see if he ever landed in America." Ailsa went to get her laptop and returned to investigate online. The other two chatted about the good dinner they'd had – teriyaki chicken Ailsa picked up on their way home – while Ailsa dove into online ship manifests from the late 1600s.

"Yippee!" Ailsa turned her laptop around and pointed to a name on the screen.

"Ky-yay," Innis Bree added.

"Ha. Funny. Okay, look at this."

There, on a list written in old-fashioned calligraphy, was the name Duncan Campbell, Kenmore, Scotland, 1690.

Ailsa explained, "He went to the States through Philadelphia. I have nae idea where he went from there. I could keep looking, but he's gone from here and out of our story. We already know Innis Bree MacIntyre didn't leave Scotland, at least naw as far as I can find. She simply disappears off the map in 1690." She closed the laptop and set it down in defeat.

"Maybe she married someone in another part of the British Isles," Innis Bree speculated, "and those marriage records are stowed away in a small church there, never to be found by us. She might be buried in any one of the hundreds of small graveyards. Garia, did Ailsa tell you about my ghost?"

"Aye. He's heartbroken o'er naw being able to find his beloved who disappeared."

"Yes. What if he was totally smitten with her, but she wasn't having it? I've only heard his side of the story."

"We do know from the kirk record that showed us the blessing o' their betrothal that they were going to get married." Ailsa tried to put the disparate puzzle pieces together. "We dinnae ken if she was forced to agree to that or if she wanted to marry him. Then he says she disappeared. He eventually recuperated from the loss o' his love, obviously, because he later married and had a son. He and his wife are buried right here in Kenmore in the graveyard."

"Maybe Innis Bree was forced to agree to marry him, like a family thing or something," Innis Bree proposed. "Or maybe she did want to marry him at first but changed her mind. In either case, she may have snuck away to be rid of him. She was only fifteen, we figured out, at the time of her engagement. He was ten years older. Maybe she hated him, although that's hard to believe if my ghost is really him. He's gorgeous."

"Or," Garia added, staring into the fire, "what if 'tis something far more sinister?"

"What – " Innis Bree started to ask a question, but Ailsa motioned for her to shush.

They didn't disturb the maven as she became hypnotized by the flames. Her hands clenched the arms of her wheelchair. She leaned forward as if to better hear what the fire had to say. The flickering light danced in her gray eyes. Time passed as the rain outside pitter-pattered on the windowpanes.

"Innis Bree o' auld is here in Kenmore. She ne'er left the home o' her birth." Garia's eyes stayed transfixed on the fire. "She ne'er wed. She's glad yer here, Innis Bree." She looked at the contemporary woman, surprised at the revelation. "She wraps you in her love. Although she hopes you'll help her, her love is unconditional e'en if you cannae. After all, she's part o' you."

Innis Bree took a minute to unravel her tangled thoughts. When she spoke, it was in a stunned whisper. "Help her how?"

Garia shook her head helplessly as she took Innis Bree's hand in hers. "That, I fear, I dinnae ken."

The young woman placed her other hand on top of the delicate, intricately veined hand that held hers. A surge of something she couldn't quite identify passed between them. Knowledge? Life? Love?

"Thank you, Garia. I can feel her love. Yours, too."

That brought a huge smile to the old woman's withered lips, revealing surprisingly white teeth for having existed on earth for more than nine decades. The wise maven and the untried lass hugged.

"Hey, naw without me." Ailsa joined the huddle.

"BRUCE! Come on, Bruce. Where are you?" Innis Bree spun around in her bedroom at the hotel, taking in every nook and cranny. "I know you're here somewhere. I want to talk to you. Bruce, come here! Please? I know you're mad at me. Regardless, we need to talk."

Nary a sound came her way. Plopping down to sit on the side of the bed, she waited. One minute later, she was up again, too antsy to sit and do nothing. She went to the window to look at the clear night sky with its resplendent swath of the Milky Way. A movement by the river caught her eye. There he was, leaning against a tree.

She wrapped a blanket around her pajamas to ward off the inevitable night chill, stuck her feet into her fluffy white slippers, and scurried downstairs. This time, she pulled a chair over to hold open the door to the deck so she wouldn't lock herself out. Chair firmly in place, she strode across the lawn to his side. He didn't look at her, his head turned toward the flowing water.

"Hello, Bruce," she said as gently as possible. "I'm glad to see you."

"Och, poppycock. Ye don't love me anymore. Dinnae go telling lies aboot being glad to see me."

"I am glad to see you. I promise."

He glanced over at her, his eyes taking her in from head to toe. "Bloody hell, what have they done to ye, those villains who took ye and taught ye such wicked ways? What's that on yer feet? Have you kilt two poor rabbits fer no good reason, only to cover yer toes?"

She looked down at her slippers and wiggled her toes up and down, which animated the faux fur. "No, no. It isn't real fur. It's fake."

His brow furrowed in total confusion.

"I promise it isn't real fur. I would never kill two rabbits for shoes. Although we use leather for shoes, so I guess one is as bad as the other."

"Ye know animals must only be killed fer good purpose. Leather shoes and meat to eat are good purposes. This is naw." He pointed disgustedly at her feet.

"This is what women wear now at nighttime to keep their feet warm when they're not in bed under the covers. And they're not real animals. I promise."

"Making a lot o' promises on this eve, eh? What aboot yer promise to be me bride and love me till the end of time?"

"About that – I have some questions. You see, I, um ..." she wavered, having been thinking about this all day and knowing she needed to take a new tack "... I don't remember anything from that time. You see, my mind is a blank when it comes to that time."

"Lassie!" He grasped her shoulders in concern. "Ye've lost yer memory then? 'Tis true? I've heard tell o' such things. That explains so much. Did ye fall and bump yer heid or such?" His tone switched from concern for her to anger toward imagined kidnappers. "Nae, they hit ye on the head when they kidnapped ye?"

"Um, not exactly. I don't remember you and me together."

He embraced her, moaning miserably. "Here I am accusing ye, and all this time ye've naw remembered me." He stepped back and took her hand. "I'm so sorry."

"Bruce, please remind me of what happened. I know you got married and had children. So I'm thinking that when I disappeared, you were okay. You went on with your life."

"It must have broken yer heart when ye heard I'd wed. No wonder ye don't want anything to do with me. I waited a year, love. Fer a whole year I searched fer ye. But ye know a man has needs. I had to plant me seed fer offspring."

And for good frolics in the hay, she thought but kept her mouth shut. Deciding to forego an argument about women having "needs" too, as that would undoubtedly get very messy with this he-man from another era and she'd had enough of talking with men she didn't really know about sexual matters, she forged ahead.

"Ah, your 'needs,' of course," she said, pretending to understand and agree with him. "Why do you care about me if you had a wife?"

"I ne'er loved her as I love ye. If ye dig down deep into yer heart, me love, ye'll find that to be true."

"Okay, well, I still don't know what happened to me."

His voice softened with remorse. "It was the day o' our wedding vows. Everyone gathered in the kirk. Yer faither came running in, saying he cannae find ye, try as he might. The whole village went out and searched. Ye were gone. Vanished like the wind o'er the vale."

"I'm so sorry, Bruce. That must have been terrible for you." She took in the expansive night sky for strength. Surely an answer lay somewhere in the universe, and she wanted to find it. Her gaze falling back on him, she said, "Bruce, was there anybody who hated me who would have done me harm?"

"Ah, lassie, I've mulled that o'er in me mind until going mad as a March hare. Duncan Campbell accused ye o' being a witch because he was furious when ye refused his advances. A cheeky brat was he, used to getting his own way. When ye rebuffed him, it settled nae well in his arrogant mind. His wife must have hated ye, also, being that her husband insisted on trying to bed ye. However, Duncan's faither sent him to America, ne'er to be seen again. His wife stayed here and joined a nunnery, they claimed. Although everyone in the village doubted that, kenning her nature as we did. Apart from her, everyone in the village loved ye and would ne'er harm a raven hair on yer bonny heid. At least, none that I ken."

She turned that over in her mind, considering it from different angles. She'd become obsessed, she realized, with finding out what happened to her namesake. It was more than the connection to the long-dead woman, although that was strong. It was Bruce's connection to one Laird Blyth, the ghost's direct descendant. The connections were long and tangled and fascinating. And, she wondered, fated? Did they lead somewhere that was meant to be?

She let the thought drift away. She was, after all, a historian who worked in facts, not fantasies like "fate." Yet here she was, standing next to a ghost. Her neat little world of facts had been shattered all to hell ever since arriving in Scotland.

"Bruce, the Fenella that you married. Did I know her?"

"O' course. She was yer friend. But Innis Bree, she was a poor replacement fer ye. Dafty in the heid, she was."

Exhaustion suddenly overwhelmed Innis Bree. Unable to make sense of any of this, she bid her ghost good night.

"And, by the way, Bruce, you need to stay out of my bed."

His face took on a come-hither look, hooded eyes, tipped chin, and the corners of his mouth almost curved. By God, he was a gorgeous man. Her resolve to keep him out of her bed wavered.

"Aye. If ye dinnae remember me, I must stay away, scunnered as

I may be. A fine, Christian lad would ne'er bed a lassie who cannae remember him."

She nodded and started to walk away until he called out to her, his sultry dulcet voice irresistible.

"Ye like it when I am there with me body pressed up against yer's, do ye naw?"

She couldn't suppress a snicker and walked away mumbling, "Yeah, I like it a lot."

CHAPTER 12

The next morning as they sat at their usual spot on the hotel deck, Innis Bree updated Ailsa about Bruce's story. None of that, however, helped them figure out what had happened to the original Innis Bree. Giving up on their amateur sleuthing over a three-hundred and twenty-two-year-old mystery, Ailsa produced a first draft of the family tree she'd made for the contemporary Innis Bree.

"Oh, Ailsa, it's wonderful. Look at all these names and dates. You've noted when Gillimichell went to America." She ran her finger over her many-times great-grandfather's name and did the same for his sister Innis Bree, who didn't make it to America or anywhere else that they could find. They spent the morning with Ailsa filling in more information she'd discovered about ancestors down the line from Gillimichell, right up to the point Innis Bree knew from family stories about her great-grandparents and the grandparents she knew.

They were preparing for lunch when Jeffrey showed up at the side of their table, holding two boxes. "Hello, ladies. These are for you." He smiled broadly, something Innis Bree hadn't witnessed him do since he'd been with his friends in the pub.

"Sit down," Ailsa greeted him. He sat down and she asked, "What's all this?"

Innis Bree's heart pattered. Jeffrey and Laird were friends. Had Laird sent them something? "Who's all this from?" she asked excitedly.

"Open them to find out." Jeffrey was cute in his coyness. He slid the larger box over to Ailsa while Innis Bree got the smaller, heavier one.

Ailsa tore hers open first and stood up to peer inside. She started to laugh. And laugh. Wiping tears from her eyes, she swished aside tissue paper and picked up the black leather chaps they'd seen hanging on a peg in the sex dungeon. She held them up to her body and did a cowgirl bow-legged prance, hollering, "Yippee-ky-yay!"

Innis Bree and Jeffrey whooped and laughed along with her. A Dutch couple who also sat at a table on the deck joined in, even though they weren't privy to the inside joke. When Ailsa looked in the box again and discovered the matching whip and swung it around, another round of raucous laughter ensued.

"Heavenly days," Ailsa said. "Rory Skeffington has a sense of humor. Who knew?"

The teenaged server came out to the patio. "Hey, where'd all this come from?"

"Och, it's a long story that's naw fit for a young thing like you," Ailsa insisted.

"Huh. Us young things know more than you think." She winked and left with their teapot for a refill.

"Come on." Ailsa plopped into her chair and coaxed Innis Bree, who'd stopped unwrapping her package to enjoy her elder's little performance. "Let's see what you've got."

"Wait," Jeffrey said. "You have one more thing. Look under all the tissue paper."

Ailsa dug in and came up with the blue sequined couture gown they'd seen in the clothing room of the castle. Full-length with crystals scattered across the fabric like stardust, it had a tasteful scoop neckline and form-fitting body. Gently, almost afraid to touch it, she ran a palm over the alluring garment then held it up, tears misting her eyes. "It's ..." in her amazement, she stumbled on her words "... it's the most beautiful item of clothing I've e'er owned. I'll have to find someplace to wear it."

"Yes," Innis Bree agreed. "It'll be gorgeous on you."

The Dutch couple applauded and agreed, "Ja, ja!"

"Enough about me." Ailsa folded her items into the box and gave the Dutch couple an appreciative little wave to indicate the end of her show-and-tell. "Open yours."

As Innis Bree unwrapped, Jeffrey said, "Mr. Skeffington sent me to Edinburgh bright and early this morning to be at the book-shop when it opened. He called the shopkeeper and asked her to pick out what would be best. I hope you like them."

Innis Bree brought out the first of three books and read the cover. "*A Sinner at Highland Court, A Highland Ladies Always Book 1*, by Celeste Barclay. Ha. It's a spicy romance. He figures I don't read spicy romances."

"Do you?" Ailsa asked.

"Well, no. But it's time to start. This one looks really good." She couldn't help being amused as she pulled out a second book. "*Wild Scottish Knight, The Enchanted Highlands Book 1*, by Trisha O'Malley. Huh. Another good one." She picked up the last book. "*Highland Princess* by Haywood Smith. That Rory thinks he's so funny. But I'm going to love these."

"He's expanding the breadth of your reading material, my love," Ailsa noted. "Go with it."

Innis Bree found herself being intrigued by the kind of fiction she'd never been interested in before. She ran her fingers over the enchanting covers and discovered she couldn't wait to start reading.

Jeffrey picked up *Highland Princess* and read off the back, "'Action, adventure, and romance combine ....' Well, looks like everything a woman could ever need."

"Yes, indeed," Innis Bree agreed, finding herself delighted. "Thank you for going to all the trouble to get these for me."

"No problem. It's my job. But naw for long, though. I have news about Rory Skeffington." He wiggled his eyebrows mischievously.

"What?" the women queried in unison.

"When I returned from Edinburgh a while ago, I was shocked to find that he was packed and ready to leave. He flew out fifteen minutes ago, ne'er to return. That's exactly what he said."

Jeffrey cleared his voice, stretched his spine, and took on Rory Skeffington's air of arrogance. In a pretty good imitation of an American accent, he said, "'I don't ever want to return to this godforsaken place. Jeffrey, you're in charge of taking care of things.'" He grinned and dropped the accent. "I'm naw sure what that meant, but I like it. He had me drive him in his Mercedes to his airplane, he said I could drive the Mercedes all I want, and he made a last-minute request that I remember to deliver your gifts. Then he boarded along with his minions and a boatload o' baggage and boxes. Off they went." He gestured flying away. "Left me right there, stunned. I drove the Mercedes o'er here, by the way. It's parked out front." He jabbed a thumb toward the front of the hotel. "And! He had his staff pack up all the equipment from the dungeon to take with him. It's gone and he's gone. Good riddance."

The women were stunned into silence for the few seconds it took them to fall all over each other's words.

"What'll happen to the castle?" Innis Bree wondered. "Will he sell it?"

"What'll you do with the place?" Ailsa wanted to know. "Can we go see it again?"

"One thing at a time," Jeffrey said. "What will happen to the castle? Well, this morning he called the president o' the company that wanted to buy it last year when he outbid them. They're still interested. They want to turn it into a golf course and resort. What will I do with the place in the meantime? Apparently, anything I want. Aye, you can come visit anytime you want. And you're the first to hear any of this. I'm sure the Blythes and everyone else in the village will be pleased to hear it, as well."

Ailsa's phone rang. She looked at the screen, held up a finger, and answered. "Hi, Jenny! …. Sure. We'll be there. Six o'clock. What can we bring? … Righto. See you then."

She'd no sooner hung up then Jeffrey's phone rang. He answered to a repeat of Ailsa's conversation.

When he hung up, he said, "Looks like we're all invited to Jenny and Clyde's tonight for dinner."

"You, too," Ailsa added, pointing at Innis Bree. "She wants you to see the family Bibles with the family trees."

Innis Bree paused. She'd no doubt be seeing Laird again. She'd have to concentrate on acting human instead of acting like the sex-obsessed animal she'd become, lusting after a male who didn't even like her. She wasn't sure she had it in her at this point to try to act normal.

"Okay," was all she could come up with in response to Ailsa's relayed invitation.

After a bit more excited chatter about the parting of Rory Skeffington, they parted ways. Jeffrey drove his newly acquired Mercedes back to his castle. Ailsa went home to take her mother to a doctor's appointment. Innis Bree had the afternoon all to herself. Ailsa had suggested she visit the Crannog Centre less than a mile away on Loch Tay.

Innis Bree had seen the ancient-looking dock that was attached to a large, round, thatched-roof hut that jutted out onto the loch. She'd read how 2,500 years ago it had been the home of Iron Age people called Crannog Dwellers. There were guided tours and historical exhibits, right up her alley.

Back in her room she looked at the inviting romance novels sitting on her nightstand. Historical site or romance novel? Which would be best for spending an afternoon by herself? She decided on the site. A romance novel at this time would only remind her of the guy she didn't dare let herself fall for, the one she'd have to deal with at dinner that evening.

A cloud moseyed across the sun, emphasizing her gloom, as she went out and trudged around the loch, determined not to feel sorry for herself. She considered taking out her Air Pods to listen to some good-old country music but decided that would only be more depressing. After all, she liked the same kind of music as what's-his-name. Besides, the sound of the water lapping along the shore soothed her.

Along the way, three cars stopped and asked if she wanted a ride. She thanked them but declined. The exercise felt good, especially since the clouds refused to mosy on, obscuring the sun.

Once she arrived at the Crannog Centre and became immersed in the history of Iron Age people from 2,500 years ago, her melancholy lifted. This was her world, the world of the past. She took the guided tour, absorbed every word, and enjoyed herself immensely.

As she started to leave, a frail old man asked if she wanted to ride with him on his boat to the village. He'd dropped someone off, he said, and it would be no trouble to take her back. She'd not been out on the loch yet and found the invitation to ride with him in his small motorboat to be delightful.

Once on the water, they chatted amicably, and she discovered he'd been in the pub the night she went out with Rory.

"May I ask you a question?" she posed.

"Aye."

"Does everyone in the village know all about me?"

He chuckled in a way that warmed her to the marrow of her bones. "Aye, miss. Yer a college professor from America, yer looking into yer heritage with Ailsa, you had a dud date with that dafty Skeffington, and Laird has been looking at you like a man possessed."

Surprised yet somehow entertained, she said, "Is that all?"

"Well, no, there's also gossip you might be talking to a ghost."

"Ah, I see. Do you believe in ghosts?"

He chortled, "O' course. Doesna everybody?"

Not in my world, she thought.

"You sort of make me feel like a celebrity," she told him. She didn't add that the part about Laird being a man possessed spurred her hopes considerably.

"Och, you are a celebrity, I can assure you o' that." His smile displayed a gold incisor.

They arrived at the dock on the edge of town. She thanked him and offered to pay. He flatly refused. "Nae. 'Twas a pleasure to keep company with the new Sassenach in the village."

He tooled away in his boat and she sat on the bench on the beach watching the clouds roll by when her phone sang its Face-time song. She pulled it out of her purse and was pleased when Kathryn's name popped up on the screen.

"Hey, Kathryn," she answered, holding it up to frame her face. To her surprise, on her screen she saw Kathryn, Rama, and Delina with a bunch of other faculty members dancing around behind them in Paddy's Pub. Loud music played. It looked like a raucous early-lunchtime happy hour. "It's a little early for happy hour, isn't it?"

Her three friends merrily toasted her with beer and margaritas.

"It's going so great you won't believe it," Kathryn said. "We have good news!"

Rama burst in, "Dean Monica Smith was fired this morning! Escorted right out of her office."

"What? No way. Really?" Innis Bree was aghast with delight.

"Really," Delina chimed in. "I wasn't there, of course, but that's all I've heard about for the last hour."

"Yeah," Kathryn said. "Somebody went above her 'skull' and she's kaput."

They all laughed so uproariously Innis Bree could tell they'd been celebrating heartily. They clinked glasses, cheered, and drank up.

"I can't believe it." Innis Bree shook her head in wonder. "Thank heaven, nobody will have to work with her anymore. I'm so happy for you."

Delina was the first to set down her glass. "Maybe you can get your job back," she said while swiping a dribble of booze off her lip.

"Oh. My job. Huh. Yeah. Wow. That would be great." The proper words came out of her mouth. However, she didn't know if she believed her own utterances. What was wrong with her? Of course she wanted her job back. She forced herself to think more clearly.

Kathryn squinted and stretched her neck until her scrunched up, distorted face filled Innis Bree's screen. "Hey. You don't sound too excited."

"Oh course, I'm excited." It struck Innis Bree that she lied like, well, like Rory Skeffington. "That's only speculation, though. Right now, I'm thrilled for all of you."

More revelers showed up behind her friends, other faculty members from the history department, drinks in hand as they sang something about walking out the door, not turning around, and not being welcome anymore. They fell into a cacophony of mumbles as no one remembered the lyrics from an old soul song, leaving Innis Bree in a fit of laughter. She'd never seen some of these otherwise staid professors so happy.

"I'm gonna let you go and celebrate," she said to her friends. "Go. Have fun. I miss you and I love you. Say hi to everybody for me." She air kissed the camera and clicked them off.

She went to her room contemplating all she'd learned about the history of the area at the Centre, how nice people were here, and how lonely she felt. She didn't seem to belong back home with her friends anymore now that she was no longer a part of their world. She surely didn't belong here in the highlands of Scotland. A "Sassenach," the old man had called her. A word made famous by the *Outlander* series, it meant an outsider, a foreigner.

She didn't belong anywhere anymore.

Even her ghost had abandoned her. Of course, she'd told him to do so, but now she missed him. Trying to nap only resulted in a twisted-up blanket on her bed. She got up and put on her AirPods to listen to music. When Marc Broussard came on with *Cry to Me*, she burst into tears. Finally falling into fitful sleep, she dreamed that Bruce came after all, stroking her hair to soothe her troubled soul.

Had he truly come or had she dreamt him?

Perhaps a fantasy world from the past was where she belonged because being in the real world of the present sure wasn't working out for her.

CHAPTER 13

*L*aird's finger grazed her hand as he passed the rolls. As soon as she had hold of the bowl, he snatched his hand back as if scorched by a hot coal. Daring to peek at him, she found he hadn't so much as glanced her way.

Jenny had seated Innis Bree and Laird side by side at the table in their farmhouse dining room. Jenny and Clyde sat on either end. Ailsa, her mother Garia, and Jeffrey filled the rest of the chairs. The hosts' two young kids, a girl and a boy, had been sent to Clyde's parents for the night.

So far, it had been an amicable evening. Innis Bree learned that Jenny was a seamstress who tailor-made women's gowns and men's kilts. Clyde had been a construction worker before quitting that to help Laird on the farm and to manage his driving business. The couple also managed a large organic garden, selling to restaurants in nearby towns. These were industrious, hard-working people.

Their house was the one she and Laird had been raised in, so this had been home to them all their lives. Their parents had surprised them when Laird came home to roost, handing over the family farm and moving, although not too far away, to become rangers in Cairngorms National Park, which had been a secret lifelong dream.

Ailsa had decided the dinner group should save the family tree in the *Bible* for after their scrumptious meal. As they ate, Jeffrey filled them in about Rory Skeffington, which brought cheers from Jenny and Clyde. Then Ailsa updated them on Innis Bree's genealogical research. The conversation flowed naturally amongst this friendly group of hometown folks.

Innis Bree envied their camaraderie, their deep connections, their acceptance of one another. Except for Laird, who'd once again become the crabbit she'd first met. He answered questions curtly and otherwise didn't participate in the exchange. It reached a point where his sister wasn't having it.

"Laird, brother dear," Jenny drolled, "you're quiet tonight. Is our charming chatter too much for you this evening?" She ate a bite of roast off her fork then pointed the tines at him as if she might stick him with it.

"Nae, sister dear," he retorted, "it's just that I should be out there in the barn. We still have a pregnant ewe ready to birth at any time."

"Ah, I see." Jenny studied her brother as if trying to decide if he needed a good talking-to or a spanking. Maybe being grounded. "Your dedication to your flock is admirable. You'll be able to get out there soon enough. We have dessert. Jeffrey brought crème brûlèe made by the castle chef. Your favorite."

He brightened slightly. "Aye. Thank you."

A few things about that surprised Innis Bree. She hadn't figured him to be a crème brûllè kind of guy. Interesting. And he had no more to say. Even his favorite dessert couldn't pull him out of his gloom. The dessert was obviously what she and Rory were going to have the night of their date. They never got to it, and she was glad for it now.

It surprised her even more when Laird, Clyde, and Jeffrey started clearing the dishes when they were done eating. Jenny insisted the women sit while the "gentlemen" did a "wee bit of the work." Innis Bree could see that was common practice in this household, and she liked this Jenny more and more with each passing minute.

When Laird set her dish of dessert in front of her, his hand once again touched hers, sending a shock up her arm and straight to her heart. Their eyes met, and she could have sworn she saw wanton desire there. His gaze quickly averted. Dejected, she admonished herself for being wrong about him once again.

"Innis Bree," Clyde said after all the dessert plates had been served and the men sat down to dig in, "we've heard about your dead ancestors. Anyone in your family alive?"

She smiled. "Yes. Very. I come from a pretty average American family. My parents still work in the jobs they've had forever. My dad's a plumber, and my mom's a store clerk. I have one brother who's married with one son. I'm an aunt." She swallowed a spoonful of her creamy dessert with its crusty top. "Ummm, this is yummy! Anyway – my family." Innis Bree powered down another bite. "We all live within an hour of each other in North Carolina, in the southeastern part of the States. We didn't have much growing up, but our parents supported us in every way possible to get good educations. My brother and I both worked admittedly crappy jobs ..." she chuckled "... to get through college. He's a lawyer and, as you know, I'm a college professor. At my level, it's officially called an assistant professor. I would've qualified to get promoted to associate professor this year and in four years I would've been a full professor. That was always my goal. Now that I've been fired, I suppose I don't have a goal."

She'd not heard herself say those words out loud before. They stung.

Awkward silence filled the room until Clyde gamely held up his wine glass. "Well, here's to getting fired by arseholes who don't deserve you in the first place. Cheerio!" Everyone joined in, even Laird.

That brightened the mood, and Innis Bree took a cue from Ailsa, who, reading her mind, nodded. "I want to tell you one more thing," Innis Bree announced. "We told you all about our research and how we're trying to find out what happened to the first Innis Bree. What I haven't told you yet is that I've been seeing a ghost named Bruce Cieran Blyth. Not only did Ailsa and I find the church record that said he and Innis Bree were betrothed, I've also been seeing him. Like in the flesh. He thinks I'm her."

She skipped the part about Bruce's frisky nature and her sexual attraction toward him. Holding her breath in fear they'd think her bonkers for believing she'd actually seen a ghost, she was relieved when Jenny and Clyde excitedly pummeled her with questions, most of which she couldn't answer. She had no idea how the man came and went or what he'd been doing in the long interval between the time of his death and now.

They finished dessert, and this time the women cleared the table. Jenny brought out two large family Bibles, one far more worn than the other. She opened the older one. "Here he is, our direct ancestor, Bruce Cieran Blyth." She pointed out the flowery handwriting on the family tree in the front pages of the book and slid it over to Innis Bree, who examined it and passed it across the table to Ailsa.

The genealogist adjusted her glasses and devoured the historical writing. "This signature may well be his very own handwriting," she marveled. "Look." She tapped it. "His wife's name, Fenella, and their son's, Andrew, are in a different handwriting, probably hers."

Everyone leaned over the table to examine it, and all agreed that was the case.

"That son was his only child, and thank goodness he had him,"

Jenny said, "or we ..." she pointed at her brother and herself "... wouldna be here."

"That son," Innis Bree noted, "means Bruce didn't spend all his time pining away for my ancestor Innis Bree."

"Maybe naw," Jenny said, "but if he's still looking for her, she must have been his long-lost love. How fascinating. Our many-times great-grandfather may have been married for convenience alone. He needed a son to carry on the family name."

"Or he may have married in his grief o'er a broken heart." Laird's voice surprised them, riveting their attention to the dour, heretofore silent man. "Perhaps Innis Bree's disappearance broke his heart, and the poor sop married another to salve his wounds. Howe'er, he's ne'er forgotten his true love, and he's been drawn to the one who feels like her." He gestured toward Innis Bree and finally stared into her eyes. "True love lingers in our hearts and souls forever."

No one else spoke.

Garia, who sat on the other side of Laird, took his hand. He did not slough off his elder, instead gently squeezing her delicate hand.

"Spoken like a true romantic, Laird," she softly said.

His face softened the tiniest bit in what was his first sign of affability that evening. "And now this romantic sop must go back to work. Excuse me, please." He got up and rushed out of the room. The conversation didn't resume until the door shut behind him and he could be heard calling Maisie.

"Well," Clyde declared, "that was interesting. Who knew the lad was such a sook?"

"What's a sook?" Innis Bree asked.

"It's a softie, love," Ailsa told her. "Someone with a loving heart."

"Laird has more than a soft heart," Garia said. "He fears his soft heart will get the better of him, so he's protecting it as best he can."

"After his divorce from that viper," Jenny said, "it's no wonder."

"I think I'd best go help him with the ewe," Jeffrey said. "He's fretting over this last one who's overdue." He got up and politely pushed his chair in. "It's been such a pleasure. Thank you so much." With that, Laird's friend left the house, supposedly to help with the lambs. Everyone knew it was to support his best mate during what was obviously a sour time in his life.

The evening wrapped up pleasantly, with Jenny refusing to accept help with the dishes. Clyde carried Garia out to the car, like he'd carried her in. He reminded Innis Bree of the superhero Thor, even schmoozing with the old woman about how she was light as a feather and pretty as an angel, which brought a big smile to her lips. Ailsa folded up her mother's wheelchair and hoisted it into the boot, adept at doing so after years of practice.

Ailsa drove, dropping Innis Bree off at the hotel. When Ailsa's car pulled away, Innis Bree stood outside, studying the old building. Bruce was in there, no doubt, and she needed a good talk with the haint. This time she wanted answers, and she wouldn't quit until she got them.

LAIRD SAT IN THE STRAW, leaning up against the wall of the barn, a ewe in labor ten feet away. Maisie sat at his side, silently, protectively, homed in on the ewe. Laird had taught Maisie not to get too close during labor, as that might make the mother-to-be nervous. Sheep, as well as most farm animals, were very good at letting nature take its course. Unless there was trouble, like if the lamb got stuck with one leg behind it rather than emerging with its snout, Laird would stay out of the way. If there was trouble, he'd put on his work gloves and pull the lamb out of its mother's womb, something he'd done more times than he ever imagined when he took on this venture of raising animals.

Low music played from the wireless speakers he'd set up, seeing that he insisted his sheep enjoyed Andrea Bocelli, Ed Sheeran, and Bette Midler. He admitted, however, that it soothed him, too, as he shepherded his fluffy white flock of two hundred and fifty. He hoped to grow to at least five hundred, and he had plenty of land to accommodate all those hungry bellies. Shearing season would begin in a week, a two-and-a-half-month frenzy of shaving, bailing, and selling wool. He'd be having an entire crew coming in to get the arduous task done.

Which meant, he told himself, he didn't have time to be fretting over an American woman who would be leaving in a matter of days. Innis Bree MacIntyre and her ancestry quest – bah! He appreciated his forebears for bringing him to life, but he recognized that they were long gone, dead and buried. Well, except for Bruce, who apparently still hung around.

Jeffrey showed up and sat down on the other side of Maisie. "Hey. How's she doing?"

"I didna hear you come in. She's in deep labor, so it shouldna be long."

Right on cue, two white feet and a snout crowned. The ewe gave a big push. Nothing happened. Tension mounted as she pushed several more times. Then, as easily as if sliding on butter, the lamb came into the world.

"Ah ha! She's a beauty!" Laird rejoiced, ignoring the fact he said that every time.

"Aye, that she is," his friend agreed as he always did.

Both men sat still to let the mother do what nature had conditioned her to do. She licked her newborn with fervor, making certain every inch of her offspring came clean. The afterbirth emerged from her, leaving a mass of blood in the straw. The lamb cried piteously as it struggled to stand on its spindly legs to no avail. It would almost make it up, fall on bent front knees, then topple over. Mam wasn't concerned, refusing to relinquish her clean-up duty.

"That always reminds me o' how my mam used to scrub my face till it hurt," Jeffrey snickered. "Ne'er was one speck o' dirt to be left on her scroungy kid."

"My mam did the same. I still always managed to have a dirty face."

The newborn struggled several times before finally standing precariously and glaring out at the world in total confusion.

"That's a good girl," Laird encouraged the baby. "You can do it."

And she did, finding her way to her mother's teat, which she suckled greedily until toppling over again.

The men chortled at her antics, knowing from experience she was good and healthy and would be fine, in a few hours walking alongside her mother and nursing heartily. Her mam had already demonstrated good parenting skills, and the babe would grow up to be a good mam herself in a little over a year.

Knowing the mother wouldn't leave her newborn so he needn't worry about her trying to shove him away, Laird got up and grabbed the spade he had on hand and shoveled up the afterbirth. He carried it outside, added it to the compost pile, and returned. Jeffrey stood by the door, and once Laird put the shovel away, Jeffrey turned off the music while Laird got the lights, and the three of them, Laird, Maisie, and Jeffrey, left the barn.

"How about a beer?" Laird asked his guest.

"Have I e'er refused?"

"Nae. Naw that I can recall."

They walked the path to Laird's croft, the small stone farmhouse that sat on the opposite side of the barn from Jenny and Clyde's bigger farmhouse. Two wooden chairs sat outside the front door, and Jeffrey sat in his usual one while Laird fetched the bottles of Tennent's inside. He came out, handed one over, and took his chair, rocking it to balance on its hind legs. He slugged down his brew.

They drank in silence, but Laird knew a scolding from his best friend was inevitable. It finally came.

"You were a total arse tonight at dinner," Jeffrey said after drinking down most of his bottle. "But you dinnae need me to tell you that, do you?"

Laird's eyes didn't waver away from the night sky. "I'm naw a total eejit." He gulped his beer. "I did it, so I ken what I was."

"All right." Jeffrey finished off his bottle and set the empty on the ground. "Well, I need my beauty rest. G'night."

"'G'night.'"

He watched Jeffrey get in his truck and drive away.

"I've never been a total arse with you, have I, girl?" He looked around for Maisie. She was nowhere to be seen. Then he saw her halfway down the path toward the barn, crouched down, keeping an eye on the place where her new charge now resided.

Laird whistled. Maisie popped up and looked at him. She didn't come. His dog always obeyed. But not this time.

"Feck. E'en my dog hates me tonight."

He whistled again and Maisie finally came, giving Laird hope that not all the world hated his guts. Only most of it.

CHAPTER 14

"*B*ruce, I need to ask you some very important questions. Pay attention, please."

"I always pay attention, me love."

She sat on the bed while he roamed the room and settled on looking out the window.

"No, you don't. You don't listen to what I'm trying to tell you. Okay. This is it. Tell me about being married to Fenella. Here's why – I'm wondering if she could've had anything to do with Innis Bree's – my – disappearance."

He roamed again, his hands clasped behind his back. "Fenella? Why would ye think that?"

"Think, Bruce. Did Fenella have a crush on you? I mean, did she want to be with you while you were in love with, um, me?" Innis Bree struggled to remember to tell this in the first person, otherwise she wouldn't get anywhere with her besotted ghost.

"Aye, o' course. All the lassies wanted to be with me. Can ye naw see why?" He pranced around with a cocky grin, puffed up chest, and arms out wide, like a male stripper peddling his wares.

"Okay, okay." She motioned for him to stop. "Yes, I see." He was indeed drop-dead – oops, she realized that was all too true – he was gorgeous, a real stud. She probably would've jumped his bones if she'd lived in his lifetime, and she simply wasn't a bone-jumping kind of gal. Well, at least not yet, but that was mostly due to lack of opportunity. "So Fenella wanted you to be with her? Even marry her?"

"O' course." He sat down beside her, his anxious concern apparent.

"And Monica Campbell, Duncan's wife, might have hated me, too. Right? Because her husband made advances toward me."

"If ye mean he tried to bed ye, aye."

"So, is it possible that one of those women did something to... me...to make me go away?"

He shrugged. "Or both. They were sisters, after all."

"What? They were sisters?"

"Certainly. Ye know that as well as I. Or ye did 'afore yer poor heid lost its brains, me love."

"Holy moly, Bruce. What if they did me in together?"

"I dinnae ken this moly o' which ye speak, but I suppose it's possible the sisters harmed ye to get ye out o' the way. I did, after all, eventually relent and marry Fenella."

She forewent a snide remark about "eventually" only being six months. Instead, she said, "What was your marriage like?"

"Ye obviously were naw here in the village, or ye would've heard us fighting. Everyone else did. Such a shrew ne'er existed 'afore, naw e'en in a Shakespeare play. Once we had a son, I had nae more use fer her than she had fer me. I'd say we hated one another enough fer each to want to beheid the other."

"Whoa. I know beheading was common then but that's a radical thought. I suppose divorce was difficult in those days."

He shrugged. "It was easier to bed other lassies than to get a divorce."

"You had affairs?"

"Affairs? Does it hurt yer tender heart that I found comfort at the bosoms o' other lassies when ye were gone, mayhap even deid?"

"No, no. That's okay. My heart is fine. Bruce, I think it could have been those two women, Monica and Fenella, who did me in."

"Ye mean me wife, Fenella? And her sister, Monica? Och, I should've known. They kidnapped ye and mottled yer brain and somehow yer finally free."

"No, Bruce ..." She stopped.

He stood up, lost in a trance of memory. "Remember, me love, when yer brother Gillimichell, me best mate, and I came home from France?" He walked back and forth and gestured as if acting out a scene in a stage play. "We'd worked so hard fer two years helping build that beautiful cathedral in Leon. We went to the pub, and the whole village 'twas there to welcome us home. I asked Gilli whate'er happened to his ragamuffin little sister." He gestured toward the door. "At that very moment, ye appeared, all grown up, the most beautiful lassie e'er to walk the earth. Me heart leapt oot o' me chest and into yers. To me utterly delighted surprise, ye walked straight up to me, reached up to place a hand on either side o' me thick skull ..." he put his hands on the sides of his head, his voice cracking "... and ye said, 'I've been waiting fer ye to come home so we kin wed.' And ye kissed me with all yer might!"

His smile at the memory lit up the room, and Innis Bree couldn't help feeling happy, too. To think her ancestor had been such a strong, determined woman. It gave her pause – and promise.

"Remember what happened on that very same night? Ah, remember? 'Twas a beautiful starlit night. Everyone in the village gathered in the meadow and built a big fire, and we drank and sang and danced." His chortle belied his enjoyment at the memory. "Gilli had learned to play waltz music on his lute in France. No one in Kenmore had heard that kind o' music or seen that kind o' dance 'afore. But when he played and I took ye in me arms, ye followed me lead as if our hearts were already one. Innis Bree, me love, it was heaven on earth to hold ye in me arms that first time, and every time after. Remember?" His voice became smooth and dreamy, like a beau serenading his lover, whispering sweet every-things in her ear. "That night we stole away to a private spot by the river. I put me jacket down on the ground, and we mated fer the first time that very night."

His gaze veered away from Innis Bree as he went to the window again. She imagined he looked out toward the spot on the river where he'd first made love to his beloved.

Lost in the memory, he said, "'Tis the moments o' joy that matter in life. All the rest falls away as long as there is love to carry ye through."

"That's beautiful, Bruce."

"Mayhaps, but then," he said, his voice raw with emotion, "only a week later, on the day we were to wed, ye were gone."

Innis Bree was caught entirely off guard when big, brave, bold Bruce Cieran Blyth started to cry like a blubbering baby.

She reached out for his hand and pulled him down to sit beside her, coddled him into her chest, and let him cry it out. After grab-bing tissues off her nightstand for him, she cradled his head in her hands and kissed the wavy hair on the crown of his indeed thick skull.

Something troubling happened at the same time. His spectral body felt more ethereal than before, as if he was losing his ability to remain a solid entity.

His tears spent, he wiped his eyes a final time, quizzically eyed the tissues in his hand, and finally looked at her. "I swear to ye, me love. Had ye been here, there ne'er woulda been another. Our home woulda held naught but laughter and love, singing and danc-ing, and tender touches and words. We woulda had many happy bairns. Our bond woulda endured fer a lifetime and fere'er after.

There was none like thee, Innis Bree MacIntyre, so bodacious and bold, and by God, so beautiful."

He stroked her hair, ran a finger down her cheek, and studied her from head to toe. A faint frown line whittled its way between his eyes. He was beginning, she realized, to accept the truth of the matter. She wasn't his Innis Bree.

"G'night, me love." He placed a kiss as soft as a brush of a butterfly's wings on her forehead and disappeared into the dark of night.

THE SPECTACULAR SUNRISE went unnoticed by Innis Bree as she peddled her way down Blyth Lane. The pinks and yellows and lavenders that lit her way only heightened her need to reach her destination. She crested the hill to see his truck near the mansion. He was nowhere in sight. Scanning the sheep in their pasture, she found him there, standing on a knoll watching his flock.

Maisie herded the sheep, making certain they stayed within her parameters. But even when surrounded by the strong scent of raw wool, the dog's keen sense of smell caught a whiff of Innis Bree. This time the canine didn't wait for her master's command; she flew to her new friend.

"Hello, sweetheart," Innis Bree said as she dropped her bike and took long, measured strides across the field toward Laird.

He turned and froze.

She closed in and came to within a foot of him, and without hesitation, reached up to place a hand on each side of his face and pull him down to plant a sumptuous kiss on his lips. After a moment of stunned disbelief, Laird Blyth kissed back, his powerful arms wrapping around her waist and frantically drawing her into his body.

This time their kiss surpassed wanton need. It became intentional, consensual, and sensual desire.

Their lips parted, and they gazed into each other's eyes. They dove in for another coming together that took hold of their hearts and seared their souls.

Her arms encircled his body, and she ran her hands up under his tee shirt to stroke his muscular back. Finally! His bare skin was in her hands.

Dazed now by the glory of her touch, he fondled a breast through her tee shirt and moaned when he found no impediment of a bra. Taking his cue from her, he ran a hand up under her shirt and cupped her bare breast.

"Are you sure?" he rasped.

She didn't let him finish, hopping up to wrap her legs around his waist and kissing him again.

Laird thrust his head back and laughed in unabashed joy, a sound she'd had yet to hear. She joined him, letting her happiness overwhelm her for the first time she could remember since being a playful child. He flung her around to hold her like a bride and carried her all the way across the field to the side of his truck where he set her down to stand beside him while he opened the door. He yanked his tee shirt off over his head and cast it aside.

She did the same.

His features became voracious as he scanned her nakedness, then kneaded her pliant breasts. The roughness of his work-warn hands sent a shockwave of urgency throughout her body. She moaned and held onto his thick hair for dear life as he bent his head to nip and suck until she knew she would soon explode with ecstasy.

Reading her mind – and her body – he shucked his shoes and did away with his jeans. It aroused her even more, which she'd thought impossible, to find he wore no briefs and a glorious treasure had been released. He groaned with agonized pleasure as she wrapped it in her hand. Without a second to spare, he assisted as she yanked off the rest of her clothing, and he picked her up to slide her onto the seat of his truck.

There in the highlands of Scotland, driven by lust, longing, loneliness — and love? — Laird Blyth mounted Innis Bree MacIntyre. Unbeknownst to them, they were meddling with history and muddling up their futures.

Not that they cared.

INNIS BREE MARVELED at the interior of the mansion. When they'd finally emerged from their bout of unbridled passion and dressed, he wanted to show her the part of the house that remained intact.

"Laird, it's so beautiful." She ran a hand over the massive oak beam mantle of the enormous fireplace in what he called the main reception room, which he said would now be called a drawing room or parlor. "What do you intend to do with the place? I asked you before and you said you weren't sure, but I get a feeling you know." When her eyes fell on him, she found that he stared at her.

He blinked and looked around the room as if only then aware of it. "Why, I'll live here. I've already had modern plumbing and electricity installed. Lights work. Loos function. The structure on this side is very stable, safe and sound. The roof needed a wee bit o' repair but is good now. The kitchen is on this side, so that's good, although I'm working on upgrading it. I dinnae ken for sure when that was put in the house because when the house was first built, the kitchen would probably have been a separate building out back. There're some outbuildings, one that coulda been the kitchen. One was the stables. The other a work shed o' some kind. There are six bedrooms upstairs and three loos, and one loo down here. The loos, thankfully, have been added within the last hundred years. The whole place will be quite livable with a wee bit more work."

She couldn't imagine living in such a beautiful place, having been raised in a typical, small, American ranch home in a suburb and living in apartments ever since leaving home. "It's spectacular. It'll make a wonderful home." She didn't mention it was sized for a big family, not knowing how he'd take that.

He took care of that. "I'd planned it as a family home when I was married. I thought we'd have children. You ken, the whole adult life thing. She had other ideas. Here, look at this pattern in the marble floor."

He obviously rushed to change the subject upon realizing he'd fallen into personal territory. Perhaps fearing a quagmire?

She didn't press. "The floor is stunning. May I see the kitchen?"

He led her through the dining room with its long panel of windows on one wall and a long oak table without chairs. The home was sparsely furnished with only a few antiques from its original days and subsequent owners. It wasn't live-in ready yet, although he'd cleaned it up to be pristine.

Upon reaching the kitchen in the back of the house, she gravitated to a large, black iron, wood-burning stove. "Oh, Laird, look at this! It's so cool." Curious, she opened the oven door and peered inside. "It's from the 1800s, isn't it. Does it work?"

"Indeed, it does. So I'm keeping the stove and will install a modern one, too. Handier for putting the kettle on. Come …" he held out his hand and took hers "… let me show you upstairs."

They returned to the main hall where she pointed to the corner by the front window. "That's where I tried to hide from you on the day you saved me from the storm."

He guffawed. "And you hated me for it."

"No, I didn't," she countered with a tug on his arm. "I didn't hate you at all. I didn't know you and was sorta afraid. I did know you hated me."

He stopped, his eyes locking on hers. "Nae. You were an enigma to me. A bother, for sure. Another American tourist who didna ken what she was doing. But from that very first second I saw you all lost and brave all by yourself at the train station, I wanted to shag you."

"What? No!" she teased. "You acted like you hated me."

"I had to. So I wouldn't grab you and beg you for a shag." His cheerfulness was infectious.

She laughed. "You're full of it."

He shrugged mischievously, then led her by the hand up the stairs. The five bedrooms were large and clean and bare, the three bathrooms had a twenties' flare, and she could imagine a family there.

Back downstairs in the main hall, she paused in front of a narrow table, one of the few pieces of furniture, that sat below a cracked and mottled mirror. Her filmy reflection showed her a woman who was happy. Sex, she knew, would do that to a gal.

Laird came up behind her, wrapped his arms around her waist, and slid his head alongside hers. Their faces side by side, his the epitome of masculine strength and hers a picture of feminine force, looked perfectly paired together in the glass. She turned her head so their lips could meet. His hands roamed up to her breasts as he kissed her neck. She reached up to run a hand through his hair as she bent over, arched her back, and brazenly nuzzled him with her bum in an instinctive, primitive mating call. Never did she take her eyes off his chiseled features in the looking glass as he took her from behind. He took, and she gladly, uncharacteristically, gave everything she had. The breathtaking intensity, the driving need, and the desire to be wanted culminated in a frenzy of shrieks and moans that left them both gasping for air when they were done.

He held her tight with one arm around her waist and laid a palm on the table for stability so they wouldn't melt to the floor.

Having been on her tippytoes, she grounded herself, too. They stared at one another in the looking glass.

Wondering what she'd just done, for the second time that morning no less, she reveled in his tenderness as he helped her adjust her clothing. She turned around and helped him do the same. They were small gestures and yet some of the sweetest she'd ever known.

"You're a treasure, Innis Bree MacIntyre," he whispered in her ear as he placed his hands on her hips and swayed with her as if ready to dance.

"No one has ever talked to me like that before. I confess, Laird, I don't know what to do next."

"Ah, you do ken what we've been doing, though." He threw her a cockeyed grin. "That's enough for now, nae?"

Relieved that she didn't have to know where to go with this … what was it? Certainly not a relationship. A tryst? A fling? Whatever it was, it was a first in her life and she didn't want to spoil it by overanalyzing it or trying to manipulate it. She simply wanted to let it be.

"I need to check on my sheep, although Maisie will have kept them well, no doubt. How about you come with me."

She adored him for not expecting any more from her than a drink. No mulling over whether what they'd been doing was folly or fortune. "I'm afraid I must decline. I meet with Ailsa soon. What time is it? I've lost all track."

"I dinnae ken. I think you'll be okay."

He walked her to her bike and asked if she would have dinner with him at the pub. She agreed, they kissed goodbye, and she rode to the village, her body reinvigorated with each turn of a peddle. Her mind felt surprisingly calm. For the first time in her life, she'd let her emotions rule and she'd discovered a part of herself buried deep within that she'd never known existed. With her former fiancé, lovemaking had always been measured, planned, organized, and careful. Now she felt like a wild bohemian minx, and it felt wonderful.

She mused that perhaps the original Innis Bree had come to life within her.

LAIRD WHISTLED FOR MAISIE. She ran up to him, stopped, sniffed, and laid down, apparently unwilling to get involved in whatever it was the humans had been doing.

"Aw, come on, you'll always be my best lassie." Even as he said it, Laird wondered what it was he felt for Innis Bree. His mind swirled with disbelief at the amazing, unexpected morning he shared with the American. Surely, they didn't know one another well enough to claim to be in love. Yet what had all that frolicking been about? It hadn't been about platonic friendship, to be sure. He had no idea what to call what they had. Lust? Aye, indeed. But it was more than that. What, he had yet to figure out.

The dog finally came to him for a good petting. "That's my lassie. Let's get back to work. Whadaya say?"

Maisie barked assent.

They went to the truck and drove to the cottage with fantasies spinning in Laird's head about the night that was yet to come.

INNIS BREE HAD time to grab a quick shower before her meeting with Ailsa. She threw her hair into a ponytail and put on her other pair of jeans but had no time for so much as one swipe of makeup. She went down to the deck looking about sixteen years old.

"Good morning," she greeted Ailsa cheerily as she sat down.

Ailsa eyed her up and down without a word.

"What's wrong?" Innis Bree asked.

"I'd say naught." Ailsa smiled.

The teen server appeared with the basket of baked goods, took one look at Innis Bree, and said, "Huh. Yup." She left the basket and sashayed away without another word.

Ailsa said, "This could get complicated." Innis Bree didn't interrupt, instead picking out a scone, slathering it with butter and orange marmalade, and taking a big bite while Ailsa talked. "Naw that I'm saying anything against it," the older woman continued. "God knows, I'm naw against two adults being …" she swished a hand "… together. But we might need to talk about what comes next. You ken? A plan."

"A plan? For what?" Innis Bree poured tea for both of them from the dainty pot that sat on the table in a flowery cozy.

"You and Laird. Do you want to extend your stay here in Scotland? If so, it might be best to call the airline soon. After all, you're only a few days away from your scheduled return. Correct?"

Innis Bree swallowed the bite of scone she had in her mouth and took a quick sip of tea. "I hadn't even thought about that. I mean, I guess I've been living in the moment. With Laird, that is. How do you know?"

"Love, look at you. You're glowing. Plus, you rode out there again this morning. Nobody believes you went out to help herd sheep."

Innis Bree sighed, then an unexpected belly laugh began to roll. Once she'd settled down and wiped her eyes, she said, "Oh, Ailsa. The absurdity of it all. The only time in my life I've ever done something reckless and wanton, and I've done it in quite a public way. The joke's on me."

"I doubt it's a joke. Tell me, shall we continue to try to find out what happened to the Innis Bree of auld, or are you going to spend the rest o' yer time, um, elsewise occupied?"

"Oh, yes, we must find out about Innis Bree. I'll never rest until I know. Let me tell you what I learned from Bruce last night."

She filled Ailsa in about Bruce's wife Fenella being the sister of Monica Campbell, wife of the Duncan who'd been rejected by Innis Bree. "I think it's possible the two sisters got together to do Innis Bree in."

"That certainly is a possibility." Ailsa warmed to the notion like an amateur sleuth coming upon a juicy new clue. "Let's see what we can find in the records about either woman." She opened her laptop and started clicking keys.

After she'd worked for a bit, Innis Bree interrupted with a question she'd been wondering about once she forced herself to stop swooning in her head about something other than that swarthy sheepherder down the way. "Did your mom find anything else in the Gaelic papers we got at the library?"

"Nae. I'm afraid it was mostly house records. Interesting in its own way but naw what we seek." Ailsa went back to her laptop.

Not wanting to break Ailsa's concentration again, Innis Bree realized she was famished. She ordered scrambled eggs, bacon, and fried tomatoes and mushrooms to go along with the basket of goodies she'd already half devoured. When her food came, she gobbled it down. As she finished and the server took her plate, Ailsa came up with a hit.

"Ah! Here." She turned the laptop around to share the screen. "We thought Monica Campbell might have joined a nunnery based on one of the documents we found. If this is correct, that might have been a cover story because here she is, entering Virginia with her husband. I trust this manifest. She slithered away to America after Innis Bree disappeared, after saying she'd ne'er go to that heathen land."

Innis Bree stared at the screen. "She was running away. From what?"

"From murdering our Innis Bree?"

"Holy moly. I need to talk to Bruce again."

"When you do, call me right away to tell me what he says."

"I will if I can find him. Last night I think he started to accept the fact I'm not his Innis Bree. I don't know if he'll come back."

Ailsa studied her young friend. "He will, my love. I can feel it in my bones."

∼

"I'M DEID."

The tone of helplessness in Bruce's voice ripped Innis Bree's heart to shreds. The way he so sorrowfully said that word with such morbid finality, pronouncing it in his strong Scottish brogue – "deid like deed" – made her realize how long he'd existed in denial. She couldn't imagine the horror of such a realization.

He looked at her. "'Tis true, 'tis it naw?" He pointed at his mossy, mildew-stained headstone. "It says so right here. 'Bruce Cieran Blyth, Loving Faither, 1670-1715.'"

They stood in the church graveyard where Innis Bree had found him after she'd searched her room and the hotel yard. His shoulders slouched as he shrunk in hopelessness, his body having suddenly aged. His handsome face lost its vibrancy and took on a sick pallor. Even his beautiful lake-blue eyes, the same color as Laird's, clouded to smoky charcoal.

"Yes. Aye, Bruce. I'm afraid it's true."

She approached him slowly, not wanting to scare him away. Stopping six feet short, she waited for him to say whatever it was he needed to say.

"How long?"

"Three-hundred and eight years. It's the year 2023."

"Feck! I've been a ghost that long?"

"Apparently."

"It hasn't seemed long a'tall. It's as if I sleep, awaken, and look fer me Innis Bree. When I can't find her, I sleep again."

"You understand now that I'm not your Innis Bree?"

He sat down atop his very own headstone. "Aye. But she's part o' ye, that I ken."

"She's my eight-times great-grandaunt." She came closer and leaned against a tall headstone so covered in moss she couldn't see a name.

"Ye look like her. Aulder, mind ye, yet the same in many ways. She was fifteen when she vanished. How auld are ye?"

"Thirty-two."

"Ye have her black hair and green eyes. Those arched eyebrows, soft skin, and pretty mouth. And yer body is hers all o'er again." Sorrowful longing laced his voice. "Yer a spittin' image o' her, as bonnie a lassie as e'er lived and breathed."

"Thank you."

"And ye've been bedded by a man today. Me Innis Bree winnow do that with anyone but me."

"Wait. Did you see us?" She panicked. Were there ghosts watching as she and Laird so flamboyantly had sex?

He chuckled heartily, and she relaxed as color returned to his cheeks in his merriment. "Nae. Don't worry about that. I believe ye were at the manse. At least that was where ye were headed on that contraption last time I saw ye."

"Yes. That's where I went. Do you ever go there looking for your Innis Bree?"

"Nae. Ne'er. I built that house after I was wed, hoping a big home would warm me wife's ice-cold heart. As it turned out, there was naught that could soften the evil that dwelt within her. Now I only go where Innis Bree, me Innis Bree, might be. She ne'er knew the manse."

"So she lived between the hotel and pub, the kirk, and the rest of the village?"

"Aye. Her mam died when she was twelve. Her mam's sister owned the hotel with her husband. They took her in, and they were good to her. After all, she was a great help to them, what with being the kind-hearted, hard-working lassie she was. And her faither John and brother Gilli lived right across the street behind John's blacksmith shop. I see that's gone now and those other buildings stand in its place. She saw her faither every day o' her life. He loved her dearly but thought it best she lived with a woman in such a nice place."

"So the mansion came later. Huh. I wondered if something might have happened to her there."

"Nae. I often think o' what a warm and loving manse it woulda been had she been me bride instead o' Fenella."

"I was there this morning, and it was a place of warmth and love." She tingled at the thought. "What makes you think I was with a man there?"

He chortled in his usual way of being amused and teasing at the same time. "Were ye naw?"

"Yes. Aye. I was," she fessed up.

"I can see it in ye. Feel it. Smell it. After three-hundred and how many years?"

"Eight."

"Three hundred and eight years since I died, and I still ken well that enticing scent, like wild animals in heat." He returned to full bloom, dancing around and chuckling. "Ye've been bedded by a very eager man."

"Bruce, it is your descendant, Laird Blyth."

"Really?" He came closer with a spring in his step, intrigued by this development. "What's his name?"

"Laird."

"Nae, his given name."

"That's it."

"That's a title."

"Not anymore. Now people use it as a first name."

He slapped his knee in delight. "So anybody can be a laird?"

"Yes." Caught up in his glee, she laughed, too.

"Are ye in love with him, lass, this spawn o' mine, many generations down?"

"I … well, I don't know. We don't know each other very well, and I have to go home to America soon. I admit, I'm a little embarrassed that I've been with a man I hardly know."

"Why?"

"Why what?"

"Why are ye embarrassed? Didn't ye both want to join together?"

"Yes. We did."

"So there's nae problem, eh? Tell me, dinnae be shy, did ye enjoy each other?"

She blushed. "Very much."

"Well then, that's all there is to it. It does me heart good to know that in 2023 folks still enjoy shagging. Especially with two people who descend from me and me love. Do ye think ye'll wed? That would make me heart swell with joy to ken that even though me love and me cannae wed, our bairns' bairns can."

"Oh, we haven't got that far. We're just, um, getting to know each other."

"In the best way possible!"

He laughed again, and his happiness gave Innis Bree that sense of freedom she'd felt with him before, like it was okay to be happy without guilt or constrictions, which wasn't how she'd felt most of her life.

"Bruce, will you stay around while we try to find out what happened to your Innis Bree? We're still searching."

"Ah, love, I'll try. But this knowledge o' me own demise is making me feel weak."

"Please stay as long as you can. When it's time for you to go, go in peace, my friend, and know that your attention has meant the world to me."

He embraced her, a feeling not as physical as a sharing of ethereal affection. "And ye have given me hope."

They stepped apart. "Bruce, we always hear about dying people seeing a light they go into when death overcomes them. Have you ever seen that light?"

"Jay-sus, that damnable light. I avoid it. It keeps trying to make me go where I'm naw ready to go. Me Innis Bree is naw there. I can feel it in me bones. Well, what used to be me bones. I cannae leave here until I ken I will be with her in the hereafter. I must take her with me."

"Okay. We'll work as fast as possible."

He started to fade then revived slightly. "I have one question 'afore I sleep again."

"Yes?"

"How do those fast, noisy carriages go without horses?"

The question caught her off guard. Of course, she realized, automobiles would be a total mystery to a man from the 1700s. "They have motors, these mechanical things inside them that have a, um, tiny charge like fire that gives them power to make them go."

"Aye? How strange. What do ye call them?"

"Cars."

"Short for carriages? Well, if I were still alive in this year o' 2023, I'd get me one o' those cars, a red one that would go very fast!"

He faded away, leaving Innis Bree to marvel at the deep friendship she'd formed with a very interesting ghost. Her adoration for him prodded her to find her many times great-grandaunt, the first Innis Bree MacIntyre, as quickly as possible.

SHE MULLED over what to wear – her new summer dress or new blouse with her jeans. She'd had her clothes laundered by the hotel staff, so at least one pair of jeans was clean. Deciding not to overdo it with the dress, at least not yet, seeing that Laird and she would be in public view while having dinner at the pub and would no doubt be causing gossip anyway, she dressed, put on a tad more makeup than her usual daytime fare, and fluffed her loose hair around her shoulders. A spritz of lavender cologne finished her off. Right on cue, a text came from Laird saying he had a table at the pub. She bounded down the stairs to find him at the table where they'd been the night Rory interrupted them. Two glasses of Tennent's beer sat at the ready, one for her.

He stood when she approached. They ignored all the eyes aimed at them, no longer caring what others thought. They sat down with her across from him, like before.

"Hello," she said, surprised at the sultry tone of her own voice.

"Hello, Innis Bree."

His sexy baritone sent a shiver of desire down her spine, alighting a fire at the apex of her thighs. This much lasciviousness in a public place hit her like a thunderbolt. The way he sipped his beer made her jealous of the glass that felt the touch of his hand and lips. She ached for that hand and those lips to grasp her and smother her ....

Slow down, girl, or you'll hit pure bliss right here without him so much as touching you. It'll be a scene right out of When Harry Met Sally, *except for real ...*

Her phone rang in her purse. Snapping out of her sex-crazed daze, she pulled it out and answered.

"Oh, hi, Ailsa." Laird drank his beer, watching as she listened. "What? Oh my word! Really? .... Yeah. Let me tell him and call you right back."

When she shared Ailsa's news, Laird agreed they needed to leave right away. He finished off his beer, she gulped down a third of hers, he paid, and they left.

What Garia discovered couldn't wait.

CHAPTER 15

The warmth of the home washed over Innis Bree as soon as she, Laird, and Maisie entered the living room of Ailsa and Garia's house. Flames crackled in the fireplace. A plump lavender-scented candle glinted on the mantle. Lamplight softly lit the space. Mouthwatering cooking smells drifted in from the kitchen.

"I'm so glad you could come." Garia held out a hand for Innis Bree to take.

Laird, who'd known this family all his life, bent down to peck Garia's cheek. "Hello, Mrs. Adair," he said, his voice gentle with respect for his elder.

"Come, lassie," Garia entreated Maisie, who pranced up for a pet.

"You won't believe what she found." Ailsa motioned for them to sit while she took a chair next to her mother. The couple sat on the loveseat facing them.

Garia used both hands to carefully hold up a wilted piece of paper. "It was stuck behind another piece o' paper, so I didn't see it at first. It's in Gaelic and is a note from Clovis Campbell to his son

Duncan. It says, 'Duncan, as ye hath failed at all else, seeith if thou can privy what yer sister Tess does in that room she hath secreted away behind her chamber. She thinks me a dobber who owns such a large castle I dinnae know what a mere lassie had built there while I was away. I am nae dobber. Find me a key and deliver it to me by the time I return from me hunt on the good morrow. Yer lord and faither.'"

"Wow." Innis Bree relaxed into her seat after being tense during Garia's reading. "A warm and fuzzy daddy Clovis Campbell was not."

"That was par for the course in those days." Laird shook his head.

"But a secret room!" Innis Bree added.

"Exactly." Ailsa popped up, gesturing as she spoke. "We're thinking that secret room might have diaries or letters or who knows what. We want to try to find it."

"Aye," Garia said, "she was our letter writer from before. She may have written more. Maybe that's what the secret room is all about."

"It could be many things," Laird speculated. "That or a hiding place for something nefarious, like witchcraft."

"Oh, my word! We have to find out." Innis Bree's mind churned with possibilities.

"Here's who can help." Laird pulled his phone out of his pocket and spoke into it. "Call Jeffrey." It only rang once before the man answered. Laird put it on speaker so everyone could be privy to the conversation. Shortly, the sleuthing was set to begin.

Jeffrey closed with, "Give me thirty minutes, then meet me at the main door to the castle."

Ailsa motioned them into the kitchen. "That gives us the perfect amount of time to eat the chicken and rice casserole that's in the oven. It's ready right about now. Come on."

Twenty-five minute later, casserole devoured, dishes soaking in the sink, and extra boiled chicken fed to Maisie, they set out on their mission. Ailsa and Garia took Ailsa's car. Innis Bree, Laird, and Maisie took Laird's truck. Both vehicles headed for the castle.

On the way, which only took ten minutes, Innis Bree filled Laird in on her conversation that afternoon with Bruce. They agreed that the crunch to solve the mystery of the original Innis Bree intensified as Bruce's strength waned.

Jeffrey waited for them at the door of the castle. After greeting them warmly, a far cry from his behavior the first time Innis Bree met him in the same spot, he ushered them inside. "Maisie," he called, "you can come too, lassie." The dog followed them in, tail wagging cheerfully.

Once in the parlor, Garia showed Jeffrey the note she'd found from Clovis Campbell complaining about his daughter Tess having a secret room.

"There are twenty-five bedrooms in the castle," Jeffrey told them. "There were thirty until the owners 'afore Skeffington had private bathrooms installed for each one. If there was a secret room, they may have destroyed it while renovating. We'd have to go through all of them to try to figure it out, except I found something a month ago that didn't mean anything at the time. Now it does. 'Tess' is scratched into the windowsill in one of the bedrooms. I'm guessing that's where we need to start."

Turning on lights as they went, Jeffrey led them upstairs. Laird carried Garia, and Jeffrey toted her folded wheelchair.

Innis Bree asked Jeffrey if he only recently moved in, since he wasn't there the night she came with Rory. He told her he always stayed in the castle when the owner wasn't in residence, a matter of security. However, Rory didn't want a local around when he was there. Soon there would be new owners, and Jeffrey hoped to find a job with them.

They went down a long hallway lined with fancy wood doors until they came to the last door. The hall ended twenty feet away with a long window. Jeffrey opened the door, switched on a light, and took them into an exquisite bedroom. He unfolded Garia's wheelchair, and Laird gently set her down.

The women gaped in wonder at the room.

"Jeffrey," Ailsa said as she looked up at the twelve-foot-high coffered ceiling, "did Rory Skeffington have this room redone the way it was originally?"

"Nae. Unfortunately, the last Campbells to live here sold or took everything they could. It was theirs, after all, and had been for generations. Most o' the rooms in the house, except the front vestibule, were empty once they were out. No one's e'er had a hint of what the place may have looked like originally. Skeffington spent a fortune on a London decorator who did the downstairs and ten o' the rooms up here. I don't know why he had so many bedrooms remodeled. He ne'er brought anybody to the place except one woman at a time and his staff. The staff stayed in the servants' quarters on the third floor. He had those rooms done much less extravagantly than this."

A crystal chandelier hung from the center of the ceiling. Crystal sconces circled the walls of silvery flocked wallpaper. Three soft gray-and-white Persian carpets covered the plank wood floors. A satiny white comforter covered the four-poster bed and half a dozen lacy white pillows leaned against the tufted headboard. Filmy gauze swooped from post to post. The bed sat between enormous windows, wide and tall, hung with scalloped lace and sheer draperies. A sitting area in front of the fireplace consisted of a divan and two chairs covered in silk brocade.

Most striking, however, was the fireplace with its silver and white marble tile in a fanciful checkered pattern. A large mirror above the embellished white mantel tipped forward, reflecting the bed and anyone privileged enough to occupy it.

Innis Bree marveled, "A woman would feel like a princess in here."

"Aye. That was the idea," Jeffrey scoffed. "This is the room where the female guests slept. Skeffington's room is at the other end o' the house." He pointed in that direction. "He liked sleeping, actual sleeping, alone."

"O' course, he did," Laird said, his scorn evident.

"This is what I wanted you to see." Jeffrey went to the window and pointed at the sill. Everyone gathered around to take a gander.

"'Tess,'" Garia whispered in awe. "The lass who wrote the letter we found earlier. She carved her name into the sill."

Jeffrey went to the fireplace wall and rapped on it. "I've been thinking about this ever since you called. It sounds hollow behind here."

Laird ran a hand over the wall and knocked, too. "Aye, as if there's another room there." He pointed at the opposite side of the room. "That door o'er there is for this room's private loo?"

"Correct. That loo backs up to the loo for the room next door." Jeffrey said. "We have the outside wall with the windows ..." he pointed "... and the wall on the hallway. This is a corner chamber, the last one up here. There should be windows on either side o' the fireplace. Unless ...."

"Unless there's another room." Laird pushed and prodded around the fireplace, searching for an entrance to a secret room. Jeffrey, Innis Bree, and Ailsa joined in while Garia watched in anticipation.

After a fruitless search, Laird had a suggestion. "There's a window at the end o' the hallway outside. Jeffrey, go out there and knock on the wall in this direction. I'll knock where the wall on the hallway ends in here. We'll see if our knocking is back-to-back."

Jeffrey hurried out. A muffled knock could be heard but not on the bedroom wall.

Laird knocked at the corner facing the hallway.

Jeffrey returned. "I could hear you about six feet up the hallway. There's definitely space between the bedroom wall and the outside wall."

They continued to look for a hidden switch that would open a secret door to no avail.

Laird stared up at the top of the fireplace. "This young woman had a secret room made while her father was away. The fireplace wouldna have been moved. So the other room was already there, like a closet or something."

"It could've been a closet, or more likely a small room for her chamber pot," Ailsa suggested. "Rich folk in that era sometimes did that, so they didn't have to contend with the smell. It was a precursor to a bathroom."

"Yet she went beyond that and made it impossible for anyone else to enter." Innis Bree shoved on the immovable wall. "Why?"

"We need to think like a young lass who wants privacy for a reason we don't know," Garia noted.

"Maybe," Ailsa said, "she wanted to hide from somebody."

"Yeah. Maybe," Innis Bree furthered the thought, "she wanted privacy from Monica, the sister-in-law we know she hated. She said so in the letter. Maybe she had this done when she found out Monica would be marrying her brother."

"Oh, that's good." Ailsa patted her on the shoulder. "You should write mysteries."

While the amateur sleuths speculated, Laird ran a hand around the panel trim on the wall. "This might be it!" He pushed and a collective gasp went up as a panel slid open with a rusty squeak.

Musty air assaulted them. Garia coughed. Ailsa groaned, "Eee-www." Innis Bree was the first to stick her head in. Pitch dark prevented her from seeing anything other than spooky striated shadows from floor to ceiling. She stepped inside, and her world took a turn she'd never in her wildest dream imagined.

~

TWO HOURS LATER, four of them sat around the fireplace mulling over what to do next as they sipped wine. Jeffrey had gone into the wine cellar and brought up a bottle of Dom Pérignon Rose.

Garia had enjoyed her glass of wine and fallen fast asleep. Laird carried her into the bedroom next door and tucked her in as gently as if she were his child. Jeffrey had already invited them to stay the night so they could get back to the secret room as soon as the sun came up and gave them light through the windows. That room had never been fitted with electricity, most likely because subsequent inhabitants hadn't known it was there.

They initially entered with the flashlights on their phones to discover a dank, narrow room with shelves between two long windows, loaded with classic books from the 17th century. Innis Bree and Ailsa dusted off the spines and were stunned by what they found.

"*Don Quixote. Twelfth Night. Paradise Lost. The Tempest.* Wow." Innis Bree fingered the delicate tooled leather spines. "These are pretty racy for a teenaged girl. How on earth would she have had access to them, do you think?"

"Howe'er it was, she wanted it to be a secret," Ailsa speculated. "Look here. This shelf has *Anthony and Cleopatra, Romeo and Juliet,* and *The Diary of Samuel Pepys.* That last one is racy indeed and terribly grownup, although the last diary we found would've been when she was sixteen. Most lassies were married by then."

"Here's a *Bible*," Laird noted.

"She was well read and well educated for a lass in that era." Ailsa swung her light around looking for anything else. "It wasn't unheard o', but it was unusual. That English tutor she disliked somehow managed to teach her a lot if she was this kind o' reader."

"Look here," Jeffrey said from the farthest, darkest end of the room. "A desk with stationary, quills, and bottles o' ink. A candle in a candleholder. It's as if she left suddenly without a chance to collect her things here, things that meant a lot to her."

"Aye," Laird agreed. "That leads me to believe she got into trouble for knowing more than somebody wanted."

"Somebody like Monica," Innis Bree added.

"Hey, here's a key." Jeffrey pulled a key out of a tiny slot in the desk. He tried it on the desk drawer, and it opened. "Diaries!"

That was how they ended up in front of the fire, diaries in hand. Even though their Tess – they'd become very fond of the lass from so long ago and had come to think of her as "our Tess" – obviously read in English, she wrote her diaries in Gaelic.

They'd brought the diaries out into the light of the bedroom. Before falling asleep, Garia interpreted the first diary from 1690. Eleven-year-old Tess wrote about new dresses, the weather, her horse, and the English tutor who bored her "to bits." Sweet, the entries of a child.

With her mother snuggled into bed in the next room, Ailsa attempted to read the next year's diary but struggled, her Gaelic not proficient enough to translate most of the writing. They wanted desperately to know what their Tess had written but decided they had to wait until dawn when their beloved translator would awaken. By midnight, they decided to call it a day. The wine was gone so there was no point in staying up.

That was until Jeffrey commented on all the desserts in the fridge. "Before Skeffington and his crew left, the chef told me to eat them up. There's enough for an army. I need help."

Ailsa checked on her mam, who slept like a bairn, and the four of them trotted downstairs to the kitchen, which had been refurbished with modern appliances and stately finishes. Before long, a moist black forest cake, savory custard and strawberry tarts, and yummy banana crème eclairs sat on the marble-topped island. They had no problem devouring some of everything.

On their way out of the kitchen, Laird commented that he'd like to explore the castle. Jeffrey had shown him around before, and now he wanted to do it with Innis Bree. Jeffrey told them to nose around all they wanted, but he was going to bed, his room being at the top of the stairs. Ailsa also went back upstairs. She opted to sleep with her mam, not wanting to leave the ninety-five-year-old alone lest she awaken and not remember where she was.

Innis Bree and Laird found themselves with the entire first floor of Bridgmoor Castle to themselves. She showed him into the vast ballroom where her disastrous date with Rory had begun.

They didn't turn on the lights, instead mesmerized by moonlight streaming in through the windows, enveloping them in a magical bluish glow.

"It's a beautiful room," Laird commented, the engineer in him apparent as he took in the tall ceiling and mirrored walls. "Opulence like this is rare in these parts, e'en in a castle. Can you imagine the parties and music and dancing that went on in here?"

Innis Bree turned to the mirrors and watched him standing behind her, admiring the structure of the room. Then his gaze fell on her. He stepped up beside her and held out his hand.

He addressed her reflection in the mirror. "Miss MacIntyre, may I have the honor o' this dance?"

"Aye, kind sir," she answered his mirror image, "you may."

He took her in his arms, and she discovered she'd been right when she thought they'd be perfect dance partners. Their bodies fit together as if each had been waiting for the other to mold to it so they could move to music.

He twirled her across the room and sang from *Once Upon a Dream.*

She fell into irrepressible laughter. "You're a fabulous singer! And you know the theme song from *Sleeping Beauty.*"

He waltzed her around and she felt as if she'd fallen into a fairytale. How appropriate for him to sing from that particular Disney movie. She felt as if she'd been sleeping for years and only here in Scotland had begun to wake up to life.

When he ran out of lyrics he could remember, he said, "I have an eight-year-auld niece. I babysit. Next time I'll sing *Frozen* for you."

"Ah. That explains it."

"Do you feel like a princess here in the castle?" he asked, moving both hands to her waist and swaying to and fro as she wrapped her arms around his neck.

"Hmmm. Only because you're here to be my prince."

"Aw, feck, that's the perfect answer."

They kissed rapaciously.

When they parted, she ran a finger down the side of his face. "I know the princess and prince never share a bed in Disney movies, but what do you say we write our own ending to this fairy tale?"

"I say aye. Let's conjure up a finale that would scandalize those wee Disney folk."

"Even the evil stepmother?"

"Especially the evil stepmother."

They scurried up to Tess's chamber to make their dreams that were a wish their hearts made come true.

LAIRD SUPPOSED most men didn't think in terms of living the dream in a fairy tale. But here he was, living the dream. A castle. A crackling fire. Lights out. Winking candles. A beautiful woman. Great sex about to begin.

He stripped naked and hopped in bed while Innis Bree was in the loo. She'd taken with her a pair of silk pajamas she found in the dresser drawer. The sheets were silk, too. That promised to be very interesting.

She came out of the loo looking pretty as a picture in the pink paisley silk pajamas. He enjoyed the view while he could because he knew those PJs wouldn't last long.

He folded down the covers in invitation, and she playfully trotted to the bed and jumped on, only to slide off onto the floor.

"Whoa!" she yelped, arms flailing in the air.

Silk on silk proved slippery. He bent over to scramble to the side of the bed at the same time her head popped up, and they bumped noggins.

"O-o-ow!" They echoed each other, holding their heads.

"You okay?" he asked first.

"Yeah. You?"

"Aye. Here, take my hand and let me pull you up." She took his hand, and to his surprise, she yanked as hard as she could and pulled him off the bed onto the floor with her. He landed straddling her.

Laughter overtook them as they writhed on the carpet while Maisie, assuming they were tussling like she and her master sometimes did, fell into the mix, jumping on them and yipping in glee.

"Nae, lassie. Nae." Laird tried to push the dog off them, fell sideways in the process, and tumbled onto the floor. He delighted in watching Innis Bree play with Maisie, the dog licking her face and bouncing her paws off her new friend's belly.

"Okay, girl," Innis Bree commanded in a firm yet kind tone. "That's enough for now. Sit. Stay."

To Laird's surprise, Maisie obeyed, going to sit a few feet away with her head cocked as she did when trying to understand something that wasn't quite clear to her.

He climbed atop Innis Bree again.

"Are you talking to me or the pup?" He slithered his hips from side to side, the silk of her pajamas titillating his bare skin.

"Oh yeah. You can sit and stay right there. You're allowed to keep moving like that though." She wiggled underneath him in a blatant tease.

He found himself holding her wrists onto the floor with her arms up above her head. "Is it okay if I restrain you like this?"

"Oh, yes. As long as I get a turn." She nudged his legs with her knee and flipped them over to take hold of his wrists above his head.

Her dominance pleased him. The pajamas came off as they made love on the carpet. When finished, they mused at having ignored the fact that they had a comfy bed right there they could have used.

Half an hour later as they snuggled in bed, Laird stroked her hair as she slept. This woman was still an enigma to him. He'd not anticipated any of this when they first met. His attraction to her then had been so intense, he thought he might implode. That first kiss, och, he was so sorry for that at the time. Afterward, if she hadn't come on to him, he wouldn't have let himself make another pass at her, just another American woman who thought Jamie Fraser lived in the hills of the highlands. Besides, how could there be a future in starting a relationship with someone who'd be leaving to go home?

And that was his conundrum now. She was set to go home the day after next. He wanted her to stay. She had no job back there. Yet she hadn't mentioned staying. Should he ask her to stay? To what end? Another rejection? He'd had his share of that.

So this must be a fling, a highland fling, no less. Whatever it was, he intended to enjoy every bit of it for as long as it would last.

He'd certainly never known anyone like Innis Bree MacIntyre. Sex with her was the most satisfying he'd ever known and sheer fun, as well. God knew, he'd been in need of some pleasure in his life.

There was a problem with all this, however. He was falling in love. Nae, he corrected himself. He was beyond falling. He was in. Deep.

He placed a soft kiss on her forehead where they'd bumped. It took a while, but he eventually willed himself to sleep.

CHAPTER 16

"June 17ᵗʰ, 1695. Me faither is furious,'" Garia read from a page in the last diary. "'Apparently, he charged me brother Duncan with finding a key to this secret room. Poor rattled Duncan dinnae stand a chance. He cannae find his own arse.'"

That elicited a chuckle from the small gathering that sat by the roaring fire in Tess's chamber. Innis Bree and Laird sat on the divan while Ailsa and Jeffrey each took a chair. Garia sat nearest the fire, in her wheelchair. Rain fell outside, providing a perfect setting for the reading of a diary that was over three-hundred-years old.

They'd arisen at daybreak, and it had already been a full morning. As soon as he awoke, Laird called Jenny and Clyde to fill them in, and they offered to take care of the sheep. Maisie had become antsy, ready to do her daily job of herding, so Laird took her downstairs, let her out the door, and said, "Go home, lassie. Jenny'll get your breakfast. Your sheep are waiting." With that, the devoted Sheltie took off running in the direction of the Laird farm.

Innis Bree followed Laird downstairs in her spiffy new pajamas. They came upon Jeffrey on their way back up.

"Excuse me, Innis Bree, for being so bold," Jeffrey said, "but you and the others might be interested in the fresh undergarments available for women guests."

"Absolutely. That would be grand."

"There are tee shirts, too, although I'm naw sure they're anything you'd wear. At least they're brand new and clean."

He led her and Laird to the clothing room where the gowns in all sizes hung on racks and showed her drawers where new women's undergarments were kept. She chuckled at all the lace and padding and thongs while Laird took in the dresses.

"He really had a system going, eh?" Laird said. "The cad."

"Aye," Jeffrey agreed. "'Twas a pleasure to see the door hit his arse on his leaving."

Laird came over, picked up a thong, made a face, and said, "Doesna that annoy the hell outta … och, never mind." He tossed it down.

"Yes, it does. That's why I don't wear them." She shoved the thongs aside and came upon something reasonable in pink lace in her size and the smaller sizes she guessed Ailsa and Garia to be.

Jeffrey opened a chifforobe, and Laird took the initiative to check out the neatly folded tee shirts. He held one up for her to see, his eyebrows raised in humor.

She read, "'Woke up sexy as hell again.' No."

He tossed it back and held up another.

"'I licked it so it's mine.' Gross."

Jeffrey left the room, and Laird held up yet another one.

She nodded approval. "Plain black. No smarmy writing. Okay. That one in medium and two smalls."

When they delivered the items to Ailsa and Garia's room, the mature women giggled like schoolgirls over the lacy panties and thanked them. They appreciated the clean shirts, too.

Seeing that the bathrooms were equipped with everything imaginable a guest without luggage could need, everyone cleaned up in their private bath. It was the first time the two lovers showered together. He told her he adored getting down and dirty with her. She teased that they were supposed to be getting cleaned up.

As they all gathered in Tess's chamber, rain fell outside, softly at first and then whipping itself into a rampaging storm. Laird held his phone and read a text from Jenny that said Maisie made it home in time to herd her flock to shelter to protect them from the weather. The dreariness outside didn't allow much light into the windows in Tess's secret room, making it difficult to see much in there. They decided on a bite to eat before tackling it again, even though they were anxious to investigate.

Jeffrey and Laird went down to bring back English muffins and scones with orange marmalade, more banana crème eclairs, and orange juice. When finished, Innis Bree and Ailsa took the dishes down to the kitchen and returned with trays of steaming hot coffee and teapots, a full creamer, a bowl of sugar cubes, and five sets of cups and saucers. Innis Bree, Laird, and Jeffrey took coffee, while Ailsa and Garia drank tea.

Once everyone settled in with their morning cuppas, the translation of Tess Campbell's diaries began in earnest.

Garia donned her reading glasses and started with the next book in succession, when their Tess had been twelve. After a few pages, she put it aside. She moved on to the last one when the lass would've been sixteen, which most likely contained what they sought. If there were references to the sisters, Monica and Fenella, they might glean information about the first Innis Bree MacIntyre. After all, they suspected the sisters of having something to do with her disappearance, based on what Bruce told the contemporary Innis Bree about how much they resented his love.

Garia flipped through a few pages. "She's making more fun o' Duncan. Nae love lost there. Hmmm … here it says, 'Today witch

Monica upbraided me fer being too fanciful. She hates me fer being free while she's tied to me eejit brother. She's pure evil, that Monica. Her sister, Fenella, as well.'" Garia took a sip of her tea. "She goes on to write about her horse again. Its name was Lady Lily. A mare. She loved that animal and must have been an excellent rider." She silently read a few pages, then said Tess wrote at length about how there had been rain followed by steamy heat. "That's rare fer the highlands." She turned more pages and stopped. "Sweet Mary and Joseph," she gasped. "Here 'tis."

"What?" four voices yelped in unison at the same moment a blinding shock of lightning lit the room, causing them all to jump. Without pause, deafening thunder rumbled, the storm directly on top of them.

Garia took a calming breath and continued more loudly to be heard over the chaos outside. "'I dinnae ken what the evil sisters did oot in the forest but suspected nae good. I followed them one day, hiding behind trees, and saw them picking poisonous mushrooms, death caps, the very ones we've all been taught all our lives ne'er to touch.'"

Her audience sat in total silence, rapt with curiosity.

"'Then yester morn they invited that nice lass, Innis Bree MacIntyre, to the castle to give her a gift, as she was to wed that very afternoon. Fenella had been pretending to befriend her, and the poor simple lass thought her sincere. She dinnae ken that the sisters carry the devil's heart in their chests. When the lass came, I wiznae invited into the parlor with them. I peeked in and saw them give her the beautiful lace veil Monica had worn to her wedding. I knew it was nary a gift but a ruse. The lass was so grateful, saying, "As ye well know, me family has little money. Although I appreciate the wedding frock me aunt has made fer me, it is a simple affair. I want so dearly to be beautiful this afternoon fer me Bruce. I cannae thank ye enough fer this beautiful veil."'"

Garia's voice trailed off as the implications within the diary began to sink in. She cleared her throat and went on in a louder voice, although the words trembled on her lips.

"'I waited, hoping me suspicions were wrong and they would let the poor lassie leave without harm, veil in hand. Nae. They served her tea. It was then I intended to run in and warn her lest the witch sisters poison her. But Faither appeared at me side, asked why I was spying on me sister-in-law and her guests, and grabbed me arm and dragged me to me chamber.

"'Along the way, I told him I feared fer the lass's life and he laughed, telling me I am naught but a fanciful imp. "How will I e'er marry ye off when nary a man wants yer trouble?" he scolded me. He shoved me into me chamber and locked the door until the lass had left. At least, the sisters said she left. But I ken naw.'"

Garia turned the page and took time to scan it. Her audience was enthralled, like a jury waiting for the accused to appear as a witness in a murder trial.

The old woman adjusted her glasses and continued. "'Alas, I was aboot to find oot what truly happened. God save me soul, I write the truth here as a confession o' remorse fer naw telling what I saw to anyone except me priest. I believe God deplores me fer cowardice. I should have ridden Lady Lily through the village streets declaring with all me might the sin I witnessed at the hands o' the wicked sister witches. Me only excuse is that I feared fer me own sweet life.'"

Garia stopped. The rain ceased. No one moved.

"They poisoned her." Tears brimmed in Innis Bree's eyes.

Laird put a comforting arm around her shoulders.

"What else does it say?" Ailsa asked, eager for more.

Garia turned the page and tilted the diary so they could see. "Naught. That's the end." She flipped through the remaining pages. All blank.

"Oh my word, we have to find out what she saw," Innis Bree insisted.

Jeffrey got up and went into the door of Tess's secret room, which remained open. "There's a lot more in here we haven't investigated yet. We cannae stop now. The sun has come out. There's a bit of light coming in the windows. We can see well enough to carry on."

"I agree," Ailsa quickly added. "Let's go through everything. There could be notes tucked into books. Hiding places. Anything."

"It'll be an hour before I'm knackered and need me morning nap." Garia laid down the diary and turned her chair around. "I kin help."

"Me, too," Innis Bree said, "but I need to take a quick visit to the hotel to see if I can talk to Bruce again." Her eyebrows knitted in quandary. "I wonder how he died."

"Oh lordy, the sister witches may have poisoned that poor sot, too." Laird put the clues together.

It was agreed that Ailsa, Garia, and Jeffrey would intensify the search inside the secret room while Laird dropped Innis Bree off at the hotel. He'd run out to the farm to check on the sheep. He trusted Maisie explicitly. However, she couldn't always do it all alone. Jenny helped as best she could but seeing that she had two young kids and a husband wearing a big boot, she had her hands more than full. Once Laird knew everything was settled, he'd pick up Innis Bree and they'd rejoin the search, hopefully within forty minutes or so.

They rushed out of the castle to finish their errands so they could get back to Tess's room.

"Bruce, are you here?"

Her bedroom remained as still as a picture.

She went to the window to check the yard. No Bruce.

"Okay, if you can hear me, come with me to the graveyard. That's where I'll look next."

She hurried out of the hotel. The rainswept street glistened in the sun. As she passed the road to the loch, steam hovered above the water, humidity rising and being hit by warm sun immediately after the storm. The intoxicating smell of rain and wet earth and window-box roses heightened her senses. By the time she reached the graveyard, she felt totally attuned to the earth and its inhabitants, dead and alive.

He stood there, staring down at Fenella's headstone. A slight breeze caused the boughs of the tall trees to sway, dappling the graveyard with frolicking droplets of light. It was a peaceful, pastoral scene.

"Bruce."

He didn't look up. "She murdered me Innis Bree, didn't she?" When he finally lifted his face, Innis Bree witnessed heart-wrenching suffering.

"Yes. We believe so."

"How?"

"Poison. She and Monica invited her to the castle with the promise of a gift for your wedding that day. They gave her a veil to wear with her gown. And then they gave her poisoned tea."

"They were wicked. She didn't stand a chance with her trusting heart. She went on the morn o' the day we were to wed, ye say?"

"Yes. Aye, apparently so."

"When they told me she'd run off, I ne'er believed it. I ken a haver when I hear one."

Innis Bree assumed a "haver" was a lie but didn't interrupt to ask.

He looked past the headstones and out to Loch Tay with its water glowing in the sun. "She was strong-willed, that one. It wiznae possible fer me to tell her to stay away from them had I known. She had a mind o' her own. But she was also innocent as a bairn. Trusting as a nun. Kindhearted as Mary Mother o' Jesus. Yet strong-willed as a queen." He shook his head and took in Innis Bree. "That was what I loved most aboot her. Are ye strong-willed, lassie? Did ye inherit that from her?"

"I, well, I hope so."

"Ken it in yer heart and soul. Ye have it within ye to be as strong as she. After all, she lives within ye."

"I'll try."

"Dinnae try. Dae it."

She approached him and touched his arm. "Bruce, thank you for being my friend."

He patted her hand on his arm. "We're family. I ken, I ken. I tried to bed ye a'fore. I dinnae ken back then. I was besotted, thinking I'd found me love after all this time. Now I ken yer the offspring that would be mine if I'd wed me Innis Bree. I love thee, lassie."

"I love you, too."

"Well now, aren't we a coupla sooks?"

"Yes. We are a couple of softies. I suppose that's why I'm still trying to find your Innis Bree's remains. She needs to be buried here with you."

"Aye. That would be nice. But there's another reason to find her."

They were interrupted when Laird's truck pulled up out front. He jumped out and jogged to them. It only took a few seconds for Innis Bree to realize that the living man couldn't see or hear the dead one. But Bruce could see and hear Laird.

"This is the lad who descends from me own seed?" Astonished, Bruce put his hands on his hips and eyed his progeny.

"Yes," she said. "Aye. This is Laird Bartholomew Blyth."

Catching on, Laird stared into the space she addressed.

"Bartholonew? Jay-sus. That's a gawdawful name. Tell him to be oot with it."

196

"He doesn't like your middle name," she informed Laird.

"I don't either." Laird shrugged.

"I suppose he thinks himself handsome?" Bruce huffed.

"Yes, he does. So do I."

"Pfft. Mayhaps. Certainly naw as handsome as I."

"Surely not. There could be none as handsome as you."

"Hey, hey, hey," Laird jested, "what about me?"

"He has me blue eyes."

"Yes, Bruce, he does. Beautiful eyes," she said.

Hands clasped behind his back like a general inspecting his troops, Bruce circled Laird. Although he couldn't see the specter of his forebear, Laird could sense the interrogation, turning around himself, the two of them inadvertently performing a comic dance.

"He's me height." Bruce nodded approvingly. "He has me dark hair. He's strong, that I kin see. I wouldna be wanting those retched breeks or that ungainly shirt." He pointed at Laird's jeans and plucked at his tee shirt. Laird flinched. "Can he ride and shoot?"

"Um, I don't know. Laird, he wants to know if you can ride and shoot."

"I can, although I do neither very often."

"How no?" Bruce scoffed.

"Bruce," Innis Bree said, "you need not worry. He went to university. He's built big buildings. He even fought in a war."

"A Jacobite war? Although, I suppose those are o'er by now? I fought in many a Jacobite uprising. I was quite the hero meself."

Innis Bree sighed. This was going to be difficult. "Laird, I know you can't hear or see him, but he can hear you. Can you explain to him what happened to the Jacobites?"

She was struck by the kindness and brevity with which Laird explained to this old Jacobite warrior that his war had been lost and his land had been taken away.

"Me manse was stolen away by the English? Argh! O' course

'twas." Bruce barreled into a rant of cursing so clipped and rushed, Innis Bree had no idea what he was saying. When she explained to Laird that Bruce was swearing, he nodded understanding.

"Bruce, sir," Laird finally interrupted, "I was recently able to buy the land and your manse. It's back in the Blyth family. I'm a sheep farmer there."

"Truth be told?" Bruce looked at Laird in amazement. "Tell him … tell him I am proud o' him. Thank him fer saving our land."

Innis Bree relayed the message. Laird told the apparition he appreciated being given life. "I thank you and am proud to be part o' your family."

"He's a good lad, then," Bruce proclaimed. "Ye have no idea how deeply moved I am to see ye two together."

She repeated that to Laird, and he put an arm around her waist in a display of affection. "It means a lot to us, as well," he said.

"Bruce," Innis Bree said, "you were about to tell me something when Laird drove up."

"Aye. Let's sit. He knows this well; ye dinnae." He led them to a bench where they sat while he told the tale of an ancient Scottish myth that made finding his love more urgent than ever. As he finished his story, an angry charcoal cloud rolled in and rumbled overhead, casting a menacing shadow over the tombstones, emphasizing the gravity of this tragic situation.

"I kin smell the rain. Ye best go." Bruce shooed them away with a swish of his hand.

"I'll find you again," Innis Bree promised. "Hopefully with news."

The shower hit hard as the couple ran to the safety of the truck. In the graveyard, Bruce Cieran Blyth evaporated into heavy air.

"We Scots ken well the story o' which he speaks. In fact, I saw it in a book here." Garia wheeled herself closer to the bookshelf and reached up to finger a row of volumes. "Here 'tis, right here in this anthology o' Scottish folk magic." She pulled out the book and opened it to the table of contents, running her finger down the list. "Ah, ere." She turned to that page and scanned it carefully.

The five of them were in Tess's small secret room inspecting every book, searching every nook and cranny, and even checking the floorboards for a possible hiding place. As they searched, Innis Bree relayed her conversation with Bruce, including the story he'd told that made it imperative they find his Innis Bree. When Garia said she knew the story and found it, they all stopped what they were doing and turned their attention to her. Jeffrey had been sitting at the desk at the only chair already in the room so he could look for a secret compartment. He got up and gave the chair to his elder, Ailsa. The others leaned against shelves or the wall and settled in to listen to the wise woman who had become their guide. Sallow light meandering in through the windows fell upon Garia. The ninety-five-year-old was the perfect image of a goddess with her striking white hair and life etched into her pleasing face.

"It's called *Scottish Folk Magic*, published in ..." she had to search for a date "... 1678. The myth about the dead is written in Gaelic. I know it well and will simply tell it to you in English. I'm sure this is what Bruce referred to." She laid the book on her lap, reverently laying her gnarled hands on the open pages. "The easiest way to explain it is to say that the Scottish, and many other cultures, have a long history o' believing the dead cannae peacefully rest unless certain death rituals are followed. This predates Christianity and the concept o' heaven, a time when Celtic people believed that after death a soul was taken by the sith, good folk, fairies. That soul went away to exist contentedly and would leave the living alone, unless the living failed to ... Let's see. How shall I say this?

Unless the living failed to send them off in the right manner. Therefore, death rites were extremely important."

"That's essentially what Bruce said," Innis Bree added. "If his Innis Bree was murdered and the body disposed of improperly, she had no way of leaving this earth. Her soul is imprisoned."

"Aye, that's it exactly. When a person died, there was a wake that lasted eight days. The departed was wrapped in a shroud and laid out at home on a wood plank that would later be used for the coffin. Windows were shunted open to remind them they would be leaving the house, although I suspect that was to release the smell, too. Clocks were stopped, and mirrors were covered with white linen because time and vanity were o' no use to the corpse. If the family kept bees, they were told o' the death and their hives veiled until the wake was o'er."

"They believed the bees mourned, too," Ailsa said. "I've always found that fascinating."

"Aye, 'tis." Ailsa continued with her tale. "Two people had to sit with the body at all times, day and night, for the entire eight days. They were called the 'dead days.' Pairs would take shifts. Family and friends and e'en strangers would come and go. Apparently, it became a wee bit boring, as singing and dancing and card games were common."

"And drinking and fights, from what I've always heard," Laird snickered.

"Aye. That, too. Sometimes there were professional keeners. In other words, it was quite an ordeal. There's much more to the superstitions. The chairs the coffin had set upon in the house had to be turned o'er when the coffin was lifted to be taken away because the dead might take the opportunity to get out and sit in an open chair. When the casket was being taken to the kirk, they had to use the correct road since passing by a crossroad was dangerous because the dead could escape. Cairns for luck were built along the way. Any deviation from common practice meant the soul could escape and would remain restless on earth, causing destruction and disease and unhappiness. The goal was to appease them so they wouldna cause any trouble. Even with all those precautions, the dead could escape if they had a strong enough will to do so."

"Like Bruce." Innis Bree knew all this to be more than superstition. Her ghost proved it.

"Aye, like Bruce. Poor soul."

Laird chimed in, "Except he doesna seem to have harmed anybody in his wanderings."

"Nae, he has naw," Garia agreed. "I believe he's a much gentler soul than he'd e'er admit. But there's a difference between him and his Innis Bree. He is free to roam. She is trapped because there was no wake."

"So," Innis Bree put the pieces together, "if his Innis Bree was murdered and buried without proper folk magic rituals, her soul has no way of escaping to where it needs to go."

"Correct. Bruce, also," Ailsa concluded, "will ne'er be able to find her and go with her into the light, as we think about it now."

Garia nodded solemnly. "He may eventually fade away to aimlessly roam the purgatory between heaven and earth fore'er if we don't find her."

"We must find her," Innis Bree insisted.

Everyone looked around the room as if wishing hard enough would magically produce an answer.

And it did.

THEY SCOURED the contents of the room for another hour before Garia's discovery. They'd taken some of the books out to the sitting area by the fireplace where there was better light. Working slowly, as they'd become demoralized by the lack of any more writings from their Tess, they took interludes to read from the old books or to peruse her earlier diaries, which produced nothing of use.

That was until Garia wheeled her chair into the secret room, lit a candle on the desk, and scanned the walls and ceiling in silence. As if a fairy's hand guided her head, her eyes fell on the candle. It was a fat stub, well used in its day, in a silver holder, now tarnished to a dull green, the size of a dinner plate. She picked it up.

There laid two tattered, yellowed pieces of paper folded together. She set the candle down on the other side of the desk, took the pages in hand, and gently opened them. Her eyes widened in disbelief as she read. Placing them on her lap, she returned the chamber.

"Here it is," she announced.

CHAPTER 17

"'*M*e hand is shaking so hard I pray ye who finds this kin read it! Faither is in the hall outside me chamber, angry as a raging bull, screaming at me to come oot. I am to go at once to Denmark to marry a wealthy auld souse and bear his milk-and-water bairns. God save me!

"'I fear this is me punishment fer me sin o' naw letting poor blacksmith John MacIntyre ken the whereabouts o' his daughter, Innis Bree. He has been bereft since her leaving. Her brother, Gillimichell, is also distraught beyond repair. And her intended, Bruce Blyth, is inconsolable. Most insidious o' all, I watch as Fenella tries to wile her way into Bruce's bed. Try as she might, she will ne'er be taken into his heart.

"'Why, dear God in Heaven, why have I naw told me tale? Because I fear they will murder me, too. Monica and Fenella suspect me. If I speak up, me soul will ne'er know peace at their hands, same as the soul o' poor Innis Bree.'"

Garia took a breath. "The poor lassie. What a terrible burden this was for a child. Believing in witchcraft and thinking that if she too was murdered and hidden and didn't get a proper wake, her soul would ne'er get to heaven."

"She was sixteen at this point, correct?" Jeffrey clarified.

"Aye," Ailsa reminded him. "Most were married by then. It wouldn't have been unusual for her father to arrange a suitable marriage."

"Suitable," Laird sneered, "naw being who she loved but who could bring the most money into his coffers."

"Sadly, 'tis so." Ailsa shook her head in sorrow. "As soon as we get this all sorted out as best we can, I'm going to do research on our Tess. I've quite fallen in love with her."

Everyone agreed they had, too, and were curious to know what kind of life she ended up living.

Garia continued reading. "'I kin only pray me confession here will save me soul from the eternal damnation o' hell. There was nae sleep fer me that night Innis Bree was here, tossing in me bed like a bat. I heard a noise and crept oot o' me chamber to see. They were there, in the dark o' night, dragging the poor lass's dead body toward the dungeon stairs ...'"

Garia held up the page for them to see. A squiggly line ended the missive.

"She must have felt threatened enough by what her father was doing," Ailsa said, "to hide this and rush out o' her hiding place."

"We must search the dungeon." Innis Bree was already out of her seat and at the door. "Innis Bree must be buried there."

"Garia, do you want to come?" Laird asked. "We can take you."

"Nae, loves, go. I'll await here. Go find Innis Bree!"

Once on the main floor, the women waited while Laird and Jeffrey went to the garden shed to fetch digging tools. They returned quickly, each with a spade and trowel as well as a trowel for each woman. The group hurried through the rooms and down the hallway to the stairs that led to the belly of the beast.

Even with the lights on, the narrow, curved stairs down to the dungeon seemed ominous. They went directly to the torture room, what had been Rory Skeffington's sex dungeon. Empty now and well lit, it no longer felt quite so menacing, although an attack of claustrophobia once again struck Innis Bree. She shook it off. This was too important for that. This wasn't about her; it was about the first Innis Bree.

"This room has a stone floor." Jeffrey ran his foot over the stone.

"That means she's naw in this room." Laird headed out the door and everyone followed.

Jeffrey sidled his way to the front of their troupe. "Follow me. The rooms in the side hallway have dirt floors."

Once in that hallway, he reached out to open the first door when Innis Bree remembered something. "Wait. The end room. There was a bump in the floor. I stumbled over it."

They rushed down the hall as Ailsa asked, "If someone was buried there, would there still be evidence of it after so long?"

Laird replied, "If they did a poor enough job, aye."

They reached the heavy wood door at the end of the hall.

"Ready?" Jeffrey asked, his hand on the rusted doorhandle.

Three nods answered.

He opened the door with a creak of its hinges and flicked a light switch. The room became alarmingly illuminated. Empty, with stone walls and ceiling and the dirt floor, it seemed innocent enough.

Innis Bree went to the spot where she'd stumbled. "Here it is." She pointed, her finger quaking.

The four of them gathered around and stared at the slight hump in the dirt, about three feet wide and five feet long. No one spoke. The disturbance in the floor was the size of a human being.

The men dug, rapidly at first, then slower when they reached a foot down. They didn't want to harm the remains, should there be any.

"Wait! What's that?" Innis Bree pointed.

An inch of rotted lace poked up from the dirt. They stopped digging.

She stooped down and used her trowel and hands to gently dig around the piece of fabric. "The evil sisters lured her here with the promise of an exquisite veil to wear to her wedding that afternoon. Then they buried it with her as a final taunt."

"Evil murderesses!" Ailsa snarled.

Laird said, "I have more descriptive words, which I'll refrain from using in mixed company."

Three of them got on their knees, and Ailsa, whose knees were older, sat on her bum as they meticulously worked to uncover the skeleton of the first Innis Bree MacIntyre. It was a shallow grave. More disintegrating intricate lace came up first, followed by the fetid smell of decay. The diggers gasped and coughed.

"There shouldna be a smell after so long," Laird noted.

"Aye," Jeffrey agreed. "'Tis as if the poor lassie fought off death as best she could."

Even though they labored slowly out of respect for the remains, within an hour the lassie's entire skeleton laid bare, her empty eye sockets staring up at them.

Innis Bree used her bare hand to wipe a final bit of dirt off the departed's foot. As if she'd pushed a button, a rush of cool air washed over them, so intense it almost knocked them over. The fetid smell evaporated as the sweet scent of heather and roses infused the room, the smell Bruce said reminded him of his lassie.

Innis Bree stood up unsteadily. "Innis Bree?" she whispered, dropping her trowel to the ground.

The ghost of her eight-times great-grandaunt materialized in front her, ogling her, confused and terrified. Either way, each saw her own face, as if looking in a mirror. The ghost reached up in confusion to stroke the face of her descendant, who marveled at the vibrancy of the touch. Innis Bree copied the gesture and stroked her ancestor's lovely face, eliciting a smile.

A spectral image of her fifteen-year-old self, the first Innis Bree's beauty could not be denied. The lush, raven black hair, the luminous green eyes, the alluring figure. No wonder Bruce had been, and still was, totally smitten. Although rotted remnants of her clothes clung to her bones in the crude grave, the ghost herself wore a long, clean, plain blue dress with a white petticoat. A knitted wool shawl wrapped around her shoulders, crisscrossed over her chest, and tucked into her belt. Her luxurious hair flowed halfway down her back. She would have made a stunning bride.

The ghost looked around, twisting from side to side to take in her surroundings as she raised her arms out to her sides in wonderment. Awareness struck as she joyously realized she was finally free. Her exuberant smile radiated exultation. That expression morphed into confusion, as she sought a way out.

"Oh! This way," Innis Bree instructed. "Follow me."

The others watched in amazement, unable to see the ghost, yet it was clear to them what was happening. They didn't interrupt as their Innis Bree led her great-grandaunt out the door, down the narrow hallway, and up the winding stairs. They followed close behind, sensing the presence of the deceased.

Innis Bree could see that the ghost floated behind her, hovering above the ground, excitedly seeking her way to freedom. In the main part of the castle, she hustled her follower through the many rooms it took to get to the vestibule with its front door. She swung the door open wide, and warm summer air wafted over them.

The ghost Innis Bree hesitated and drew a long breath, energized by the fresh air. She flew out the door, thought better of it, and circled back to place a kiss on her successor's cheek.

Innis Bree put her hand to the apparition's cheek in awe. "Innis Bree," she whispered, "your Bruce is looking for you. He's out there searching." She pointed toward the village.

The ghost nodded understanding, blew a kiss of sparkling golden dust, and vanished from sight as she fluttered away.

Innis Bree couldn't move. She could hardly breathe. Stupefied, she stared at the spot in the distance where the ghost had disappeared.

"We did it!" Ailsa squealed.

"Did she look like you, love?" Laird wanted to know.

"Yes. Exactly like me. It was as if I looked into my own face from over three hundred years ago. I can't believe it! We did it!"

"Thanks to Tess," Jeffrey said. "Love that lassie."

After a giant group hug, they dashed upstairs to tell Garia.

It was quickly decided that Jeffrey, who volunteered, would collect the bones of the skeleton, secure them in a cloth bag, and replace the dirt to fill up the hole. Later that evening, in the dark of night, he, Laird, and Innis Bree would sneak into the graveyard and bury them over Bruce's grave.

"That's against the law, o'course," Garia cautioned, "but this isna a legal matter. 'Tis a matter o' the heart and soul. There's one more thing, me friends. We must keep this a secret. Even in the year o' 2023, there are those who would call us evil witches for communicating with the dead. They could try to make our lives hell. This I know from experience."

"Yes," Ailsa said. "Mam used to work as a medium, sharing her gift o' sight with the world. Unfortunately, there were wee-minded people – naw from our village but others in the highlands – who considered her to be a threat. 'Tis best we keep this whole experience amongst us, along with Jenny and Clyde because they're family and we ken they'll understand."

"What say ye?" Garia asked, surveying those gathered around her.

Everyone agreed wholeheartedly.

They decided they would hold a private celebration at dinnertime. Jeffrey offered up the castle, but the others admitted they'd had all they could take of Bridgmoor Castle for the time being. When Laird suggested his manse for a cookout, it seemed the perfect place.

As they gathered their belongings to go to their respective homes and hotel, Innis Bree quickly realized she was exhausted and in much need of a nap before the evening's events. Laird needed to get back to the farm, so they went their separate ways for the few short hours until they'd meet again. He kissed her goodbye and was off. Ailsa gave her a ride to the hotel, where the desk clerk and rainbow-haired server chatted at the registration desk and greeted her heartily, teasing that they hadn't seen her much the last couple of days. She liked them but wasn't about to reveal any secrets about what had transpired on that day. And she certainly wouldn't tell them about the last few nights.

In her room, she collapsed on the bed. As much as she loved her ghosts, dealing with them drained her strength. As she drifted off to sleep, she mulled over the influence Innis Bree and Bruce's love had on her. Was it merely fanciful imitation to fall in love with Laird? Was she doing it only to bring the romance of the couple from the past to life?

No. Her ancestor's love affair presented an enchanting correlation to what she felt now, but the past didn't determine her present. She was madly, gladly in love with Laird Bartholomew Blyth. Of her own free will, her heart and soul had interlaced with his. Had the other Innis Bree and Bruce never come into her life, she still would have fallen in love as if it was always been meant to be.

She fell asleep, fantasizing Laird in her arms … and more ….

LAIRD BLYTH HADN'T BEEN this happy since … He couldn't remember ever being this happy. The ghost of Innis Bree MacIntyre was finally free to join the ghost of her beloved Bruce Blyth so they could journey together to the hereafter. And the real-life Innis Bree MacIntyre seemed to be as smitten, nae, as *in love* with him as he was with her.

"Lassie," he said to Maisie, who cocked her head listening to her master as she laid on the bedroom floor, "I said I'd ne'er fall in love again. I said I'd ne'er let myself be a chump again, victim o' a woman's wiles. I was going to love 'em and leave 'em." He sighed. "That was before we met Innis Bree, eh?"

Maisie chortled assent.

"She's perfect, is she naw?" He reached down to ruffle his pet's ears, then went about the task of picking out a tee shirt. He was gathering clean clothes to wear that evening. "This one?" He held up a dark green one. Maisie didn't seem impressed. "Naw that one. Okay. Perhaps a dressier shirt? Nae. We'll be outside. How about this one?" He held up a deep rusty red. Maisie got up and nosed that one. "This one it is. Thank you, my love."

He stripped naked and warbled *Can't Help Falling in Love* as he padded into his bathroom, turned on the shower, waited for it to steam, and stepped in. He'd never paid much attention to the local soap he used, a manly scent of thistle, pine, and heather. Now he was glad to have it. He grinned at his erection that appeared at the mere thought of what the night had in store. "Wait for it, my friend. Your time will come. More than once."

Shower done, toweled off, and standing at his sink looking in the mirror, he ran a hand through his tussled hair to slick it off his forehead. Examining the stubble on his face, he said to Maisie, "Let's surprise her with smooth skin, eh. It's time to be done with this." He shaved, then tossed aside the towel he'd wrapped around his slim waist to inspect himself in the mirror. "Lassie, 'tis fair to say I ne'er preen o'er my own body, is it naw?" He traced the Celtic tattoo on his arm as he talked. "But we must admit it is indeed an impressive thing to see."

Maisie had seen it all before. Unimpressed, she didn't bother lifting her head off her paws as she laid in the doorway.

Laird knew he was what women considered to be a "hunk." He never thought about it. He simply went about living his life of hard work that bulked up his muscles, kept fat at bay, and rendered him strong and healthy. Now, how he looked mattered because he wanted to appeal to the woman he sought. He smiled at himself, realizing that seemed to be a done deal. So far, this body had brought her back more than once and hopefully would do so for a long time to come.

He faced his dog and in all his naked glory made a confession. "I'm in love with Innis Bree. Hopelessly, madly in love. And tonight, my lassie, I'm going to tell her."

With a bounce in his step, he dressed and took Maisie with him to prepare the manse for the adventurous evening to come.

The intrusion of her phone startled Innis Bree out of a Rip Van Winkle nap. "Okay, okay. Shut up." She grappled for it on the nightstand, fumbled, knocked it off, and had to stretch over the side of the bed to retrieve it off the floor. She squinted at the screen, had to turn the contraption right side up, and finally swiped to answer. "Hello?"

Her friends from home popped up on the screen. "Hello!" Kathryn, Rama, and Delina greeted her cheerfully.

"How are you?" Kathryn asked.

Innis Bree blinked in disbelief and shook her head to try to wake up. "I'm ... I'm fine. How are you?" It was a weird time of day for them to be calling, not quite noon in North Carolina. Delina should be at work in the hospital, and the other two should be in their campus offices. Instead, they sat in Paddy's Pub with drinks in front of them.

"We're great!" Rama's face filled the screen like a cartoon character, then he sat back and all three were visible again.

Kathryn brimmed with excitement, bopping up and down in her seat. "We have good news!"

"Really good news," Delina reassured in between sips of her margarita.

"On top of the fact that the dean is gone," Kathryn reminded her.

Rama nodded vigorously. "When the vice-president got the paperwork she needed to endorse your dismissal, she refused to sign it. You're not fired! You still have your job, plus the promotion you've been waiting for."

"You, my friend," Kathryn picked up the story, "are going from assistant to associate professor at the beginning of fall semester. How's that?"

"That's … that's great. I can't quite believe it. Um, gee, who'll be acting dean until they conduct a search?"

Rama raised his hand, and the women pointed at him as they did a merry little jig in their seats.

"Rama! Congratulations! That's awesome. You'll make a fantastic dean. Will you apply for the permanent position?"

"I will." He placed a hand over his heart. "I'm thrilled to have been asked to fill in until they find someone, who I hope is me."

To follow the law and not be accused of favoritism, the college, a state institution, had to conduct a formal search, inviting applicants to submit resumes and conducting interviews even if they knew who they wanted to hire. Then, if someone inhouse was hired, they needed documentation that it was the best person for the job. Rama wouldn't have any trouble fulfilling the requirements.

"Oh, Rama, I'm so happy for you." A stab of FOMO, fear of missing out, struck as she wished she could be there to celebrate with her best friends. That world seemed so far away, now that she'd been immersed in the happenings of the living and the dead here in a small town in the highlands of Scotland. She felt torn, missing her old life while reveling in what she had here.

"And happy for yourself, right?" Kathryn asked.

"Sure. Yes. Of course."

She caught the flash of doubt that crossed Kathryn's face. That woman was no fool.

"When will you be home?" Delina asked. "You fly out day after tomorrow, correct?"

"Yes." Day after tomorrow! It'd come up so quickly. How could it be possible that she'd have to leave? Yet how could she possibly stay?

"We'll have a proper celebration when you get back." Rama tipped his glass of Coke at her. Apparently, he thought it imprudent to drink booze early in the day now that he held an elevated position at the college.

"Sounds good. Congratulations again, Rama. I'm so happy for you. For all of you. Life is going to be a lot easier now without the Fuhrer and with our Rama in charge."

"Easier for all of us, right?" Kathryn questioned.

"Yes. For all of us."

They bid her adieu, and she clicked off. Sprawled out on her bed, she felt paralyzed. What in hell was she going to do? Go? Stay? Stay where? How? She needed a job. She needed … she didn't know what because the only thing she wanted was Laird.

She grabbed a pillow and held it to her face as she screamed and kicked in frustration. Throwing off the sheet that had wadded up around her legs, she snarled at the mess.

"Shit. I'm screwed. And not in the way I'd like."

CHAPTER 18

The cookout became a wake of sorts for the Innis Bree of so long ago. Laird grilled chicken and hot dogs on the barbeque he'd brought over, and Ailsa and Garia brought au gratin potatoes and steamed veggies. Jenny contributed homemade sourdough rolls to die for. A cooler held water and beer. Jeffrey brought what was left of the desserts from the castle, including butterscotch pudding, triple fudge brownies, and cherry turnovers. He also provided the wine.

Laird had set up his wireless speakers and country, pop, and Scottish classics played in the background. His taste in music was eclectic – rowdy, sweet, romantic, and fun. A perfect mix for this gang.

Jenny and Clyde and their two kids had been invited, although the ghost stories were kept from the seven- and five-year-olds. The kids ran around enough, playing with Maisie, to afford plenty of time for the parents to be filled in on the events of the last few days regarding the first Innis Bree and her Bruce. The couple was aghast and fascinated as the story unfolded about their own village where they'd lived all their lives.

The group sat in the open-air part of Laird's manse at a long folding table covered in a crisp white linen tablecloth with lace edging, compliments of the castle. Laird had cleaned up the rubble to lay bare oak and marble flooring, outdoors now but once part of luxurious rooms they could only imagine. As the gloaming began and gray shadows reached out to envelop them, Laird lit a fire in the fireplace even though the weather remained pleasantly warm.

When nine o'clock came, Jenny and Clyde left to take their children home to bed. After they'd gone, Jeffrey asked everyone to gather by the fireplace while he got something from his truck. They pulled their chairs into a semi-circle and waited, wine glasses in hand.

He returned with a bundle covered by a lovely pink silk quilt gathered together at the top and tied with a wide white ribbon. As gently as if it were a bairn, he set it down between them and the fire. "This is she."

Innis Bree, Laird, Ailsa, and Garia stared in silence. It was surprisingly small. Bones alone didn't take up much space.

"I thought she deserved silk," Jeffrey explained. "I took it from the castle. 'Twas the least the place could do, seeing it held her in captivity for so long. She deserves this kind o' luxury, which she never had when alive."

Garia bowed her head and without preamble prayed aloud. "Holy Father in Heaven, Our Lord Jesus Christ, and Mary Mother of Jesus, take into thy arms this loving young woman who did naught wrong in her entire life except trust the wrong folk. She is an innocent bairn who deserves all the abundant grace and love you have to give. Let her finally rest in peace alongside her beloved Bruce. May they walk arm in arm together for all eternity. Amen."

"Amen," the others echoed.

Respectful silence ensued until Innis Bree said, "We need to wait until later to bury her, so no one sees us."

"I suspect anyone in Kenmore," Laird said, "who learned o' their love story would simply help us."

"Aye," Jeffrey agreed. "Folk around here have no problem believing in long-lost loves and the ghosts who seek them out."

Soon after, Ailsa and Garia called it a night. On their leaving, each woman took a hand of Innis Bree's, and Garia said, "Dear lass, you have honored your ancestor in the best way possible. You gave her freedom to love. She lives on in you. May you always know in this lifetime the kind o' love that was stolen from her."

"God bless you, Innis Bree," Ailsa added. "I'll see you tomorrow." She referred to their final morning meeting, as it would be the American's last full day in Scotland.

Innis Bree wiped the tears from her cheeks and hugged them. "Good night. Thank you so much for everything."

An hour after that, with the table and chairs folded and stashed in Jeffrey's truck, the three of them – Innis Bree, Laird, and Jeffrey – headed for the graveyard. They took both trucks, and the ride with Laird was rightfully solemn for the task at hand. Even Maisie remained silent and still, aware this was a solemn occasion.

In the graveyard, with a three-quarter moon shining down, Jeffrey and Laird used their shovels to lift the sod off the top of Bruce Cieran Blyth's grave and lay it aside. Digging as quickly as possible, they made a hole the size of the bundle. The men looked at Innis Bree, she nodded, and Laird picked up the silky casket and gently laid it in the ground.

"Rest in peace, my great-grandaunt Innis Bree," Innis Bree said. "Thank you for being such a touching and important part of my life. I've learned so much from you. Even though we never knew each other on this earth, I know you in my heart. I love you. I hope you've found your Bruce and that you two are together in love forever." She looked around, expecting to see both of the departed.

No one appeared.

She picked up a handful of dirt and sifted it through her fingers onto the silk. Each man did the same, then they refilled the hole with most of its dirt, leaving off the amount of the bundle of bones. That got tossed over the side of the hill the graveyard sat on. Methodically, they replaced the strips of sod, leaving the grave looking almost untouched. Jeffrey commented that after one good rain, the grass would thicken and no one would ever know it'd been disturbed.

Jeffrey got a hug from Innis Bree and from Laird, with the men doing the typical male version handshake with one pump, pull in, and one tap on the back. Maisie twirled around until Jeffrey patted her head.

The trucks parted ways, one headed to the castle and the other returning to the manse, where Laird had a big surprise for Innis Bree. An even bigger surprise, however, turned out to be for him.

BACK AT THE MANSE, Laird pulled an air mattress out of the bed of his truck.

"What's this?" Innis Bree took one side to help him carry it.

"On a night as beautiful as this, we cannae sleep indoors. Eh? It's a wee bit chilly, but we can keep each other warm. I've spent many a night out here under the sky."

They reached the fireplace and plopped the mattress down in front of it.

"I love it!"

He grabbed her around the waist and pulled her in for a kiss. "I thought you would. Bedding is in the truck."

By the time they finished setting up, a fitted sheet covered the mattress; a flat sheet, a handcrafted quilt, and a comforter provided covers; two fluffy pillows awaited; soft music played; and the cooler still had bottles of water, beer, and wine. Laird preferred the Aberfeldy Scotch Whisky he pulled out of a bag. He asked if she wanted a wee dram, and she said yes, this night called for whisky. A bowl of water sat at the ready for Maisie, too, who lapped it up noisily.

He threw a couple of logs on the fire, sparks flying and crackling in a spurt. The calming smell of burning wood permeated the air. Innis Bree couldn't imagine a more romantic setting. She loved the way the flames played with his eyes, causing them to sparkle with warmth. Or, better yet, heat.

They undressed and sat on their makeshift bed cross-legged, facing each other. As a nod to modesty they knew wouldn't last, they pulled the quilt over to cover them from the waist down.

He took a sip out of his bottle of scotch and handed it over. She took a hit and coughed, eyes watering as she wiped her mouth with the back of her hand.

"Lassie, my love, have you ne'er had whisky 'afore?" He took the bottle from her.

"No." She coughed again. "But I like it." Her scratchy voice didn't seem to agree.

"You needn't drink it. Shall I get you some water?"

"No. Really, I like it." She took the bottle. "It was a surprise, is all." She took a small sip this time and swallowed hard. "That's good. What's in it?"

He smiled. "I fear I'm a bad influence on you. Introducing you to hard liquor." He chuckled and took another swig. "It's aged whisky with heather honey and herbs and spices, made in Scotland. I've been drinking it since I was fourteen." He took another gulp.

"Fourteen? That's a little young, isn't it?"

"Nae. Naw for highlanders like me and Jeffrey. He introduced me to it."

They passed the bottle back and forth, with her taking small sips and him drinking heartily.

"What's the deal with Jeffrey? Has he ever been married? Does he have a girlfriend?"

His quizzical expression showed his surprise. "Ah, I thought you woulda guessed by now. Jeffrey is gay. He had a male companion, but they broke up last year. Understandably, he's been quite morose since, until now with all the goings-on around you and your ghosts. You've been good for him."

"I didn't realize he was gay."

Laird shrugged. "When we were mates in primary school, bullies teased him for being a 'priss.' I was the strongest o' any o' them so one day I punched one o' the arseholes in the nose. They left Jeffrey alone after that, and he and I became friends."

She stared at this gorgeous, bare-chested, tipsy man sitting there with her. Was this a dream?

"Are you really this good a person?" she asked. "It's like you're out of a wholesome Hallmark movie and a juicy romance novel all in one. Which reminds me, I have a stack of swoony romances I haven't had time to read yet. Thankfully, I have my own swoony stud right here."

"Pfft," Laird scoffed. "Me? In a love story? That I've ne'er heard 'afore. I'm a sheep farmer. Hardly a woman's fantasy man. My ex-wife regaled me often enough about the billionaires in those stories."

She shook her head. "Not for me. One disastrous date and I'm done with that."

He took a drink from the bottle and held it out to her. She took one more hit and waved a palm for no more as she handed it back. He set it down on the ground.

Slowly, he pulled the bedding off her legs, the feel of the fabric moving across her skin to reveal her nakedness exciting her. Emboldened by his move, she slowly rendered him buck-naked, too. The quilt ended up in a heap at their side.

"You're the one who's a dream, Innis Bree." He ran his hands up her thighs. "Ne'er in my life did I expect to be here like this with a lassie like you. An American, no less."

They leaned in for a kiss, the taste of liquor on their tongues intoxicating. No matter how many times their mouths met, it felt shockingly new to Innis Bree each time, always overpoweringly sublime.

It seemed they each had more to say but booze, emotions, and hormones took over as he straightened his legs and pulled her up onto his lap. Cupping her breasts, he bent his head to nip and suck. Out of her mind by then, overtaken by a primitive call to mate, her legs wrapped around him in a stronghold as she lifted her torso to take him in. Mate they did, their howls cutting through the night to mingle with those of the wildlife in the hills.

Lying in front of the fire, Maisie huffed, annoyed by the disturbance to her bedtime. Still, she was happy that this sweet-smelling new friend had come into their lives. With her around, she got more petting than ever. Besides, the lass made her master happy. That was the best thing of all.

INNIS BREE'S eyes popped open to an amazing array of stars above them. The Milky Way sprawled out across the sky in a startling display with a pitch black backdrop full of points of sparkling light. The breadth and depth of the universe filled her with wonder. She didn't know if it was because she was still woozy from the scotch, but she felt elevated to a new level of existence.

"'Tis beautiful, is it naw?" Laird's question broke into the stillness.

"You're awake, too. How nice." She nuzzled in under his arm to rest her head on his shoulder, the curve in his frame perfect for nestling. She placed a hand on his chest without taking her eyes off the sky. "Yes. It's beautiful beyond words."

He drew her in close and placed a warm hand over hers. "I love sleeping out here. When I move in, I'm putting something permanent out here to sleep on for these nights when 'tis warm enough."

"That'll be wonderful."

He hesitated, mulling over something. "You're booked to leave day after tomorrow, eh?"

The question surprised and dismayed her. She'd been putting off thinking about it. "Yes. I am."

"Innis Bree, I – "

"Laird," she interrupted, anxious to say what she'd been wanting to tell him all evening, before alcohol and sex took over her mind and body, "my friends from work called me while I was at the hotel." Afraid to look at him, she stared at the firmament. "My boss who fired me got fired. I have my job back, with a promotion."

Silence answered. An almost imperceptible stiffening of his shoulder underneath her head and cooling of his hand answered in their own way.

What she hoped was that he'd beg her to give up her worldly pursuits to stay here in the highlands with him. That he'd smother her in kisses until rendering her immobile and incapable of leaving. That he'd – yes, she admitted to herself – ask her to marry him. What a stupid romantic fantasy. She'd apparently seen far too many Disney movies as a kid. Her fantasies were just that – unrealistic wanderings of her imagination.

He let go of her hand and pulled his arm out from under her. "I suppose congratulations are in order. You've worked long and hard for that. 'Tis well deserved, I'm sure."

That was it. Her heart, she could swear, stopped beating as the devil himself reached into her chest, squeezed her lifeblood, and ripped it out.

She slid over to her own pillow, shivering as she pulled the blankets up to her chin.

At least he noticed. He got up, flaunting, it seemed, his nakedness as he cast kindling onto the fire. It flared, and he threw in a log. He stroked Maisie's head, the dog having been awakened. Maisie put her head down and went right back to sleep. Laird crawled into bed, turned his back to Innis Bree, with nary another word.

Heartbroken, devastated, furious – she felt it all but not one word came to her in response to his reaction to her news. It was as if she'd never held an argument before in her life. Why bother to argue? There was nothing to argue about, apparently. He'd been honest with her right up front. He'd told her he'd had his heart broken and hated women. She should have taken him at his word. Instead, she'd foolishly fallen in love while he'd happily been having a fling. She'd be gone soon, so he was ready to move on. And why not? What was the point of going on together? Their lives had nothing to do with one another. She wanted to cry but refused to let him see her crumble under his cruelty.

She thought about that. Was it truly cruelty? They'd never set any boundaries for their relationship. They'd been too busy enjoying sex. Realizing she needed to be as angry with herself as she was with him, she looked into the sky and silently pled for her ghosts to show up to help.

Bruce? Innis Bree? What should I do?

No one answered.

After a couple of hours of fitful dozing, she roused to find Laird dressed and sitting on the hearth. A gray day had begun, casting a gloomy dawn over them. Still, she could see the empty Aberfeldy bottle at his side.

Maisie hopped onto the mattress to plop down across her chest and give her a sloppy kiss on the face. Laird scolded the dog, but Innis Bree hugged Maisie in appreciation. Apparently, that was the only kiss she'd get that morning. Or maybe ever.

She sat up, holding the covers up to her shoulders.

"I need to get to work," Laird insisted. He stood up and swiped his palms on his thighs as if wiping his hands clean of this whole affair. "I'll give you a ride."

"I'll walk."

"Fine."

He was ten feet away when she got up the nerve to say, "Will I see you tonight?" She shocked herself with the question, having no idea where it came from. Proud that she'd finally found her voice, at the same time she cowered at the rejection that was about to hit.

He stood still as a statue staring at the sky, hands in his pockets. When he looked at her, his answer was another shock. "Seven. My place. I'll pick you up."

"Don't bother," she asserted. "I like walking. Remember?"

"Suit yourself."

He headed for his truck and whistled at Maisie, who didn't know what to do, switching back and forth between her two people. She ran to her new friend for one more kiss, whimpered, and followed her commander. They got in the truck and away they went.

Innis Bree sat there in the cozy outdoor love nest all by herself.

"Some honeymoon," she grumbled once again, right back where she started when this whole Scottish highland debacle began.

CHAPTER 19

*H*er psychology professor colleagues would no doubt call it avoidance when she slept like a rock for three hours in her hotel room. After her night of spasmodic slumber, the early morning coma-nap was much needed.

Up, showered, and dressed for her mid-morning meeting time with Ailsa, she arrived on the hotel deck first and ordered coffee. Tea wouldn't do it for her today. Not even close.

She wished she had some of that Scotch whisky. If she was going to wallow in self-pity, sheer escapism would be better than mere avoidance.

The teenaged server brought the usual basket of baked goods, orange juice, tea, and a whole pot of coffee. This time, she didn't question her customer, who was too ill-tempered to be crossed.

Ailsa brightened up the day as best anyone could, dressed in another flowery dress, accessorized with long earrings and her playfully noisy bracelets. The two women hugged, and the seventy-four-year-old immediately said, "What's wrong?"

Beyond crying at this point, angry instead, Innis Bree told her woeful tale of disenchanted love. She drank three cups of coffee and ate half a scone and a whole cream-cheese-filled Danish in the telling.

"Mam says you two are meant to be together. Mam is never wrong," Ailsa insisted.

"This must be a first."

"Will you see him at all before you leave tomorrow morning?"

"Oh, sure. We have a date tonight. At his house. He's not picking me up. I'm walking. It's only a mile. If we don't kill each other first, he'll probably want to have some wham-bam-thank-you-ma'am highland fling sex and say adios. So I'm thinking I'll go and be smarmy and show no interest in sex, seeing that I hate every damned dude who ever walked the earth."

Ailsa pulled her glasses down on her nose and squinted at her companion. "I think yer thinking isna thinking straight. You're naw talking about the Laird Blyth that I ken or that anybody else kens."

"I know him like that."

"This conversation needs to end, love, because it makes no sense. We'll talk about it later, when we're done with this. Here ..." she pulled a thick-papered scroll out of her tote bag "... let's look at this and get back to Laird later. This is, after all, what you paid me for."

Feeling upbraided like a child, Innis Bree helped as they shoved everything to the far side of the table to make room. Ailsa unrolled what turned out to be a detailed family tree full of color and illustrations and embellishments.

"Oh, Ailsa, it's so beautiful. Look! Every name and birthday and where and when they lived and died. It's wonderful! Thank you so much."

"At least 'tis every one I could find. It starts with what we discovered here and goes all the way to you in America."

"Here's John MacIntyre, his son Gillimichell, and his daughter Innis Bree." She ran a finger over the precious names. "Oh, Ailsa,

I'm so glad we found her and so happy she's at rest with her Bruce. I've been so obsessed with my own pitiful love life I've almost forgotten to be happy over theirs. I may have been dumped, once again, but at least they have a chance to be together."

"Have you seen them?"

Innis Bree looked out at the river, thinking that over. "No. Truth is, I've been so preoccupied, I haven't been open to them. I've been too busy either being ecstatically happy or wallowing in my misery."

Ailsa patted her hand. "I'd lay odds you won't be miserable for long."

"I wish I could believe that, but I feel like I don't dare let myself believe I can be permanently happy. I'll only be disappointed again."

"Would you like to come home with me and Mam for the rest o' the day? You can hang out with us auld lassies and soak in our wisdom. And our love, Innis Bree."

Innis Bree was tempted, but decided otherwise. "I'll stop by for tea this afternoon. How's that? I want to spend some time alone looking around the village one more time."

"That's a good idea." Ailsa stood and gathered her things. "I'll see you at four?"

"Yes."

Her friend left, and Innis Bree drank a fourth cup of coffee. No need to let the nectar of the gods go to waste.

SHE TOOK ANOTHER NAP, a short one this time, then took a final foray around town. There were locals and tourists milling about, reminding her this village belonged to more folk than merely her and her friends. It had felt like her private homeland all week. She wondered if any of the other visitors would experience anything like she had. When two pretty women about her age walked by, she cattily wondered if Laird would be having a highland fling with one of them. They smiled at her but she scowled in return, hating them on sight.

A last visit to the church and graveyard reminded her of the gravity of life and how important it was to live it as well as possible. She would need to work on that because right now her life was crap. As she stood beside Bruce and Innis Bree's grave, the realization struck that she did have what she'd always thought she wanted, what she'd worked so long and hard for – a professorship at a college, teaching what she loved. On top of that, she'd always wanted to be a wife and mother, too. Now, because of them, she wanted more. She wanted what they didn't get a chance to have.

She wanted a soulmate like they had with each other. She never would've had that with Walter. Good old Walter. Thank God, he abandoned her. As devastated as she'd been on the day of her disastrous wedding, now she saw it as a blessing. If she was here on her honeymoon with him, this week would've gone very differently. Bruce wouldn't have come to her. She wouldn't have had a date at the castle and would never have found Innis Bree, who may never have been freed. Laird certainly wouldn't have been in the mix.

She waited for a couple of other graveyard visitors to walk out of earshot before saying, "Bruce and Innis Bree, I pray you've found each other. If you haven't yet, don't stop searching. Bruce, she's free now! You're both right here in Kenmore. You need to be together. You have a kind of love that is so rare. You're true soulmates. I don't know if you ever called it that, but it means you are perfect together. Thank you for teaching me it's possible to find someone to love forevermore. I thought maybe I'd found that with your descendant, Bruce, but apparently not. Don't worry, though. I'll keep searching until I find it with the right person someday."

She kissed her fingertips and placed them on the headstone. "I love you both."

When Bruce didn't appear, she knew she'd miss him for a long time to come. Not many people had the gift of visits from their own ghost who guided them. Everything with Laird may have gone to hell in a hand-basket, but she'd made wonderful new friends, dead and alive.

Would she ever return? And no doubt see Laird with another woman? She couldn't entertain the idea. At least not yet.

She went back to the hotel and put on the lovely summer dress she'd bought in Edinburgh the day she and Ailsa went to the archives. The sandals she bought that day were already well used, so she used a tissue to rub them clean before putting them on.

The bike ride across the ancient stone bridge to the other side of town calmed her down and, right on time, she rang the doorbell for afternoon tea with Ailsa and Garia. Their time together was heartwarming and heart-wrenching. After having fresh-baked blueberry scones and hot black tea, they said tearful goodbyes. As she left, Ailsa entreated her to work things out with Laird. She did her best to nod assent even though she knew that was a lie. As she saw it, things would never work out with Laird Blyth.

Back at the hotel, she prepared for her evening with him, Mister Love-'em-and-leave-'em. She figured she had three options, considering that Laird obviously had no interest in a long-term relationship.

One was to simply not appear at his cottage that night. She wondered if he'd come looking for her. Probably not.

The second possibility was to go and have a wildly satisfying night of sex. To make that happen, however, she'd need to turn off her emotions. Could she do it? She knew the answer before finishing the question. Because of all that had happened that week with the dead and the living, she'd unearthed a depth of emotion within herself that she'd never imagined. For the first time, she clearly understood what real love could be like. So sex with no sense of connection or commitment wouldn't work for her. If she had sex with Laird, her feelings for him, as misguided as they might be, would surface and she'd only be heartbroken again.

That led to option three. An appraisal of herself in the mirror inspired a naughty plan for that one. A mischievous grin struck her face. She could turn her emotions into something naughty. Maybe even vindictive. She'd never been vindictive. Maybe it was time.

The dress came off. Her panties and bra followed. She put the dress on again. Yup. Just what she suspected. Without a bra, her nipples poked at the fabric. Good. Let him stare. Panties? Nope. Let him wonder.

This night would be her night of retribution. Getting even for bedding her and then leaving her out to dry. She'd tease. She'd let him look. But she wouldn't let him touch. She'd walk out on him with a cocky sashay of her bottom that would leave him crumbling to his knees at the sight of her going.

She'd let one man walk all over her when he walked away from their wedding. This time she'd do the walking away.

All that played on her mind as she applied more makeup than usual. Not exactly Hollywood Kardashian tacky but not her ordinarily sweet self, either. Thick eyeliner emphasized the emerald green of her eyes. Blush highlighted her high cheekbones. And she imagined her red lipstick made her lips as succulent as Priyanka Chopra's. She fluffed and primped her lush black hair until it fell perfectly about her shoulders.

Stepping back from the mirror to take it all in, she said, "Laird Blyth, you are about to meet your match."

"IF A HIGHLAND FLING is all the American lassie wants, that's what she'll get. She'll be wooed like she's ne'er been wooed 'afore." Laird talked to Maisie, who tilted her head in quandary. "Naw once has she mentioned staying here with me. All we've been through together, and she doesna want to stay. What's the song say? 'Love me or leave me in peace.' Eh?" He grabbed his phone, scrolled, hit the song, and turned it up as high as the volume would go.

Maisie left the bathroom, opting for her dog bed in the quieter corner of the bedroom.

Showered, standing in front of his mirror with a towel wrapped around his waist, Laird contemplated his plan. He tussled his unruly wet hair for a wild look. Running his hand across his cheek, he decided not to shave. Let her get whisker burn. He considered cologne but figured a swipe of deodorant under each arm would do. His own smell would suffice, that of a real man. He brushed his teeth but mouthwash? Nae. He'd have a dram of Scotch whisky instead. The taste of his liquor would coat her mouth.

He padded into the bedroom, dropped the towel, and stood there naked, looking at the clothes he'd laid out on the bed. Underwear? Nae. A new, deep blue tee shirt the color of his eyes went on first. His dark blue-and-green tartan kilt was next, the tee shirt tucked into it. He sat on the side of the bed for his socks and cleaned-up work boots. Not traditional, to be sure, but Innis Bree would like this version of a Scottish highlander. Rugged. Unconventional. Swoony.

She liked swoony.

"Come on, lassie," he called to Maisie as he turned the music down for her benefit. "Let's get everything ready."

He labored for half an hour before everything in his small croft cottage was exactly as he wanted it. Sexy. Sultry. Something she'd never forget.

"Let her think about this when she's four thousand miles away from me, teaching an American history class, eh?"

Maisie stared at her master, then whined to be let outside, not wanting to be part of whatever strange thing was about to happen in the cottage. She preferred the barn with her sheep, who were far less complicated.

INNIS BREE DIDN'T NEED to knock on the door. It stood ajar. She pushed it open and stepped inside.

It was the first time she'd been in his cottage and the atmosphere struck like landing in a charming 17th century farmhouse with cozy 21st century updates. The lights were down low. The scent of heather and roses filled the space, the flowers in vases spread out around the room. Lit candles were scattered about. The living area was a single room, a combination living room and kitchen. It was, after all, a small cottage from long ago. The walls were whitewashed. The plank wood floor and wood beams on the ceiling gave it a warm, homey feel. Music played in the background. The fireplace held a small, softly crackling blaze.

He stepped out into full view in the doorway of what she presumed led to his bedroom and the real blaze began. She felt her knees buckle and had to remind them to stay strong. He was hot! Even hotter than before, and he'd been sizzling then.

He didn't speak, instead putting his arms up on the doorframe above his head. The gesture stretched his torso and formed rocks out of his biceps, emphasizing the Celtic tattoos that peeked out of his short-sleeved tee shirt.

She glanced at the face and then the arms. Then, of their own bloody free will, her eyes glommed onto the kilt. Oh lordy, she knew there would be nothing underneath but bare skin. Bare skin on … Well, she couldn't let herself think about that. She shook her head and forced herself to focus on his face.

He was staring at the nipple bumps in her dress. She took a deep breath to inflate her chest. So there, mister highfalutin Scottish highlander hunk.

He stepped out of the doorway and took a step toward her, not even trying to hide the steamy, slow-burn appraisal he made of her body, his eyes roaming from her breasts to her face and back to her breasts where they settled for a bit, then traveling down to rest where her thighs met. Involuntarily, as her unruly body now had a mind of its own, her hips gently tilted toward him in a primitive response to his blatant invitation. His lips parted as he inhaled deeply. His scan meandered up to take in the quickening rise and fall of her chest. His gaze came back to her face where he watched as her tongue teased upon her red lips. Finally, lake-blue and emerald-green eyes locked into a fixated stare.

The song *My Guitar Gently Weeps*, seductive and slow, came on, and he held out a hand. She moved into his tight embrace, and they swayed to the tune. He lowered his head to croon into her ear, giving it a little nip with his teeth in the process. That ear, she thought, might never recover. His hand moved up and down her spine until landing on her bum. When the next song brazenly declared he wanted to "lay her down," he covered her mouth with a brash scotch-whisky kiss that left her drunk with desire. When he picked her up and carried her into his bedroom, she didn't object. She couldn't remember how.

Her mind vaguely recalled bits and pieces of something about making him want her and rejecting him – was there something about sashaying away? – and here she was, only two songs into their date and on her way to his bed. The remnants of her plan for revenge unraveled and fell away as he laid her down and straddled her, and she reached up under that kilt to find the glory she so desperately wanted. She'd have to think about sweet revenge later.

Right now she might die if Laird Blyth didn't fill her up with his sweet manhood.

He had no problem fulfilling her need and therefore saving her life.

HE DIDN'T EVER WANT to let go of her. He had his arm wrapped around her waist from behind as they laid in bed. She slept soundly and he feared that moving would wake her, but his arm was falling asleep. He inched it off her and rolled onto his back, making sure his side still touched the length of her backside. He had to keep that connection lest he disintegrate into nothingness.

His resolution to love her and leave her had been trashed in the three times they'd made love, twice to the point of exhaustion, then snacking and catnapping to renew their energy for the third time. Nae, he couldna do it, let her leave without asking her to stay. When she awoke, he'd swallow his pride and ask, e'en though she'd ne'er so much as mentioned staying, naw even to extend her trip for the summer.

When she refused, he would take it like a man. At least he would always know he tried.

But what if she dinnae say nae? What if …?

With a glimmer of hope in his heart, he finally fell into peaceful slumber.

INNIS BREE PRETENDED TO SLEEP, hanging in limbo as to what to do. He took his arm away from her waist and rolled over. They still touched. Did that mean anything or was it a mere accident of proximity?

He fell into slumber, his breathing becoming heavier. It came to her then, the only thing to do, and it must be done immediately while she had the chance. She must leave now or it would be even more painful to wait until he awoke to hear him say goodbye. Inch by inch she slid out of his bed, grabbed her dress and sandals off the floor, and took one last look at him. With him half turned over on his side, she could see the scratch marks she'd left on his back. Their sex that night had been rough, greedy, desperate. Two selfish souls, each satisfying their own needs. She touched the love bite on her breast. At least she'd be taking something of him with her. She tiptoed out of the room.

In the living room, she dressed quickly and quietly. She took one last glance around his wonderfully homey cottage. It still smelled of heather and roses. The fire had died. The candles had burned out. The dishes from the shepherd's pie they'd snacked on a couple of hours earlier sat there. He'd taken it out of his fridge and heated it in the oven, the meat and veggies topped with mashed potatoes. They'd hardly spoken, except she'd asked if he made it, and he said Jenny gave it to him. "I cannae boil an egg," he'd admitted. Finally, something he wasn't good at.

Outrageously handsome, smart, accomplished, educated, hard-working, a good singer and dancer, the best lover a woman could ever imagine – and damn, he even made a living – but he couldn't cook? Pfft. Who'd ever want a loser like that? She tried to uplift her spirits with the thought.

Once outside in dawn's gray twilight, she shivered in the chilly, damp air, her thin summer dress not nearly warm enough for this hour of the day. Steadfast and determined, she quickly walked the mile to the village. She used her room key to open the front door of the hotel, something she'd learned after she'd locked herself out that first night. In her room, she called Jeffrey. It was five in the morning, and he answered like a man in a coma. When she told him what she wanted, he said he'd be there in fifteen minutes.

Right on time, he pulled up in front of the hotel. She waited out front with her roller bag, tote bag, and purse. Wearing jeans, a tee shirt, a jacket, and grimy white sneakers, she was ready to travel.

"I dinnae understand," Jeffrey complained as he loaded her luggage into the boot of the Mercedes. "What happened? Why are you leaving?"

"I'll explain on the way. By the way, you have a terrible case of bedhead." His hair stuck out like a cobweb around his face. She hopped in, ready to go.

Reluctantly, Jeffrey got in but didn't start the car. "O' course, I have bedhead. You woke me up at five in the morning. That should be against the law. You ken that train station has trains every hour or two. You dinnae have to get there for the very first one o' the day."

"Let's go, Jeffrey. We need to leave now. Please?"

Her pitiful pleading made him turn the key and slowly drive down Kenmore's empty main street. He kept stealing glances at her, waiting for her to explain.

"I might be pathetic, but I refuse to beg. Laird didn't ask me to stay. I have my job back. I need to go home to my life. End of story. Drive a little faster, please."

He hit the gas a bit. "Back up to the part about Laird dinnae ask you to stay. What are you talking about? He's madly in love with you."

"Not that I can see. To hell with him. I'll go home, find my soul-mate, have a couple of kids who I'll love with every inch of my being, and we'll live happily ever after. So there."

"Och, you sound so-o-o convincing. Besides, what if your soul-mate is right here in Scotland?"

He turned onto the road that led to Pitlochry, and Innis Bree didn't know what she felt most – relief to be escaping or despair to be leaving the village that felt like her long-lost home.

"Let's call him," Jeffrey suggested.

"No! Don't you dare. Please, Jeffrey, if you value our friendship at all, don't do that. We are friends, aren't we?"

"O' course."

She stared out the window as she spoke, choosing her words carefully. "Jeffrey, do you believe it's possible for true friendships to form and for people to fall in love within days? Maybe even within moments?"

He kept his eyes on the road as he nodded. "Aye. The heart and soul dinnae ken clocks or time. Nae matter when it begins or how long it lasts, love kens nae bounds. Love is timeless. Laird said it at dinner. 'True love lingers in our hearts and souls fore'er.'"

She didn't respond as she stared out the window, gazing at the highland hills.

He sighed and drove on in silence. Fifteen minutes later, halfway there, he said, "I want you to ken that if I was attracted to lassies, I woulda fought him for you."

She turned her attention to him and patted his shoulder. "The way things have gone with him, you definitely would've won."

"You ken, dinnae you, I'm going to call him the second you get out o' this car."

"Go ahead. I'll be gone by then and he won't care."

"You're wrong."

"Jeffrey, don't. Please. I want to go home."

He clammed up from then on. When he let her out at the Pitlochry train station, she insisted he go. She wanted to be alone, as she needed some transition time between her fake Scottish life and her real American life.

He kissed her cheek, enveloped her in a hug, then got in Rory Skeffington's expensive Mercedes and drove away. She watched him go, her emotions swirling with all that had happened in one short week. Her life would never be the same. Whether she would ever recover, she had no idea.

~

"Wait, wait, wait! I'm confused. I thought a man should ne'er – ne'er! – ask a woman to give up her career and her friends and her family and her *life*, for kristsake, for him. They tell you that on the telly and in movies and on social media, and you my dear sister you – you! – have told me, too. I dinnae ken. I cannae keep up."

"Welcome to my world," Clyde grumbled, lifting his coffee mug in salute.

Laird paced like a madman in Jenny and Clyde's kitchen, running his hands through his hair in frustration.

"That's right," Jenny said as she calmly poured herself a second cuppa and leaned against the counter. She wore a fluffy pink bathrobe and slippers with owl heads embroidered on them.

Clyde sat at the far side of the table in his brown checkered bathrobe, staying out of the fray.

"So I didna. I didna expect her to give up anything for me. She worked hard for nine years to get that job. I cannae interfere with that. Right?"

"Och, dear brother." Jenny shook her head. "You ken I love you, aye?"

"O' course. And I you."

She bopped him in the chest with a forefinger. "Yer a fecking eejit."

Clyde lifted his mug in salute again.

"What? Why?" Totally flummoxed, Laird stood in the center of the room with outstretched arms.

"You two spent last night together. Aye?"

"Aye."

"Did you ask her to stay or to at least extend her visit?"

"Nae. If I had, I'd be the kind of domineering man you keep saying women hate. But I was going to anyway when we got up

238

this morning." His voice broke in distress. "But she was gone, already back at the hotel, I suppose."

"To avoid being an overbearing man, you do two things. One, dinnae assume she should give up everything for you. And two, you give her the choice to do so. You made that choice for her."

Clyde got up to refill his cup, and as he did so, he addressed Laird. "That was very, very bad. You dinnae make decisions for them." He looked at his wife, she nodded, and they fist bumped. Clyde went back to his seat.

"Laird, love," Jenny said, "this is your country, your village, your land, your family, your home, your sheep – hell, e'en your sweet dog." She pointed at Maisie, whose ears perked up at the mention of her name. "What was the lass supposed to do? Say …" and with this she mimicked an American accent "… Hey, big boy, I know we've only known each other for a week, but do you mind if I move in on your whole life?'" She dropped the accent. "Nae. You need to give her the option and let her decide."

"Och shite, I did it all wrong. I'm a fecking eejit."

"Aye." She nonchalantly sipped her tea. "Besides, we all ken …" she used her mug to indicate herself, Clyde, and even Maisie "… the real reason you didna ask her to stay is because you're terrified she'll say nae and you'll end up with another broken heart."

He stared at his little sister in total defeat. She'd nailed it. That was what all that bravado had been about last night, the promise to love her and leave her and the accompanying angry sex.

"What if I do get a broken heart?" he asked in a tone like a teenager afraid of being rebuffed the first time he asked a girl out.

Jenny set down her mug and hugged her big brother. "You'll survive."

Laird surrendered. "I have to talk to her. Thank you." He bussed his sister's cheek, nodded at his brother-in-law, and rushed out the door, dog in tow.

His phone rang as he opened his truck door. He pulled it out of his pocket and checked the screen, hoping it was Innis Bree. It wasn't, but he swiped it anyway. "Hi, Jeffrey. Listen, I'm in a rush …"

When Jeffrey explained where he'd been and why, Laird hopped in his truck and charged out of town. It took him twenty minutes to make the thirty-minute drive.

He pulled into the Pitlochry train station parking lot in such a hurry he leapt out and didn't take time to close his door. He sprinted toward the boarding platform at the very moment the train bolted forward, huffed like a fiery dragon, and started to chug away.

"Nae! Nae." Helplessly, he reached out to the giant beast, beseeching it to stop. It ignored him and rattled down the tracks. "Shite," he moaned.

As the rumble of the train diminished while it ambled away, Maisie's bark pierced the air. He turned, and his eyes fell upon the most wonderful sight he'd ever seen.

Innis Bree sat on a bench on the platform, scratching Maisie's ears. She looked at Laird and slowly stood up to face him. Cautiously, lest she flee, he walked toward her. He came close and stopped.

"I …" she stammered, pointing at where the train had been, "I couldn't get on."

He stepped forward, understanding that he no longer had to be afraid she would abandon him. He wrapped his arms around her and held on tight as if their lives depended on it.

Joyful relief washed over him. This hug meant more than anything else they'd been through – more than all that fabulously sweet and rowdy sex. This embrace meant they were finally where they belonged. Together.

They clung to each other for a good while as Laird stroked her hair and she nuzzled his neck. When they came apart, he took her hands in his. "Innis Bree, do you believe in fated love?"

"I do."

As her words sunk in, Laird surprised himself when a seemingly presumptuous and precarious question tumbled out of his mouth. "Do you have a mind to repeat those very words at our wedding?"

"Oh, I do!"

They kissed long and lovingly, entertaining the passengers who gathered for the next train.

Maisie laid down and watched, her world having turned right side up, too.

CHAPTER 20

The wedding took place a week after his proposal at the train station, which seemed a fitting place to have proposed as it was where they first met. It was only two weeks after that first disastrous meeting. Some might have said it was too soon to get married, but neither bride nor groom wanted to wait.

Knowing Innis Bree's family and friends couldn't make it over from America because scheduling flights on short notice would be cost prohibitive, they planned a second wedding reception for the end of the summer. Hopefully by then her folks could come over.

As Ailsa, Garia, and Jenny helped her dress for the ceremony, there was a knock at the door. They were in Tess's chamber in the castle, as Jeffrey had insisted the women all stay there the night before to help the bride get ready the next day. So far, they'd had a great time. Not able to imagine who was left that could be at the door, Ailsa answered.

Innis Bree was standing at the mirror when the knock came. Ailsa opened the door, and Innis Bree was shocked to see the reflection of her mother, Kathryn, and Delina come into the chamber behind her. She spun around and shrieked with glee.

After a round of exuberant hugs, she finally got out some words. "How did you get here?"

"Why," her mother said, "that nice man Jeffrey had that private plane bring us over. And we get to stay right here in the castle. Can you imagine? A real castle!"

Kathryn chimed in, "Your dad and brother and Rama are here, too, downstairs."

"Wait. What private plane? Oh. Just minute. Don't move." Innis Bree went to the door and stepped into the hall. "Jeffrey!" she hollered excitedly.

He instantly appeared, not that he'd been lurking nearby or anything.

"Thank you so much for arranging Rory's plane to bring everybody! How on earth did you talk him into it?"

"It was simple. I called and told him he owed it to you. He asked who you were marrying. When I told him, he freaked out." Jeffrey became animated in the telling. "He said, 'Him? She could've kept dating me and she chose to marry a sheep farmer?' I said, 'Aye. They're in love.' He was quiet for a second, then said, 'What a woman.' Then he agreed to the plane."

"You're the best." She hugged him heartily and returned to her room with her friends and family, to finish getting ready for the biggest day of her life.

Jenny helped her finish with her gown, which was a strapless ball gown they'd picked up in Edinburgh, then Jenny modified it. She'd gathered the top layer of the skirt on one side, fastened it with a floret, and sewn a lace underskirt beneath it. A dark blue and green Blyth clan tartan sash finished the decidedly Scottish look. The bride's hair was swept up with roses and heather tucked into the curls.

Her mom and Delina cried while the others beamed. Everyone was dressed to the nines, with Ailsa wearing the sparkly blue dress

Rory gave her. With everyone all set, it was time to go to the site of the ceremony, Laird's mansion.

There, in the highlands of Scotland, the land of their ancestors, Innis Bree MacIntyre and Laird Bartholomew Blyth wed. The ceremony took place outdoors in the open-air portion of his manse. They'd strung patio lights all about and fragrant flowers from townfolk's gardens were everywhere. They invited the whole village and not one person missed out.

As she began her walk down the aisle to the emotional music provided by a local bagpiper, the bride knew without a doubt this was what her life was meant to be. When she saw Laird waiting for her in his formal attire – dress kilt, shirt and tie, jacket, sporran, and even the knife in his hose – any dream of Jamie Fraser she'd ever had completely evaporated. This was better than a dream. This was her life.

The wedding was touching, with many a happy tear. Although, she suspected her parents were still dumbstruck, and her mom may have been crying out of shock. Her brother, Kathryn, Rama, and Delina were on board, though, truly thrilled for her.

The bride and groom chose not to have anyone stand up with them other than Maisie, who sat slightly behind the couple, looking up at them adoringly throughout the entire short ceremony, her tail wagging in delight.

The reception was a joyous affair. Most villagers brought food. Scotch whisky was plentiful. Everyone was in a celebratory mood, including the children.

Her dad became teary-eyed when the song for the first dance, the bride-and-father dance, was *Because You Loved Me*. When she and Laird had their dance, she'd asked him to choose the song and was deeply touched as *When I Said I Do* played.

After an hour of revelry, there were piles of shoes laying around outside the dance floor, including Innis Bree's. Everyone had let their hair down, too, including Innis Bree, whose hair had fallen down. Even though the men wore their dress kilts and women had on their best dresses or gowns, staid formality had no place here.

Jeffrey twirled Garia around in her wheelchair in time to the music. Ailsa danced with the old gent who'd given Innis Bree a boat ride. Jenny and Clyde did their best, considered his big boot. Laird and Jenny's parents were there, good dancers having a good time. Innis Bree even saw her parents dancing, something they seldom did. Rama and Delina were like lovebirds, and Kathryn pranced around in a ring of little girls. The desk clerk and rainbow-haired teen from the hotel danced together. The priest from the kirk, who'd performed their ceremony, made the rounds chatting with one and all. The man who'd offered Innis Bree a ride her first night there and warned her about the impending storm was there with the woman she presumed to be his wife.

It was during the song *The Keeper of the Stars* that she glanced at the gaggle of merry dancers, and suddenly could have sworn that in the middle of the crowd she saw a flash of a familiar blue dress and a red-and-black tartan kilt. She stretched her neck to try to see in between all the swaying bodies. Another snatch of blue and red-and-black. And another as the wearers merrily circled the dance floor. Could it be? She worked her way through the crowd and there, in the midst of it all, Bruce and his Innis Bree waltzed. They were together!

He held his love close and when she looked up into his eyes, sheer bliss radiated between them. The song ended, and they drifted hand in hand off the floor, across the driveway in front of the house, and out toward the pasture of sheep.

Innis Bree frantically grabbed Laird's hand and dragged him out to the front of the manse with her. "Can you see them?"

"Aye! They found each other after all. How wonderful."

"He never gave up on her."

"That's e'erlasting love."

"They finally got to do what he'd always wanted to do with her, dance and sing and enjoy the company of friends and family, all at the home he built."

Arms wrapped around each other's waists, they followed the ghosts into the field. She lifted her wedding gown and allowed the clover to tickle her bare feet, a sensation that made her feel like one with the land. Laird's land, and Bruce's long before him.

Bruce and his Innis Bree stopped amidst the sheep and looked around in wonder. She picked a wild posey, inhaled its sweet scent, and held it out for him to enjoy.

Innis Bree and Laird waited. The ethereal couple, hale and hearty and young and so in love, turned around and smiled at their progeny. They each extended a hand, reaching out as a sign of their lasting connection to their living family.

Their offspring smiled and reached out in return, tears of joy streaming down their faces.

All of a sudden, the heavens opened, and a beam of scintillating light rained down upon the deceased. Holding hands, the lovers floated up into the sky, their hair billowing and clothes rustling as they ascended into the light.

They disappeared, and the beam withdrew.

Innis Bree and Laird didn't move, mesmerized by what they'd witnessed.

"I'm so happy for them." Innis Bree tightened her hold on her husband.

"As am I." He kissed his wife's hair.

"While on earth, they never got to live together as a married couple like we'll get to do. It makes me want us to be happy enough for them, too, and do all the things they never got to do."

"Aye. They ne'er got to have bairns ..."

She grinned up at him. "We should be having a bairn sooner rather than later, the way we're going at it."

Her husband wrapped his arms around her waist, picked her

up, and twirled her around, overjoyed at the miraculous wonder of their lives.

Innis Bree MacIntyre Blyth felt more alive than ever before, having awakened to beauty and happiness and love like none she'd ever known. Bruce had been right when he said, "'Tis the moments o' joy that matter in life. All the rest falls away as long as there is love to carry us through."

THE END

THANK you for reading *Waking Innis Bree*. I hope it took you to Scotland as it did me while I was writing. I'm glad you came along.

Here's a quick and easy link for writing a review, which is always much appreciated:

https://amazon.com/review/create-review?&asin= B0C2T5D6R5

WOULD you like to read another of my novels that includes ancestor ghosts? The first in my Ancestor Ghost Series, *Becoming Jessie Belle, Book 1,* an Indie Book of the Day, is free on Kindle Unlimited and available for sale in eBook and paperback.

Get your copy here:

Becoming Jessie Belle on Amazon

TO RECEIVE my twice-a-month newsletter for a free book and updates on new releases and special offers, including the next installment of this series, sign up on my website at www.lin-dahughes.com I hope to see you there.

LETTER FROM THE AUTHOR

Dear Readers,

Waking Innis Bree is personal for me because I used my own ancestors and their hometown as the crux of this story. Of course, I can only imagine what their lives were like. I wonder what they'd think of what I made of them.

In 2019, I visited Kenmore in the highlands of Scotland. As I sat in the pub, I could feel the souls of my forebears, John and Gillimichell MacIntyre. If their descendants are a clue, that's where they spent a good deal of their time.

I got such a kick out of reading a church booklet that recorded John MacIntyre's accusation against his neighbor for being a witch. He was indeed reprimanded by the priest.

Here's hoping this story served as a gentle reminder that your ancestors, too, led lives we can only imagine. They laughed and cried, loved and hated, feared and persevered, and toiled and rejoiced. Somehow they survived to bring us into this world. That truly is miraculous.

If you can't visit the hometowns of your ancestors, books and internet searches can take you there. Enjoy finding them, as I did mine.

Love,

Linda

www.lindahughes.com

ACKNOWLEDGMENTS

First of all, I'm eternally grateful to my ancestors who gave me life. In my extensive ancestry searches, I've found no royalty, upper crust, celebrities, politicians, or rich folk in my family tree. I have found the blacksmith, a lot of farmers, and one small general store owner who traded snuff for home-canned goods. Most of them lived in poverty and somehow managed to get me here.

Thank you also to the residents of Kenmore, Scotland, and all the Scots I've met around the country during my several visits throughout the years. I've been greeted with warmth and hospitality everywhere I've gone.

Appreciation also to my author friend Doug Godsman, a real Scot who edited this story for language accuracy. If you haven't read Doug's wonderful highland novels yet, start with *Highland Justice.*

Andy the Highlander doesn't know he helped me, but his videos on social media gave me great advice about his part of the world.

My program manager, Maria Connor, saved the day at the last minute to finish up editing. Maria, you're the best.

ACKNOWLEDGMENTS

And there's Maisy, my Sheltie. All I had to do to include fictional Maisie in a scene was look over to see what my lassie was up to.

Thank you most of all to you, my readers. I appreciate you more than you may ever know. I do my best to show it by writing more stories for you, so stay tuned.

ABOUT THE AUTHOR

Linda Hughes has won numerous writing awards and has twenty-five novels in publication. She writes romantic women's fiction in a blend of sub-genres. You'll find family mysteries, lively young adults, wise elders, contemporary and historical timeframes, settings you want to visit, first-time and later-in-life romances, and always a promise of hope.

Learn more about her books and writing journey at www.lindahughes.com

Made in the USA
Las Vegas, NV
07 January 2025

16025827R00144